D0063363

STORM

STORM

EVAN ANGLER

BOOK 3

THOMAS NELSON
Since 1798

NASHVILLE   DALLAS   MEXICO CITY   RIO DE JANEIRO

Storm

© 2013 by Evan Angler

All rights reserved. No portion of this book may be reproduced, stored in a retrieval system, or transmitted in any form or by any means—electronic, mechanical, photocopy, recording, scanning, or other—except for brief quotations in critical reviews or articles, without the prior written permission of the publisher.

Published in Nashville, Tennessee, by Tommy Nelson. Tommy Nelson is a registered trademark of Thomas Nelson, Inc.

Tommy Nelson titles may be purchased in bulk for educational, business, fund-raising, or sales promotional use. For information, please e-mail SpecialMarkets@ThomasNelson.com.

Scripture quotations are taken from THE ENGLISH STANDARD VERSION. © 2001 by Crossway Bibles, a division of Good News Publishers.

Library of Congress Cataloging-in-Publication Data

Angler, Evan.
Storm / Evan Angler.
pages cm. -- (Swipe series ; bk. 3)
Summary: While Logan and his friends, leaders of the Markless revolution, face Chancellor Cylis's army, the Dust seeks a cure for an epidemic sweeping through the Marked, Logan's sister Lily's allegiance remains unclear, and climatic changes become ever more threatening.
ISBN 978-1-4003-2197-1 (pbk.)
[1. Science fiction. 2. Government, Resistance to--Fiction. 3. Fugitives from justice--Fiction. 4. Christian life--Fiction.] I. Title.
PZ7.A5855St 2013
[Fic]--dc23
2013002300

Printed in the United States of America

13 14 15 16 17 RRD 6 5 4 3 2 1

For Molly,
who risks life and limb
to bring these books to you

CONTENTS

CONTENTS

A NOTE FROM
THE AUTHOR

Dear Reader,

We have escaped. We're alive. But for how long?

I'm writing to you Markless now because you're the ones who question. Who think differently. Who doubt.

And under a government that Marks its citizens in the name of Unity, that swipes its own kids over the faintest sign of what might someday turn into defiance . . . *you* are the ones in danger.

It is you who will be weeded out. To be forgotten. So that all who remain will be unified.

One month ago, Logan Langly and his friends in the Markless Dust took a stand against all of this. They traveled to Beacon, the capital city of the American Union, to take back the swiped, to rescue Logan's beloved sister Lily, and to expose the truth behind the Mark at any cost.

But all was not as it seemed.

With the unwitting help of a Marked ally named Erin Arbitor, the Dust very nearly did succeed. They found Acheron, the Markless prison thought surely not to exist. They sneaked inside. They saw the place for what it was—a training ground for General Lamson's secret army of "Revised" Markless, modeled slavishly after Chancellor Cylis's in the European Union. They came face to face with these International Moderators of Peace. These IMPS. They even found Advocate Lily Langly among them.

But Advocate Langly did not *want* saving from Acheron. She betrayed her brother and his friends, imprisoning them. And while Logan did later narrowly manage to escape, his good friend Eddie did not.

Meanwhile, General Lamson and Chancellor Cylis have been consolidating their power. Under the terms of the new Global Treaty, the American and European Unions have finally completed the decade-long process of their merge. They are now, together, the Global Union, ratified in the name of peace.

But within this supposedly peaceful Union, Erin Arbitor has just discovered something else: evidence of a targeted, biological weapon—Project Trumpet—conceived by Cylis long ago and designed by the Department of Marked Emergencies to unleash upon the world just in case its Markless ever got . . . out of hand.

Well. The Markless *are* out of hand now. In the wake of the truth about Acheron, exposed by the Dust and symbolized by Logan's imprisonment, protests have risen up all throughout America, from Beacon City to New Chicago. It seems certain that Trumpet will be activated nationwide.

Yet, so far, it is not the Markless who have gotten sick. It's the Marked.

And Erin has just come down with the first signs of a fever.

Now Logan Langly, Daniel Peck, Hailey Phoenix, and Erin Arbitor are on the run. Away from Beacon. Across America and under the new umbrella of the Global Union. Fugitives wanted by DOME and the IMPS both. They've set out to find a cure before it's too late.

But this is a battle that's bigger than them. And it's one they cannot win alone.

My name is Evan Angler. This book is the third in the ongoing chronicles of the Dust's great defiance. It has surely been outlawed by now. To hold it is a crime. To read it is worse. So if you've come this far, then you and I are already in this thing together.

Welcome to the Dust.

Let's see how much trouble we can find.

Evan Angler

THE REQUEST

THE DOOR TO THE HOUSE WAS CLOSED AND locked and guarded by two men wearing uniforms unlike any Connor had ever seen. They were quiet. They held rifles and wore helmets that shadowed their faces. They stared out and didn't move.

Connor watched from the yard next door, dark under the curtain of a hot September night. The town around him was still, suspended in the thick, stifling air, and he crept through it silently.

Around him, paper cups and wrappers and colored confetti littered the dirt, dotting it with reminders of the day's celebration—and of how quickly it had passed.

A morning parade down Main Street, a town-wide feast lasting all afternoon, an award ceremony, an evening full of pomp and circumstance—after-parties with dancing and live music— all celebrating *him*. Connor Goodman, national hero, first-ever recipient of the General's Award for Marked Excellence, Promise, and the American Dream. General Lamson himself had come all the way from the capital to present it.

Yet here Connor was now, just two short hours later, stripped of all dignity, locked out of his own house, and sneaking around like some Markless burglar just to get a glimpse inside his own living room window. *Humiliating,* Connor thought. And yet he wasn't above it. He had to know what the general was telling his parents inside. He had to hear. America's newest national hero deserved it.

So when the armed guards at the door finally looked away, down the dirt path of Main Street toward Central Square, scanning momentarily for movement in just precisely the wrong direction, Connor jumped at the chance. In one swift motion, he ran from the shadow of his neighbor's house all the way into the flowers and bushes lining the back of his own, and he pressed his ear hard against its rough, brown wood siding.

The general's voice was low, muffled, and distant through the wall. But the tenor notes of his father's carried through soon enough. Connor held his breath, determined to hear.

"General . . . please. We're begging you to reconsider. What you are asking of us will bring . . . unbearable suffering to your citizens. Hardship in every corner of this Union!"

There was a pained pause from behind the wall. In that moment, Connor grabbed the window ledge above him, pulled himself up, and peeked through the glass, hoping for a better understanding of the scene inside.

The general was pacing now, his tall frame towering over Connor's parents. When he did speak, his words came slow and heavy through the windowpane.

"I am . . . aware of the consequences, Mr. Goodman. And I am sympathetic to the risks. I've taken a fair share of my own just coming here today. But the time is upon us. This threat is one that could destroy our way of life—our very *existence*—here in the American Union. We've no choice but to eliminate it.

"Ready or not, Mr. Goodman, we find ourselves here. At this crossroads. Today. And without your cooperation . . . without your patriotic commitment . . . this nation of ours will perish from the earth. The Union hangs in the balance. And that, Mr. Goodman, is *worth* this sacrifice."

Then the sound of footsteps drowned out the general's voice. Connor twisted and froze, dangling helplessly from the window ledge above the bushes, holding his breath.

The two guards were silhouetted against the midnight black. Connor swallowed hard.

Two red targeting dots found him, converging to a bright spot over his heart. Remarkably steady. The guards' hands did not shake.

Think fast. Act now. And with one quick twitch of his wrist, Connor knocked hard on the window to his right. The general came up against it, cupping his hands around his eyes and looking out into the dark yard beyond. He saw Connor there. He saw the red glow of the laser sights. He saw the guards, guns raised, awaiting his order.

General Lamson laughed.

ONE

FIGHT OR FLIGHT

1

THE FLOOR SHOOK VIOLENTLY UNDER LOGAN'S feet, its rug jumping and sliding in short, stiff bursts. The window to his side rattled, and he wondered if the whole door might soon fall off.

Logan leaned forward to the driver's seat in front of him, peering over Peck's tense shoulder at the fuel gauge, which jittered so much that the after-image of its soft green glow showed only a blur.

But he could still see the needle, pointing with certainty.

Empty.

"Can't this thing go any faster?" Hailey asked from the passenger seat.

"Not if we want it to stay in one piece," Peck said, but he pressed harder on the gas pedal even so.

Lifelessly, Erin bounced from her spot on the backseat and slid to the floor.

"She all right?" Peck asked, unable to take his eyes off the road.

Hailey turned to look over her shoulder. "Not stirring," she said. "Keep driving."

"Low on gas," Logan warned, hoping not to spark an explosion of new frustration from up front.

"It'll stop when it stops," Peck said. "'Til then, worry about what's behind us."

So Logan turned to peer out the back window, where behind them a drone plane appeared low on the horizon.

"You've gotta be kidding me," Logan said.

"Nope. Very serious. As predicted."

Not far off and closing in fast, the running lights of the drone glowed bright red, green, and white against the night sky. It flew silent and unwavering in the steady hands of its remote pilot. And on its side, branded proudly in big white letters, was the single, horrible, menacing word:

DOME.

Most of the way to Sierra by now, Logan had hoped that the four of them might enter the sprawling city undetected, that the protests they'd stirred up back in Beacon might distract authorities enough to provide some cover. But the team had made a critical mistake, and they knew it.

About twenty miles back, along the first patch of run-down outskirts near Sierra's eastern city limits, along the forgotten road that decrepit signs called "Highway 66," Daniel Peck, Hailey Phoenix, Logan Langly, and Erin Arbitor decided to make an emergency stop. Erin's fever had gotten worse, her shivering violent and her words increasingly delirious. Everyone knew she needed medicine—anything to lower her temperature, even if only for a day or two. Anything to buy her some time.

So the team decided to take the risk.

"They'll know she was here the second we buy this thing," Peck warned as Hailey stepped toward the corner store counter with a handful of nanomeds. "They'll trace her scan instantly. You know they've been watching for it."

Erin nodded in detached agreement. She was standing, but barely, and only because Logan held her up. He had his arm around her back, bouncing it now a few times, trying for a better hold. "We'll be miles away by the time they get here," he said. "And anyway, there's no way around it." If they wanted the goods, they needed Erin's Mark, simple as that. So Logan snapped his fingers in front of Erin's eyes. "Look alive, Erin. This part's all you."

And the four of them walked to the counter.

"Evening," said the store clerk. "Find everything all right?"

"Just fine," Hailey said, not looking at the man. She handed him the nanomeds and held her breath while he scanned them under the counter's Markscan.

"Your friend's not lookin' too good." The clerk nodded at Erin.

"She'll be all right," Logan said, propping her head up with his own. He grabbed Erin's hand and waved her Marked wrist under that same scanner. It beeped and flashed green. "Just fighting down a fever. These cold winter months and all, you know . . ."

"You making her pay for those meds herself?" the clerk asked, scolding him a bit.

"She insists," Logan said, but he quickly shoved his own Unmarked wrist into a deep pants pocket. And Peck and Hailey did the same.

"Well . . . bed rest," the clerk instructed. "Plenty of water." Then he pointed to the nanomeds. "And one of these pills twice a day. They won't cure anything, but they should keep the fever down."

Erin nodded distantly. Logan readjusted his hold on her. And the group hustled out without another word to anyone.

"We've sealed our fate," Peck said. "They have us now." He put the car in gear and peeled out before the store clerk could notice that these three Markless teens and their dying Marked friend had somehow gotten their hands on the last combustion vehicle in the entire Global Union.

Logan shook his head. "We're out. We're safe. That drew less attention than a robbery."

"A robbery's anonymous," Hailey said. "Markscans are not."

"No stealing," Logan said. He opened Erin's mouth and gave her two nanomed pills at once. She didn't protest. "She needed this. We had no choice. We'll deal with the next crisis when it hits us."

And Logan was right, Hailey knew. The truth was, they *didn't* have a choice. The truth was that they'd made their choice already, when each of them—Peck, Hailey, Logan—refused the Mark on each of their thirteenth birthdays, refused citizenship, refused to Pledge allegiance to General Lamson and Chancellor Cylis. They knew then what the consequences would be. They knew then that they'd never have rights. That they'd never in their lives be able to buy or sell anything, hold a job, vote, own a house, sign a contract, see a doctor, finish their education, start a family. . . . Those quaint hopes dried up the moment the world broke into its Total War; the moment it realized that Unity was necessary, that fractured cultures and incompatible views could *never* keep the peace. The kids knew all of this at the time.

But each of them knew something else too. That the Pledge was a trap. Much more than a ceremony of citizenship, it was a system designed to weed out those who didn't fit in. Flunkees were rare, maybe one in ten thousand—few enough that no one raised a fuss. DOME let families believe that their children were dead, victims of infrequent and unavoidable complications in the Marking procedure—an allergic reaction, an infection, or an unfortunate error, perhaps.

But this was not the truth. The truth was that once identified, flunkees were simply *removed*, thrown into the secret prison known only as "Acheron," where they were converted, brainwashed, crafted into soldiers . . . into the International Moderators of Peace, the IMPS, hidden enforcers of the Mark system.

Under this program, the rest of the world was free to be Unified. Protected by the very peers who otherwise might one day have betrayed them.

Logan, Peck, Hailey . . . they knew this because Logan's sister, Lily, had Pledged herself . . . and had never returned. They knew this because Peck spent the next five years piecing together what might have happened, had even warned Logan that it might happen to him next.

Peck was right. But Logan escaped.

And with all his worst fears finally confirmed, Logan had gone on to break into Acheron, had seen it with his own eyes, and had managed to break back out.

It wasn't safe for him in Beacon City any longer. It wasn't safe for any of them.

Peck, Hailey, and their friends known only as "the Dust" had used Logan as a symbol—as a martyr, willing to die in his fight against DOME. And among Markless everywhere, that symbol took hold. The news spread countrywide, through renegade radio stations and secret airwaves, and the Dust spread right along with it. The Markless were banding together. They rose up; they fought back. They brought the IMPS out of hiding. And Logan became a hero.

Erin, until that time, was as loyal to DOME as anyone,

Marked and diligent and proud of it. Her father worked for DOME, after all, was an operative for them, and until recently he and the Department had given Erin no reason to doubt their intentions. But then last month she discovered Project Trumpet . . . and everything in her world changed forever.

Erin now lay on the floor of the group's cramped car, contorted and barely conscious. The drone plane behind them encroached.

Peck pushed the pedal harder, gliding dangerously across the icy, broken road, and Logan said, "It hasn't shot us yet. It could have by now. It's close enough."

"DOME's not trying to kill us," Peck said, gripping the wheel with white-knuckle force. "They're trying to track us."

"Not very subtle about it," Hailey said. The plane blinked menacingly as it lowered to car level and followed maybe a hundred feet behind.

"They don't have to be. We're cornered."

Logan looked out over the wide-open land and the Rocky Mountains in the distance. It was a funny word, *cornered*, spoken in the middle of so much empty space.

"How could DOME even know we're the ones in here?" Logan asked. "They can't scan Erin's Mark from that distance, can they? Even if they've already traced her to the store, as far as this car goes, they'd only be guessing . . ."

Peck laughed. "Logan, they know Erin was with us in Beacon less than a week ago. And now they have her Markscan on file in a store two thousand miles away, without a single logged magnetrain ticket in between. As far as we know, this is the only private car driving on *any* road between here and Europe. What other conclusion could they reasonably come to? Of *course* we're in this car."

"So how do we hide?" Hailey asked, very nervously now. "We can't outdrive it."

Already, Logan was hunched over, grabbing at Erin's shoulders and sliding her up into the backseat. She groaned once, and her head lolled to the side. He buckled the seat belt around her. "We can try."

Hailey turned to Peck uncertainly. "Hey," she said. "Guys, seriously—"

Peck shook his head. He sighed. "Hold on," he said, and he pushed the gas pedal to the floor.

In their headlights, the broken road cast shadows on itself long into the distance. Its potholes, jutting concrete, and black, wintry ice rushed in fragments and patches toward the run-down car. Peck weaved fast between frosty cracks and scattered debris, and the drone shrunk smaller in the window behind them. For miles, it seemed they were succeeding. But Peck couldn't avoid the road's obstacles forever. Coming off a tight swerve, their back right wheel caught an old blown-out tire, and Hailey yelled, "Hold on!" as the whole car lurched forward with a panicked force.

It spun faster than it could turn. Its back wheels came up alongside its front. The driver's side plowed ahead with an ear-piercing squeal of its tires, the left wheels leading the charge against an unforgiving road, front and back together hitting a street-wide crack, catching and stopping all at once. In one continuous motion, the passenger side reared up, getting ahead of itself, flipping end over end at a staggering speed. Metal on concrete. Glass shattering. Gravity shifting. The world rolled hopelessly outside. A car full of breathless screams.

They tumbled from the road.

2

In Beacon, the citywide protests had reached a stalemate.

For weeks, Markless had marched, and chanted, and camped out on the streets. For weeks, they'd demanded rights, representation, respect, all spurred on by the truth the Dust had revealed about flunkees and Acheron and the kids who were swiped.

DOME's darkest secrets were in full view now, its Markless prison finally identified, its once-covert IMP troops forced to line the streets, make arrests, curb unrest by any means necessary . . .

For years, the Markless in Beacon had stayed mostly underground. They'd lived below the surface, huddled into communities inside an abandoned nuclear fission reactor that rested below the city, coming up only to scrounge for food or catch a glimpse of daylight. Some of them had spoken up, sure; some of them had held signs, had shared thoughts with the Marked that passed by, or gave food, or dared to stop and stare. But never before had a Markless rocked the boat. Never before had any of them surfaced with the intention of challenging the system. For years, the Markless in Beacon had been silent.

No one was silent anymore. For the first time, Markless were fighting. They were Dust. And they were not afraid.

But for each huddle that made its way street side, for each Unmarked who yelled or blocked the road, a squadron of IMPS was lying in wait. And the IMPS were fighting back.

From his quiet spot on the sidewalk hundreds of feet above, Blake leaned over, carefully considering the showdown below him. In Beacon, a five-tier system of streets connected most City Center skyscrapers at forty-floor intervals, and currently, Blake stood at the edge of Tier Two, peering over the railing at the ground level below.

From here it looked like the top of an open box of crayons: dots of colors all pressed up against one another, each one a person, each one a Markless protester. Each one Dust.

Surrounding them, completing the crayon-box likeness, were barricades—rigid right angles of makeshift hurdles and fences, put in place by IMP forces and guarded by the IMPS themselves.

Blake sighed deeply, appreciating the brief reprieve from the noise and violence down below . . . and yet Blake was on no break. He wasn't resting. He wasn't relaxing. He was preparing. And he knew the chaos would come to him soon enough.

In fact, he was counting on it.

"This one's filled with ketchup Meg swiped from the huddle, and this one here . . ." Tyler held a balloon in each hand, and he raised the right one now. "Well, I'm honestly not quite sure what's in this one. Some sludge Rusty found in the gutter between Barrier Street and the power plant, I know that much. But beyond that . . . I really couldn't tell ya. It's green, I think." Tyler frowned. "Sorta chartreuse-green."

"Chartreuse?" Jo stepped forward from behind Blake. "I wager a punch to the face that you have no idea what color chartreuse is."

"Sure I do. It's the color of what's in this balloon. You know, greeny sludge color."

"Look, will ya just drop the thing already so we can get on with this?"

"I'm trying to decide which to drop first. I'd rather see the gutter sludge splash . . . but, see, I also kinda wanna save it."

"Tyler—" Jo motioned to grab the balloons herself, but Tyler ducked quickly out of the way.

"Okay, okay—gutter sludge it is."

Tyler leaned over the second-tier railing, forty stories up, his whole torso hanging off the side, feet dangling in the air just above the sidewalk, balancing himself precariously over the ledge. He closed one eye for aim, his tongue sticking out just slightly to the side, like a master in full concentration.

"Third IMP from the corner," Tyler said. "The one with all those stupid extra badges. Don't think we've hit his squad before."

"Me neither," Blake said. "I say we go for it."

"Good game," Tyler said. So he grinned wide, and he let go of the balloon.

Blake, Tyler, Jo, Meg, Rusty, Shawn . . . these kids were the Dust. The original Dust—Peck's Markless gang—before Peck left them all to head west. Blake, fourteen years old now, had become a bit of a ringleader in Peck's absence. Joanne, fifteen, used to be Peck's right-hand girl; now she was more the enforcer. Meg, thirteen, was autistic, rescued by the Dust last July after Peck realized she was at risk of flunking her upcoming Pledge. Rusty was an orphaned six-year-old, picked up by Blake back when DOME made its raid on the Dust's old home, Slog Row, last September. Shawn was the Dust's newest member, a Markless hacker from Beacon who fell in with the rest during their Acheron breakout a month ago. And Tyler . . . well, Tyler was just a troublemaker. He grew up an orphan too, never knowing or fully comprehending life outside of Markless huddles. Then one year ago, right around the time when he could have Pledged, Tyler just sort of glommed on to the Dust for fun—and never left.

And until recently, there was Eddie, Tyler's best friend and now a painful hole in the Dust's once-inseparable group. Just a few weeks ago, Eddie was captured along with Logan and Joanne by DOME during the Dust's attempt to break Logan's sister, Lily, out of Acheron. Unlike the others, Eddie never escaped.

He was gone now.

Eddie was an IMP.

"Bull's-eye!" Tyler yelled. He jumped up and down as he did, pumping his fists in the air and soliciting high-fives from the rest of the group. "Did you *see* that?"

The balloon had hit with astonishing force, and the resulting scene down below was chaos, rapidly growing violent.

The IMP's first response, of course, had been to assume that the balloon had come from the crowd he was guarding. The sludge slathered his helmet and shoulders with a greasy green, his face smeared with goop and his uniform now looking something like pickle relish. Immediately, he'd spun around, eager for someone to hit or arrest or worse. But no obvious culprit had emerged.

Finally, the IMP's squad looked up. They stared in disbelief. They tapped their leader on the shoulder. "There," they seemed to say.

Forty stories above, Tyler stood in plain view, grinning, laughing, and waving happily as he tossed down the second balloon.

It took two and a half minutes for the IMPS to call in their underground backups and coordinate a response. This was longer than the Dust was expecting. So for about thirty seconds, Tyler was bored again.

"It better be because they're gathering *extra* reinforcements," he grumbled.

Jo sighed. "I'm sure it is."

"You ready?" Blake asked. He trained his eyes on the nearest elevator tube. It flashed red as the doors slid open. "Because here they come."

More than thirty Moderators flooded out, four full squads in total, each uniformed with precision nanocamo that flickered as it adjusted to the new environment, blending seamlessly into the colorful advertisements on the building behind them. Each sported utility belts and shoulder straps that held all types of guns, magnecuffs, gadgets . . .

The leaders—the Coordinators—wore helmets with visors that came down past their eyes and shadowed their identities. But among the rest, it was easy enough to see faces, scowls, grinding teeth, and of course, the telltale branding of an IMP—the Mark, uniquely tattooed in nanoink across each forehead.

"Freeze!" yelled the first squad's Coordinator, his uniform still goopy with Tyler's sludge. "In the name of General Lamson, we order you to stop!"

But already, the kids were running. Tier Two was the densest of Beacon's four sky levels, and the street they'd chosen as their perch was especially well connected. Blake, Tyler, Jo, Rusty, Shawn—all of them knew the plan, memorized their routes, choreographed their responses, and they moved now with the same swift certainty as the Moderators chasing them.

"Like we planned!" Blake yelled, and at the nearest intersection, he, Rusty, and Jo zigged left while Tyler and Shawn zagged right, buying valuable seconds as the squad leaders shouted commands to their troops to split in half and form two chase groups. To the left where Blake led Jo and Rusty was a narrow pedestrian walkway leading to a rare public entrance on the fortieth floor of a commercial retail building. The group sprinted straight into a multilevel clothing department store, knocking over t-shirt racks and pants and shoes as they dashed through the mazelike floors. Behind them was a trail of fabric and cloth and accessories strewn about wildly, and for all the IMPS' fancy gadgets and training, the kids managed to outrun them.

Meanwhile, Tyler and Shawn ran full-throttle through a wide alley that dead-ended against the private doorway of a skyscraper apartment building. The building was locked, but not for them. In one swift motion they ran up the wall together—one, two, three steps in quick succession—and they each grabbed with both hands onto the ledge of an open window several feet up.

"It's us!" Tyler shouted to the Markless sympathizers inside. "But the IMPS aren't far behind!" And as Tyler and Shawn pulled themselves in, the owners of the apartment darted to the window, slamming it shut and locking the latch behind him.

"Run!" they called, keeping watch through the glass, and the boys didn't stop until they were in the hallway outside and on an elevator headed for Ground Level, into the crowds, into anonymity, into safety.

Through all of this, Meg watched, focused and sentry-like, from a Tier Three sidewalk suspended even higher above. She looked on through binoculars, following all five of her friends through the streets, but paying particular attention only to the

IMP troops behind them. Meg scanned each face, one by one, scrutinizing every last detail.

This was the Dust's new routine. Seven days a week, morning, noon, and night. Tyler had made it his full-time job to torment the International Moderators of Peace. Any way he could think of, so long as he hit a new squad each time and made them call for plenty of reinforcements.

The rest of the Dust, they made it their job to keep Tyler alive.

But this wasn't just a pastime.

This was business.

"You see him?" Tyler asked Meg after the whole ordeal was over. "Anywhere?"

Meg frowned. She shook her head.

"Sorry, Buddy," Blake said, turning to Tyler. "Really—I'm . . . I'm sorry . . ."

Tyler closed his eyes. "Okay," he said, stoic and resolute. "Next time then."

Blake smiled. "Yeah, Tyler. Next time."

Because one of these days—if not this chase, then the next one, if not the next one, then the one after that . . . one of these days, the squad that they baited, or a squad called up from Acheron for reinforcement to catch Tyler . . . one of these days, that squad would include Eddie.

It had to, right? The Dust had already scanned each above-ground IMP troop they could find, and Eddie hadn't been anywhere. The only explanation left was that he was underground, out of reach but still on call for emergencies—which the Dust was more than happy to create. Because Eddie *was* an IMP now. He was one of them. And it was the Dust's job to pull him out.

The plan would work, they were sure. It had to. Because there wasn't another way to get him back. And because losing Eddie for good simply wasn't an option the Dust was willing to accept.

"Right?" Tyler asked. His eyes were red, but he refused to cry.

Blake patted his back. He smiled sadly. "That's right, buddy. We'll find him next time."

∃

Logan Langly wiped the sweat from Erin's forehead. She lay wrapped in a tattered blanket, shivering in her delirium, below a small cover of rock halfway up the side of a desert ridge.

"How's she doing?" Peck asked.

Logan frowned. "Fever just broke. For the night, at least. The nanomeds helped."

"Any injuries?"

"Not that I can tell."

"I'm fine, by the way," Hailey said, rubbing her lower back and standing off to the side. "Thanks for asking."

"I'm very glad," Peck said. He smirked, and Hailey made a face.

In the distance, the group's old car lay upside down and totaled, a good ways into the desert brush off the main road, while DOME's drone plane circled above it, lower and lower with each pass.

"It's trying to get a better look," Logan said. "Whoever's piloting that thing's not gonna be too thrilled with what's left inside."

Peck laughed. "All that tumbling, and not a single dead body. Hardly the outcome DOME could have hoped for."

"Congratulations," Hailey said sarcastically. "So we managed to trick it. For, like, five minutes. Now what?"

"Now it looks for us," Peck agreed. "It should start sweeping the area soon enough."

"We can't stay still," Erin grumbled, sitting up slowly. "We need to move."

"*You* need to rest," Logan said. "End of story." The hike here from the car had taken enough out of her already, and that was with Logan and Peck carrying her the whole way.

"I can walk," Erin said.

Logan laughed. "Yeah, right."

A few feet away, Hailey paced nervously, her hands shaking with a dull, endless frustration. "Walk, don't walk—what difference does it make? What we need is a *plan*."

"We have a plan," Peck said patiently.

"Then we need a better one."

Erin sat up, just a little. She rubbed her temples with both hands and tried hard to push back some of the pain. "Beyond this ridge is Sierra City," she said. "You can see it now. The lights, the ruins . . ." The desert to the west was black on black in all directions, but Erin was right—signs of life did sparkle among it. "And in Sierra City is Dr. Rhyne. The Trumpet documents I hacked pointed straight to him. He's there. I'm sure of it. And we need to find him."

Earlier that winter, it had been Erin who'd discovered Project Trumpet, the nanovirus designed to wipe out the Markless in the case of a rebellion. DOME had been using its Pledge process to vaccinate the Marked since the program's inception. Erin alone had hacked DOME's most secret files surrounding this, following the trail of information through one buried memo to another, all the way to the horrible truth—that Acheron *did* exist, that Logan's sister *was* inside of it, that the place was a training ground for IMPS, and that six months ago, on August 16 at 7:16 in the morning, a stealth team of those IMPS called the Trumpet Task Force had been dispatched to assassinate a group of Marked A.U. citizens already sick with the fever. Somehow, it seemed clear, Project Trumpet had finally been activated. But the experiment was a failure. Its nanovirus wasn't killing Markless. Instead, its *vaccine* was killing *Marked*. And now Erin, Marked and vaccinated herself, was the next victim to suffer the consequences.

"Dr. Rhyne was the DOME engineer who created the nanovirus all those years ago. The Trumpet documents confirm it. We're close to him now. Closer than I ever believed we could get. He *must* have a cure. He'll help us. Because it's his virus that isn't working right. It's his fault I'm sick. He'll *have* to fix it." Erin was shivering again in her blanket on the rocks. "We find Rhyne, we save lives. Millions of them. Mine included. *That's* the plan." She lay back down, fingers still pressed to her temples, absorbing the pain of a headache that wouldn't go away.

"I don't like this," Hailey said. "What if this drone is just the beginning? What if they are in Sierra *waiting* for us? What if we're walking into a trap?"

Erin shook her head. "My dad . . . he used to talk about Sierra. You know it's the tech capital of America, right? What Beacon has in economics and New Chicago has in manufacturing, Sierra has in tech. All our nano-stuff's come out of here, all our tablets, all our rollersticks and wallscreens . . ."

"So what?" Hailey said. "That just means they'll have better tools to catch us with."

"No, you don't understand, Hailey. Why is it that techies are so drawn to this place?"

Hailey shrugged.

"Less government! Fewer prying eyes. Sierra's as far as you can get from Lamson and Cylis. There isn't nearly the same level of oversight out here." Erin smiled. "My dad *hated* this place. It's practically lawless. DOME's foothold here isn't nearly what it is out east, or up in New Chicago. Same goes for the IMPS. Even without Rhyne, it'd be the perfect place for us to go next."

Peck nodded. "Many of the best minds in the world live out here, for all the same reasons Erin was saying. It'd be great for us to talk with some of them. The Sierra Library is top notch too—*chock-full* of banned books. I've been dying to check it out for years."

"DOME can try all they want," Erin said. "But once we outrun that probe down there, there's no way anyone's ever gonna find—" Erin stopped short. "What's that sound? Am I hearing things again?"

"Not hearing things," Peck said. "I hear it too."

From high in the air over toward Sierra, a low, electric hum like from some great, spinning energy ball pulsated and whirred and traveled through the sky. The four of them craned their necks back, following the soft buzz up and over to a source that must have been nearly a mile away, moving fast and just ahead of its lagging roar. The glowing blue dot lit a tiny patch of clouds as it careened up, over, and through them, and its vibration became something Logan and the others could feel just as well as hear.

"What in the world . . . ," Peck started to say, but already that soft blue dot was closing in. It seemed to travel the whole sky in just under a minute, moving fast and with the high, parabolic arc of a missile.

But it didn't *look* like a missile. It looked like an oversized blue baseball charting the course of some incredible grand slam. It wasn't flying. It was falling.

And it was headed straight for them.

Hailey turned to Erin, her expression a mix of self-righteousness and horror. "You were saying?"

"Take cover," Logan shout-whispered. "Hide!"

Within seconds, the giant ball was there, right on top of them, just a couple hundred feet above.

Logan shielded his face. Peck grimaced. Hailey held her breath. Erin pulled the blanket up to her eyes.

And then that glowing orb did something unexpected. In the last hundred feet of its free fall, short bursts of steam sprayed out from below in all directions, slowing it, aiming it, controlling the final moments of its descent. It wasn't going to crash. It was going to land.

Now just a few feet overhead, the object could be seen for what it was—a glass sphere about the size of a car, its blue glow shooting out the front like a single, huge headlight. Softly, quietly, it touched down onto the ground in the center of the rough square formed by Logan, Peck, Hailey, and Erin.

Logan held a rock in his hands. He bounced it a couple of times, preparing to throw the thing with whatever force necessary to defend himself.

A short, sliding sound escaped the giant ball, and Logan, Peck, Hailey, and Erin watched in silence as the side of it opened up.

But what stepped out wasn't DOME. It wasn't an IMP. It was a kid. No older than ten or eleven. He was tanned with dusty brown hair and freckles. He wore a nanotech tie-dye t-shirt with a pattern that swirled and moved and morphed like a vat of paint still being mixed. He took two steps forward, and promptly threw up onto the ground.

"Sorry," he said. "That always happens." Then the boy stood

up as tall as he could, balancing on tiptoes, looking down at the valley below. He squinted at the DOME probe and frowned. "You guys are the Dust, right?"

Logan stared at him. "Who's asking?"

"Oh, hey—Logan! Nice to meet you, I'm Sam." The boy stepped forward to shake Logan's hand. Logan gripped his rock tighter and made no motion to return the gesture.

The boy shrugged and pointed to Erin. "You're the hacker, right? Snooping around Dr. Rhyne's files?"

Everyone stared. For a moment, there was quiet.

"Hit a snag, I see." The boy pointed down to the car in the distance and the drone still circling above it.

"You could say that," Peck said.

The boy frowned. "A gas car. Private. Quite a useful commodity, before you went and totaled the thing." He eyed Peck and the others in succession. "Wonder where you found it . . ."

"A friend," Peck said. "It was a gift from a friend."

And in fact, this was partially true. The car had once belonged to Winston, son of the Rathbones, a megarich family out in the middle of nowhere that just two months earlier had come very close to having Peck and all his friends killed on their way out to Beacon. And they would have, too, had Winston not taken mercy on them just in time. He'd given that car—his family's one-of-a-kind prized possession—to the Dust in the hope that they might escape his family's clutches and make it the rest of the way to Beacon in one piece.

They had. But that wasn't the end of the gift's usefulness. For the past week, Peck and the others had been burning up the last of that car's trunkful of gasoline canisters like the whole thing was going out of style (which it very much had), and praying that it just might have enough life left in it to take them all the way to Sierra.

So close, Peck thought.

But the boy frowned and pulled Peck back into the present. "You *are* here to see Dr. Rhyne, though, aren't you?"

"How?" Erin asked, raising an eyebrow and trying to hide her terror. "How could you have guessed that? What exactly is it you know about us?"

The boy shrugged. "I know your best option is to come with me. I know the doctor is waiting for you. And I certainly know how impatient Dr. Rhyne can be."

"Oh yeah?" Logan said. "And what makes you think any of that?"

The boy stepped back toward the giant blue ball, inviting the rest of them inside. "Because Dr. Rhyne sent me," Sam said. "I'm the doctor's son."

4

"It's called a POD," Sam said several minutes later. "Projectile Object Delivery. Little start-up company called PopHopper began making them a couple years ago. Just a pet project, I think, but they've really caught on."

"You're not Marked," Peck said. "How are you flying it?"

"First of all, nobody's flying anything. This thing's not a plane—it's a projectile. It goes up, it comes down, and that's all there is to it. Free fall the whole time. We're a cannonball right now, nothing more.

"Second of all, this thing's not public transit. DOME has

nothing to do with it, so no Marks required. It's just a service—necessary after the earthquake destroyed all the roads around here."

"But how does PopHopper pay for any of this?"

"That's how," Sam said. He gestured around them, to the glass casing of the POD. Suddenly the whole thing fogged over, and almost the entire 360-degree interior surface became one big panoramic wallscreen. A woman walked into view, strolling through an immaculately clean household. From the sidescreen, a dog ran happily toward her, jumping up and getting paw marks all over the woman's nice, white shirt. The woman laughed, and smiled, and shook her head.

"Tired of washing your clothes? Do rubble stains get you down? Try Laundercloth—the fabric that washes itself!"

As she said it, the dog's paw marks slowly disappeared from the shirt.

"Immersive advertisements." Sam laughed. "The POD rides pay for themselves."

Below them, in the one patch of glass not hijacked by commercials, Logan could still see outside the POD. Sierra rushed by in a nauseating blur, but even from here he could tell it was like no place he'd ever seen. Ruins and new buildings intermingled, sharing the same streets, even the same foundations, as though instead of cleaning up after the earthquake, Sierra just grew through it. Like daisies sprouting from the cracks of concrete. Except here, from this height, Sierra's daisies looked awfully high tech. And the run-down concrete patches among them were simply ignored.

Below Logan and all around him, PODs sprang up from the ground like monstrous fleas, popping up and falling down, as though Sierra were the great, big back of some infested, hairless dog. Logan smiled, thinking of that. And suddenly the ground swelled up, rushing at him through the glass. Logan's stomach turned over. He entered free fall. And his first PopHopper ride came quickly to its end.

Logan, Peck, Hailey, Erin, and Sam all threw up the moment they exited the POD.

"I told you." Sam laughed, wiping his mouth. But the five of them stood now in front of the glowing blue plastic of the Sierra Science Center, and none of them gave a moment's thought to their lingering motion sickness. Before them the SSC rose only ten stories high, but its structure and context made it far more imposing than its size alone would suggest. All around it was rubble, piled two, three, four stories high in some places: enormous slabs of concrete, mounds of old brick, huge chunks of drywall, all lumped together, like a citywide memorial, a constant reminder of the earthquake that decimated the western coast ten years ago. Rising right out of those ruins was the SSC, with an architectural style all its own. With its rounded edges and bulging shape, the Sierra Science Center looked something like a beehive, complete with a honeycomb mesh that held the structure up. A glowing white pattern of wire held the building's blue-tinted, translucent tarp siding taut, but it also made the entire building supremely flexible in the case of a future earthquake or other such disaster. Even now, the building twisted and swayed a bit in the wind.

At its base, a single hexagonal tile was larger than the rest, and the tarp within it hung loosely from only a few of the wires. This was the building's entrance, and a colorfully dressed woman walked through it now.

The woman smiled at Logan and Erin and the rest. Like Sam, her clothing took on a swirling tie-dye pattern. Her ears, nose, and eyebrows were pierced and dressed with heavy rings. Her Mark was only one of many tattoos on her arms and shoulders, some of which glowed with a nanoink that shone even through the sleeves of her shirt. Her hair hung in thick brown dreadlocks, tied back with a handful of tan rubber bands.

"Thanks, Sam," the woman said casually. Then she pointed deliberately at the rest, rattling off each name in quick succession. "Peck, Hailey, Logan, and—ah, good—Erin. We are so glad you've come to join us."

Erin swallowed hard. "I'm still not sure whether we're hostages or guests," she admitted.

"Guests!" the woman proclaimed happily. "Guests in the greatest city on Earth. Please, do come in."

"And you are?" Peck asked before taking a step forward.

"Oh! Forgive me," the woman said. "You can call me Arianna. Pay no attention to the stuffy old bats you'll meet in the lab . . . no matter how many times they insist on calling me Dr. Rhyne."

TWO

CALL TO ORDER

1

*P*OP! POP! POP!

Deep below Beacon City's tangle of streets and skyscrapers and protests and politics, Acheron's training room was exploding with the fireworks of four dozen IMP-issued taser rifles. The shots crackled and whizzed and ricocheted across the space with a furious chaos, but Lily Langly never flinched. Instead, she looked on, unblinking, as Eddie Blackall gripped his own shaking gun . . . and her only emotion was shame. This boy was clumsy. He was unfocused. All around him, IMP trainees fired shot after shot of electrobullets at targets that popped out from corners, bounced up and down, rolled along on the ground . . . and through all of it, Eddie just watched.

Across the floor and surrounding him was a massive, complex obstacle course made up to look like Beacon's city streets, and on each towering wall of the place was a floor-to-ceiling projection of the City Center skyline. Superimposed on top of this was a series of scoreboards pacing each Moderator against one another by squad, ranking them all in a myriad of categories from accuracy, to firing rate, to each Moderator's ability to determine quickly the difference between Marked and Unmarked targets.

Lily's ears rang with the echoing rounds of the taser rifles before her, and she looked up at that big projected scoreboard with disgust.

Dead last. The only other trainee ever to have fallen even within spitting distance of Eddie's current score was Harry Raiman . . . and Harry couldn't even pass bed making.

"Look alive, Blackall!" Lily scowled at him as she said it, and Eddie fumbled hopelessly with the chamber of his gun. Was it jammed? Was the safety on? Lily couldn't imagine what was going through this kid's head. He reached into his shoulder strap for a new canister of electrobullets, and it rattled in his sweaty fingers before slipping out and falling to the ground.

Crack. The casing shattered. Dozens of pellets scattered across the ground, buzzing with unspent voltage.

Beside Lily, a supervising Mitigator stood, arms folded in total disgust and disbelief.

"I don't understand it," he whispered to her. "He is without a doubt the worst recruit we've had in months. What does the general see in him?"

"Moderator Blackall has a past," Lily said. "He's a catch. Right now he's our closest connection to the Dust."

"The terrorist cell? From New Chicago?"

Advocate Langly nodded. "That's the one."

"*This* is one of the great Markless traitors DOME was getting so carried away with?"

"That's correct."

The Mitigator laughed. "*Cylis,*" he said. "What on *earth* were they worried about?"

Lily looked at him out of the corner of her eye. "What does any government worry about?" She took a short breath. "Loyalty."

The Mitigator looked at her.

"These Dust kids," Lily continued. "They got swept up in something strong. This wasn't just idle dissatisfaction, not just some impudent huddle. These guys were aggressive. And, talented or not, Moderator Blackall was at the very front of that line."

Eddie knelt down to collect his pellets. They bounced and shocked him, their electric-blue lightning arcs finding his fingers and pricking them one by one.

"I've heard whispers that he's starting to doubt," the Mitigator said. "His poor performance, his attitude . . . There are Moderators that are beginning to question his very commitment to Lamson and Cylis. To the IMPS. The word they're using . . . saying he's 'backsliding' . . . except, that's impossible. Right, Advocate? No one backslides."

The Mitigator looked at her, and Lily sighed. "Technically, you're incorrect, Mitigator. Some traitors do. Over time, in certain cases, prior, misguided associations can seep back in. Memories of bad habits realign. There is a . . . a falling away. It's a terrible thing to see."

The Mitigator frowned in thought. "But . . . who do you know that's ever . . . ?"

"It doesn't matter," Lily said. "She's fixed now."

Ahead of them, Eddie's pellets sparked and popped like jumping beans as their current found his clumsy hands. And Eddie began to laugh.

Well, that does it. Lily took a decisive step toward the wall beside her. She hit a switch so hard that the impact echoed through the space. Immediately, the scoreboard overhead flickered and went out. The cityscape around them vanished. The targets froze in place. And all the lights in that cavernous room turned on in a bright, fluorescent flood of white.

"Attention!" Advocate Langly yelled, and all four squads of IMP trainees climbed out from the obstacle course and stood straight and stiff and ready for orders. Except for Eddie. Eddie was sitting on a piece of foam rubble, shaking his hand and sucking on his fingers.

"Sorry." He laughed. "They're numb. From the shocks."

But Lily was not amused. The Moderators would run laps, she ordered—two hundred of them. "One for each shock on Moderator Blackall's miserly hand."

Eddie's squad mates looked at him furiously, though none dared complain.

"Hey—last one to two hundred's a rotten egg," Eddie said, but Lily stopped him before he could take his first step.

"Not you, Moderator. You're coming with me."

Now there was a murmur among the line of Moderators. Eddie slung his rifle onto his back. For a moment he smirked, as though he'd just thought of the greatest comeback. And yet some part of him must have thought better than to share it—a rare display of self-restraint, perhaps, upon seeing the anger in Lily's eyes.

Eddie looked down and cleared his throat.

He followed Advocate Langly out of training.

2

At that same moment, on the two-hundredth floor of Barrier Street's highest skyscraper, the Beacon City Stock Exchange reeled with its own chaotic fury. It had been pandemonium on Barrier Street ever since the Union merger—what had once been capital of the western economy alone was suddenly the epicenter of the entire globe's, and the transition had not been kind to anyone involved.

No one was more aware of this than Dr. Olivia Arbitor, though it would have been hard to tell just by looking at her. Currently, Dr. Arbitor stood, resting both arms casually against the glass overlook above the B.C.S.E. trading floor, absorbing the frenzy and trying not to think about . . . well, anything at all.

A decorated professor of economics, Dr. Arbitor had transitioned from academia to public finance the moment General Lamson implemented Europe's Mark program ten years ago. Ever since, it had been her job to ensure a smooth transition between the American Union and European Union economies. For years, Dr. Arbitor had flown back and forth between Beacon City and Third Rome over in Europe, working tirelessly toward the day when the two countries might finally be one.

But just over two weeks ago, with the signing of the Global Union treaty pushed hastily through Parliament on both sides of the Atlantic, that day had arrived just a little bit too soon.

Indeed, from the perspective of the Beacon City Stock Exchange, it was a worst-case scenario: a scramble that Olivia had worked ten years to prevent. But looking down on that trading floor now, seeing the aftermath in full force, Dr. Arbitor found to her terrible surprise that frankly, amazingly . . . she couldn't have cared less.

Olivia had been fielding frantic calls all day from every corner of the Global Union, putting out economic fires and issuing press releases to what felt like every last newspaper this side of the Atlantic. "What are you doing to fight inflation?" people were asking. "What do you have to say about America's debt?" "Do you think General Lamson adequately thought through the effects this merger would have on Marked pension plans?" And on and on, the same old stuff.

In fact, unless, by some grace of Cylis, it had ended without her, Olivia was pretty sure there was another conference call going on back in her office right now, at this very minute, even as she stood out here on this quiet balcony.

So, after a few more short moments of respite, she turned around, braced herself, and walked right back into the thick of it.

"I'm sorry, what was that?" Dr. Arbitor asked as she sat back down at her desk. "'Fraid you were cutting in and out for a minute there."

The voice on the other end of the line sizzled with anger and agitation. "I said we really need you over in Third Rome—now—to pick up the pieces on Europe's end of this transition."

"It isn't my fault your Parliament pushed that G.U. treaty through before Barrier Street was ready, Bill. We'd been prepping for this merger for nearly a decade now. You're telling me you couldn't have waited another three months? I mean, what did you *expect* would happen?"

Dr. Arbitor took a deep breath and tuned out the next several things Bill said. When it seemed he was done, she shrugged absently. "Sure, Bill. Whatever you say."

"Does that mean you're getting on a shuttle? Does that mean you'll be here in the morning? Because I really need for it to mean that you'll be here in the morning, Olivia."

"I have to go, Bill. We'll talk."

"We're talking now. I'm asking for answers *now*, Liv."

Dr. Arbitor ended the call without even registering she'd done it.

And for a moment, then, she sat, staring blankly at the wallscreens of her windowless office. In front of her was a drawing, displayed electronically just as it had been every day for the past six years, sketched long ago by her daughter, Erin.

"Any word?"

The voice came unexpectedly from the doorway behind her, and Olivia jumped when she heard it. She turned in her chair and nodded when she saw him.

"Hiya, Mac. Good to see you."

"Just wondering if . . . I dunno. Just wondering if you'd heard anything, maybe."

Dr. Arbitor shook her head. She knew Mac and Erin had been close. Summers growing up, Erin spent nearly every day cooped up in this small Barrier Street office, and indeed, nearly all of that time had been spent with Mac. Mac taught Erin everything he knew about computers, about programming, about hacking . . . and he and Erin had certainly caused enough trouble together to prove it. "No sign of her," Dr. Arbitor said. Then she frowned, and she closed the door on him.

Two months, now. Erin Arbitor had been gone for nearly two full months. Just right up and disappeared.

Olivia was beginning to believe she'd simply never see her daughter again.

Charles Arbitor, the professor's estranged husband, had long worked as a secret agent for DOME. When Erin first ran away back in December, just off into the night like it was no big deal, Charles spent every last one of his office's available resources trying to find her. He leveraged every last ounce of influence, cashed in every last favor owed, tried every last thing he could think of to get his daughter back.

But then the whispers started. The rumors of Markless uprisings brewing around the country, standing up to the Union, standing up for the swiped. And those whispers became shouts . . .

And every last one of those shouts traced back to Erin.

In the end, all that effort Charles had spent getting DOME to investigate his daughter had served only to reveal one basic, horrible fact: Erin Arbitor was a traitor. By using the hacking skills her own mother had encouraged, *Erin* was the thorn that had uncovered all DOME's greatest secrets. She wasn't just gone, it turned out. She was a fugitive. And as long as General Lamson was still in charge of DOME, Charles knew she couldn't come back.

So after all the Arbitors' efforts, after all the energy they spent trying to find her, Dr. Arbitor's husband, Charles, now found himself in the unbearable position of having to *undo* his work. Of having to throw DOME *off* the trail. Of trying everything he could think of to keep Erin as far away as possible from all the people best equipped to help bring her back.

To find Erin through DOME would be to kill her.

So now a terrible race was on. The Arbitors had to find their daughter first. And through all of it, the only thing Olivia could do was worry.

Dr. Arbitor's tablet rang again, and for a long while she contemplated not even picking it up. What could one more stupid call possibly matter?

It rang seven times before she finally answered.

"Yeah?" she said. But her eyes went wide when she heard the voice on the other line. It was her husband. Not some financial something or other. Not some politician. It was the father of her missing daughter. And he sounded more worried than she'd ever heard him. Dr. Arbitor turned the video feed on. She could see his face now, over the connection. It was so stripped of life, it looked broken. Like the video connection itself was faulty.

But no. It wasn't the connection. That was just the state of things.

"Been trying to reach you for hours," Mr. Arbitor said. "You need to get better at returning my calls."

"Yeah, well . . . I've been busy."

"Look," Mr. Arbitor said. "You and I—our differences . . . they'll keep."

"What's that supposed to mean?"

"It means I may need your help on this."

"Help on what? What? What's going on?"

Charles Arbitor sighed. "Things just took a turn," he said. "We're losing."

"Losing what?"

"The race." There was a pause over the connection. "DOME's just found our daughter."

⅂

The elevator ride between Advocate Langly and Eddie Blackall was tense and quiet all the way until it came to a stop, at which point Eddie jumped, hitting the floor so hard that his knees buckled.

"Whoa!" he shouted. "That was a good one!"

Lily looked at him sharply, but Eddie didn't seem to mind.

"Have you ever noticed that? On elevators. If you're going down and you jump just as it stops moving, you'll slam into the ground. Do it as they're going up, and you'll float for a second."

Lily was silent.

"Momentum." Eddie smiled. "It's because of momentum."

The elevator doors opened to a vast room full of desks and nothing else. On each desk was a helmet.

Lily gestured into it. "Level Six."

And the smile on Eddie's face vanished at once.

"Wait, what is this?" he asked. "I've done this already. You've done—" Eddie was panicking now. "You've done this to me already."

"Last time you were here for treason," Lily said. "Level Nine. This is Six."

All the humor in him was gone. "What's Six?"

"Heresy. To disrespect training is to disrespect the IMPS. To disrespect the IMPS is to disrespect General Lamson and Chancellor Cylis. And that, Moderator Blackall, is heresy."

Lily pushed him down the path between two endlessly long lines of desks, buried far below the surface of Beacon City. The Advocate's strides were so fast and confident, Eddie had to step double-time not to fall.

"But you can't. You can't just . . . This is torture!" Eddie pleaded. "Please! You *can't!*"

Advocate Langly raised an eyebrow.

"Do you know the ranks of the IMPS, Moderator Blackall?"

"Yes. No. Wait, I'm pretty sure—"

Lily stopped him. "Moderator—that's you. Then Counselor. Then Mitigator. Then Coordinator. Those are the four levels, in order, of the subservient ranks. From there, we have Advocates—that's me—then Champions, then Presiders, and then Deciders. Those are the Controlling Ranks. They give the orders to the subservients. And last, of course, is the general. General Lamson."

"So then how come when we Pledge, we Pledge to Cylis? If our highest rank is the general, then why in the world aren't we Pledging to *him*? I mean, who's actually supposed to be in charge here? How can I be the picture of loyalty if I don't even know who it is I'm supposed to be loyal *to*?"

Lily smiled and sidestepped the question. "*You*," she said, "are subservient. You are the *lowest* of the subservients. And I fail to see what about this is confusing to you." She frowned. "*I*, meanwhile, am a Controller. There are not many of us. None have yet even made it to the rank of Decider. None in the world.

"Now, Moderator Blackall, because you were stupid enough to implicate me in your futile attempt at a break-in last month, I've been assigned the thankless task of monitoring your worthless training progress. And do you know what I've seen? I've seen a little Dusty miser who's managed to actually get *worse* with each passing day. I've seen a troublemaker who wakes up each morning a little less *fixed*. A little less *loyal*. And a whole lot less serious. You began with such promise! And now look at you—you're a worm! Writhing around, claiming small victories with each passing joke. And thinking . . . *what*? That if you backslide far enough, we'll just let you go? We'll just give up? Just open Acheron's door and let you run back up to your little skinflint friends in the Dust?"

Eddie was silent.

"No! We will *fix* you. We will *Revise* you! Just as we did the first time. Just as we'll do every time. As many times as it takes for Revision to stick. Do you understand me, Eddie?"

Eddie looked into Lily's eyes with open terror.

"I very much *can* do this," the Advocate told him. "And you very much will obey."

Eddie pointed to his forehead with a single, shaking finger. "But I Pledged. I'm Marked. I did this already. I've already Pledged!"

Lily shook her head. "A Pledge is not a promise, Moderator Blackall. It's a way of life. And you backslid. This is what happens when you backslide."

Eddie was very serious now. Precisely as serious as the situation demanded.

"Advocate. Advocate, it's me. Eddie. Your brother's friend. We came here to rescue you, back in December. It wasn't a 'break-in.' It was a rescue mission. I . . . I risked everything to rescue you. Your name is Lily Langly. You're a good person. You may not remember it. But I know that you are. And you don't have to do this!"

Lily showed no sign of hearing him. Instead, she pushed Eddie down onto an open desk, and as he spoke, she slipped the BCI helmet over his head and face. The brain-computer interface. The total immersion torture. It would last as long as it needed to last. It would last until Eddie was broken. Until he recognized the truth. That his was a great and powerful country, led by great and powerful men. And that defending this country was a very serious honor, indeed.

His final words were muffled. ". . . have to do this!" barely even made it out of the helmet.

"On Level Nine your punishment was the frozen lake," Lily said, latching the helmet's lock. "But Level Six is fire." She hesitated. Then quickly, sadly, under her breath, she added, "Be grateful. Trust me. Level Six isn't quite as bad." She closed her eyes when she turned the thing on.

She squeezed them tighter. Even the thick, metal helmet wasn't enough to snuff out Eddie's screams.

4

DOME's Beacon headquarters was not the architectural marvel that New Chicago's Umbrella was out west. There, it was a glass-floored disk atop a fifty-story spire, totally unique and imposing. Here, it was an office building, just the middle twenty floors of your average, pass-right-by-it skyscraper. Below it were a couple of poorly managed nonprofit organizations. Above it were the annex offices of a small European bank.

In Beacon, the Department of Marked Emergencies preferred to keep a low profile; its agents hid in plain sight. And it was in this way that the headquarters avoided the worst of the Markless protest's wrath, for the Markless simply didn't know where to aim.

Not all of the offices inside Beacon's DOME headquarters were as dreary as the building's outside might have suggested, of course—some had nice windows, others good light and plenty of space. But Charles Arbitor's was practically a closet.

Ever since he'd been reassigned to Beacon after the botched raid he led against the Dust back on a Midwestern farm in December, the perks of Mr. Arbitor's job had rapidly dried up. No longer did Mr. Arbitor have any agents under his command. No longer did his day-to-day activities include detective work, or even fieldwork. These days, Mr. Arbitor shuffled documents on a low-res, hand-me-down tablescreen, slogging through one menial task after another and taking orders from office men who just this past fall would have begged to serve under his command.

And then a month ago the news arrived of Erin Arbitor's treasonous crimes.

Mr. Arbitor wasn't fired. But the menial tasks got much, much worse.

For his part, Charles Arbitor never complained. He knew precisely what kind of thin ice he was on, and the last thing he wanted to do was draw attention to himself as he secretly did everything he could to throw DOME off Erin's trail. But last night, when the word came around about DOME's current lead on Erin's whereabouts out west near Sierra, Mr. Arbitor realized he couldn't keep quiet anymore. Presently, with his tie fixed and his breath held and his hair brushed carefully back, he was walking to DOME's Beacon headquarters main office. And he was knocking on the door.

"Come in," said the woman through the frosted glass.

Charles Arbitor turned the knob slowly. "I'm sorry to bother you, ma'am."

"It's no trouble, Charles. What can I do for you?"

Mr. Arbitor cleared his throat and took a step toward the desk. "Nothing, really, ma'am, I just . . . Any further update on the Erin Arbitor situation?"

Head Agent Samantha Tate looked at Charles with some strange mix of pity and irritation.

"Not since the update you received—what was it, now—fifteen minutes ago?" She smiled. "But don't worry. It's only a matter of time before we move in."

Mr. Arbitor took a deep breath. "Ma'am," he said gingerly. "You know I hate coming here like this. You know I hate even to bring this up, but . . . well . . ." He chose his words carefully. "In light of all of this . . . have you ever considered the possibility that, perhaps, there's a good explanation for Erin's criminal behavior?"

"Of course there's an good explanation," Tate said. "She fell in love with a criminal. What, you think Logan Langly and the rest of those Dust traitors haven't rubbed off on her by now?"

"Sure," Mr. Arbitor said. "Sure, yes, that's what I've always thought too. Except . . . the thing is, ma'am . . . Erin had been working *with* us. The whole time. She was *helping* us. Helping us find the Langly boy, doing everything she could to reason with him . . . right up until the moment she disappeared. I honestly believe Erin was on DOME's side." Mr. Arbitor sighed. "I guess I just don't see where her sudden change of heart might have come from, unless a good reason came along with it."

Tate shrugged impatiently. "So what are you suggesting, hm? Go on. Out with it."

"Nothing in particular, I suppose." Mr. Arbitor looked bashfully at his feet. "It's only that, when I came to work for DOME, it was my understanding that our mission here was to promote Unity and peace."

"Of course."

"And now out of the blue we're told, ten years later, that our own General-in-Chief Lamson has been assembling a flunkee army of IMPS this whole time? I mean, what kind of government builds an army with another country's leader? No matter how friendly their heads of state are, you have to agree, it's more than a little strange."

Tate sighed. "The chancellor has always been an ally, Charles. You know that. Our movement toward a Global Union has been well-known—anticipated, even—for quite some time. Its leaders' shared ownership of the IMPS is perfectly consistent, in light of that."

"Okay," Charles said. "But what does a *Global* Union need an army for? Who are they planning to fight? Wasn't the G.U. Treaty ratified in order to *end* wars and violence and conflict? Wasn't that the point of all of this?"

"The IMPS are not soldiers, Charles. They're Moderators. The 'P' stands for Peace."

"I know that," Mr. Arbitor said meekly. "But we can call them whatever we want—the fact is, they're Pledge process flunkees who have been trained to fight. *Flunkees*, Tate! I was told flunkees were a myth!"

"And so was I."

"Then both of us were duped! Right along with everyone else in this office. And the *only* reason we know that now is because of Erin."

"Everything she's done has been illegal, Charles. Everything."

"I know that, ma'am. I just . . . What *else* don't we know? What if there's more, even, than Acheron and the IMPS? And what if Erin knows it? If there's even a chance that someone within our ranks is working at cross-purposes with our department's *stated* mission of Unity and peace . . . and if Erin has discovered that truth . . . . She'd be a *hero*, ma'am. Not a traitor."

Head Agent Tate lowered her eyes and looked down at her desk for some time. "Look, Charles. I'm going to level with you. I have a daughter too. What you must be going through right now . . . I can't even imagine. And, hey—this IMPS bombshell blindsided me just as much as it did everyone else in this office. But the fact is, Charles, you're an agent of the Department of Marked Emergencies. And right now, your daughter's made her way into the middle of a very big emergency. Sitting here, hoping that her intentions are good . . . it's missing the point. Current intelligence states that Erin Arbitor has acted treasonously. I have orders to take her in, as soon as possible, for questioning. It's for the security of the Global Union that I do that, Charles. You must understand that."

"I do," Mr. Arbitor said. "I do." There was a long pause between them. "And that's why I came here today to request that I be assigned to her case."

For a moment, Head Agent Tate only stared. "Charles, you have to know that's a horrible idea. How could I possibly expect you to act impartially on this?"

"Because you know me, ma'am. You've asked me to jump and I've jumped. You sent me out west to find Peck and his Markless threat in Spokie, and I went. You called me back here, and I came. I'm as loyal to this department as any agent's ever been." He stood straighter as he said it. "At the end of the day, if my daughter's broken laws, then I expect her to pay the price for that just as much as anybody else. It's my job to protect the Marked against the Markless. That's what I came here to do."

Tate nodded slowly. "Then I admire your intentions," she said. "Even if it wouldn't be professional of me to trust them." She shrugged. "I'm sorry, Charles. But whatever happens once we have Erin in custody, I want you as far away from it as possible. My answer is no."

Agent Tate sat back in her chair, clasping her hands behind her head and leaning into them. She ran her tongue around her teeth, waiting for Charles to speak.

"Understood, ma'am," Mr. Arbitor said. "I apologize for wasting your time." But he couldn't bring himself to look at her as he went to let himself out.

"Charles," the head agent called as Mr. Arbitor opened her office door.

He stopped but didn't turn. "Yes, ma'am?"

"I will see to it that Erin's treated fairly. You have my word on that."

Mr. Arbitor stood for a moment, his back still to his boss.

He said nothing.

He closed the office door softly behind him.

5

Lily was late. Teeth clenched and eyes narrowed, she walked fast through Acheron's winding bowels as though leaning headfirst into some stormy wind. Disciplining Eddie had put her behind schedule, and she resented him for that. An assembly among the Controlling Ranks was not something to which one was tardy. For any reason. Ever.

She exhaled sharply and picked up the pace, and red lasers in the walls flashed and scanned her Head Mark as she approached the auditorium. Its entrance opened automatically. She stepped inside and quickly found her seat.

"Down to the wire, Advocate. Presider's just about to begin."

It was that smug Champion who'd said it. Seating order never changed at these Roll Rank Assemblies, and Lily had been expecting an earful. Even if she hadn't been late, this guy surely would have found something to reproach. He always did—it was a matter of what, not if. But Lily hated giving him a reason, all the same.

"I had a Moderator needing Revision," Lily said simply. "It couldn't wait."

"Acknowledged," the Champion said, as though he had any real power over her.

He didn't, in fact. Their squads' chains of command had

nothing to do with each other's, and on some level, the Controlling Ranks were supposed to be peers anyway. But the Champion sure did enjoy his title.

No matter, Lily thought. And she told herself she'd remember this when the day came that her own rank leapfrogged his.

"So anyone here have any idea what this Roll Rank's all about? It's hardly the first of the month."

Around her, the auditorium buzzed with the speculation of over a thousand eager Controllers. Roll Rank meetings—IMP jargon for the assemblies among the Controlling Ranks—had always been monthly; Lily couldn't even remember the last time a special session had been called.

"Must have something to do with the merger," the Champion said. "I'm sure Council is anxious to address the rumors."

Lily raised an eyebrow. *What rumors?*

"All right, Controllers, call to order!" the Presider boomed from the stage as the Council streamed in behind him. "Simulcasts, are you with us? New Chicago out west? Gulf Bay down south? We all together?"

On the walls of the auditorium were one-to-one scale projections of the lecture halls at Acheron's mirror sites across America, giving the impression from where Lily sat that all three audiences were assembled together in the same gigantic space. There was a general assent among the ranks in the projections. Everyone was here.

"Good," said the Presider, although this was just a formality. Lily was quite certain that Council knew full well before walking out on stage that every assigned seat in all three assembly halls was filled. The active Markscans on each seat back confirmed it. One simply did not miss Roll Rank.

"Then let us begin," the Presider said. "First of all, allow me to say that, in light of the ongoing Markless riots across Beacon and New Chicago, I'd like to keep today's meeting brief; I know how eager all of you must be to return to your positions. Marked citizens across America are thanking you for your outstanding moderation of the peace in our streets, and the last thing I want to do is distract you from your duties to them." The Presider nodded quickly, as though punctuating his own selflessness. "That being said, our Council has assembled us here today because, concurrent with these trying Markless protests above ground, there is a matter that we feel requires additional attention from us right down here below."

The Presider lifted his arms. "Controllers. The dawn of a new era is upon us. An era without borders, without violence, without the very concept of 'difference' itself. Nationality, culture, religion, perspective . . . I speak to you today from a world's stage in which all of these divisions are no more.

"Unity!" the Presider said. "Finally! Unity."

A wave of applause swept through the house, but Lily couldn't help noticing a certain shuffle among the seats around her. A certain discomfort, perhaps, accompanying each clap. What was it these IMPS knew that she didn't?

"Advocates, Champions, fellow Presiders . . . Fourteen days ago, our long-awaited Global Union became a permanent reality. The integration of East and West is now complete. And understandably, this has led many of you to wonder, 'Well? What does our new Unity mean for *me*?'" The Presider paused. "An excellent question." And the Presider stepped away from his podium, pacing down toward the front of the stage to speak now more directly with the IMPS in the audience. "First of all, Controllers, allow the

Council and me to reassure you: At the moment, our chain of command remains unchanged. Standard Operating Procedure remains unchanged. Your day-to-day activities remain unchanged.

"You will not become the subordinates of our European brethren. You will not be receiving mixed signals from your superiors on account of the impending two-head system between General Lamson and Chancellor Cylis. Your roles in the world will not be reduced to 'glorified police officers' or 'relief aid missionaries' or whatever else your peers have been saying in these last few weeks. Our new perfect Unity does *not* make our forces any less relevant today than they were prior to the ratification of this great Global Treaty.

"In fact, Controllers—quite the opposite.

"While we recognize that the Articles of Unification are a work in progress, and while it is true that they do not yet fully address all foreseeable details of the impending East-West IMPS integration, it is critical for each of you to understand that your job, both to your fellow IMPS and to the Marked citizens you have Pledged to protect, is the same now as ever. Our goals are unchanged, our stature is unchanged, our roles are unchanged—"

There was a growing murmur now, around the lecture hall.

"And, for the time being, any speculation you might have heard suggesting otherwise is baseless, reckless, and absolutely without place among our ranks. Is that clear?"

In unison, all three auditoriums replied, "Yes, sir." But it did little to cut the tension in the air.

"In many ways, Controllers, this integration is the ultimate fulfillment of every IMP's original and, to this day, fundamental purpose. Since our inception, we have always Pledged loyalty to the great Chancellor Cylis in Europe. We have always regarded him as our one true savior, as the man who pulled us up from the ashes of the Total War and the terrors of our former, Unmarked lives. And now, Controllers, finally—all of us will have the honor of serving under this great leader directly.

"We have always owed a debt of thanks to our brothers and sisters in the European Moderators of Peace. Their exemplary institutional model made our own success possible. It will be a privilege to work more closely with them. And at present, there is no evidence whatsoever suggesting that any of this will adversely affect the rank, status, or responsibilities of any Controller in this room. Therefore, the Council and I have called you here today to let it be known, in no uncertain terms, that effective immediately, any public or private display of doubt, inflexibility, or pessimism regarding the impending merger of our Union's great East-West IMP system will be classified as destructive rumormongering, and it will be heresy punishable by a stay of any length necessary in the helmets of Level Six."

A silence spread through the house like ice crystals across water.

"Now. Any questions?"

Lily expected not. The consequences, already, were clear. And yet, several rows in front of her and over to her left, one brave Champion surprised her.

"I have a question, sir."

For a moment, the Presider just stared. Already, the Council behind him was whispering, and IMP guards at the back of the auditorium began to shift and prepare.

But finally, the Presider answered, glancing down at his

podium first to see its tablescreen's display of the Champion's personal Markscan. "All right, Champion. This Council welcomes your interest."

The Champion took a deep breath, perhaps gathering his resolve.

"Presider . . . for weeks now, the official story from on high is that everything among our ranks will be business as usual. Your statements today confirm this, and I am glad for it. But the fact remains that you still haven't told us who is actually in charge here. The general? Or the chancellor?"

"As I've said, Champion, both men will be—"

"Yes, I know what you've said. And I understand that your answers will suffice most of the time. But, Presider—there simply has to be one, ultimate leader. What if there's a disagreement between the general and the chancellor? What then? Whose orders would we follow? Will the International Moderators of Peace remain neutral in cases of discordant command? Or does one vote supersede the other? How is no one considering this? It is imperative that we know the answer!"

The Presider grimaced a bit before answering. But finally, he said, "Champion, I can assure you—there is absolutely no reason to believe that Lamson and Cylis will *ever* be anything but *completely Unified*. Any suggestion to the contrary is an outrageous speculation, and there is simply no place for it in this assembly hall. There *will not* be disagreement—"

"Yes, but what if there *is*?"

"There won't be. End of story."

Behind him, the Council members nodded. Quietly, IMP guards descended upon the questioner. The Controllers around him sat rigid, staring at the ground. The Presider smiled. "Thank you, IMPS. That is all for today. Controllers dismissed." And the meeting ended as abruptly as that.

Coming out of Roll Rank, Lily found herself walking slowly, aimlessly through Acheron's winding halls. She'd been blindsided by the clear undercurrent of division over Global Unity. And even more so by the suggestion that Lamson and Cylis could ever be anything but totally United. For several minutes she walked, wondering how these developments changed things.

But her train of thought had not gone far before a lone man stepped forward, weaving in front of her against the current of Controllers as the assembly's crowd dispersed.

"Advocate Langly?" the man said.

"Yes?" Lily froze. This man was no IMP. But she recognized him, all the same. His was the last face she expected to see in these halls. Immediately, cold sweat beaded at her hairline and down her back.

"Advocate, my name is Michael Cheswick, former director of DOME's Umbrella out west in Spokie."

"I remember, sir." How could she forget the man who'd assembled the Trumpet Task Force last summer? How could she forget the man who'd personally ordered the murder of nearly two dozen innocent Marked at Lily's hands? She nodded now and saluted him, but it took much of her willpower to do so.

"Quite a remarkable few months, huh, Advocate Langly?"

Lily nodded. "Please forgive my surprise, sir. I . . . I didn't know you'd been transferred to Beacon."

Michael Cheswick nodded. "When the riots began." He

laughed. "Oh, I don't work *here*, of course, in Acheron! No, no. I work with the general, in the Capitol Building. One of several advisors, made useful by my knowledge of Trumpet, as I'm sure you understand." He gestured ahead. "Please. Advocate. Will you walk with me?"

Lily hesitated. She wanted to be very far away from this man. Slowly, she shook her head. "I'm afraid I'm occupied, sir. I have a Moderator in Revision, and it's important that I check in on him. So if you'll excuse me, with your permission—"

"Permission denied, Advocate. This matter is urgent."

Lily swallowed. "The Moderator's condition should take precedence," she said. "Excess time in a helmet can make a person fragile. My work with him, really . . . it's time sensitive. It can't be interrupted."

Cheswick looked at her, mouth slightly open, one eyebrow raised. He laughed a mean laugh. "By Chancellor Cylis, it can."

THREE

CONNOR GOODY
TWO-SHOES

1

CONNOR GOODMAN SAT CROSS-LEGGED ON his chair at the fold-up card table in his parents' basement, contemplating his next turn and thinking about how this used to be more fun.

"Your move," he said. But Sally wasn't paying attention.

"Hey, you all right, Sally?" Steve asked. "You seem pretty bummed."

In an era of virtual reality and nanotech, the three of them had always loved playing tablescreen games, and Mark-opoly in particular had long been Sally's favorite. But right now her heart just wasn't in it. She touched the random number generator and slid her avatar four spaces across the glass, but it was clear to the boys that she was only going through the motions.

"Come on, you've been quiet all afternoon," Connor said, taking his turn. And that was true. She'd even turned down the snacks Connor's mother had brought in for them. "And you *never* turn down peanut butter."

But Sally only frowned. She looked at him scoldingly. "You could've hit me hard with that move just now, Connor. I thought for sure I'd set you up."

"Yeah, why didn't you take it?" Steve asked.

"There were other good moves," Connor said.

But Sally wasn't having it. "You're throwing the game. You can't just let me win because you think you should be feeling sorry for me. It's condescending."

Connor shrugged. "I'm just trying to be nice."

"Sure." Sally laughed meanly. "Right. For a second there, I forgot I was playing Connor Goody Two-Shoes."

Connor winced when she said it. *Wow,* he thought. *Something must really be bothering her.* His name, of course, was Connor Goodman, and though many of the kids in Lahoma had taken to calling him Connor Goody Two-Shoes ever since he'd won the General's Award, Sally Summers never had. She knew how much he hated it. She was mindful of that. And anyway, she and Steve were barely any less stand-out themselves.

In school, Connor, Steve, and Sally were at the top of the heap. No one in the ninth grade—or in *any* grade, for that matter—had a better average, with Connor at a 100 percent, and Steve and Sally tied at 98.

But it wasn't just that the three of them were the smartest kids at Lahoma High. It was that their teachers loved them.

Why, just a couple of months ago, the day before winter break and the start of the Inclusion Day festivities, it was Connor who flailed his hand wildly in his seat at the front of the class. And it was Connor who reminded his teacher that so far, she had forgotten to give her class any homework assignments over break.

Steve and Sally were relieved when he said it. They'd been thinking the same thing all afternoon, and Steve had started to fidget with guilt. That was just the kind of students they were.

"Well, anyway, the boardwalk is now Marked territory," Steve said, dragging his own avatar across the tablescreen and trying feebly to lighten the mood. "Better pay up if either o' you land on it."

This was the closest thing to trash talk that ever went down in the Goodmans' gray-carpeted basement. But Sally still wasn't having it.

"So what's your big General's trophy doing hidden away down here?" she said, pointing to the corner and stubbornly pressing forward with her Connor Goody Two-Shoes line of attack. "I mean, what gives? If *I* had that thing, I'd sleep with it under my pillow."

Connor laughed sheepishly. "Well, it's really not that big a deal," he said.

But the truth, of course, was that it *was* a big deal. The truth was that Connor's General's Award was a very big deal, indeed.

It should be no surprise, perhaps, that a kid nicknamed Connor Goody Two-Shoes would be a model citizen, famous all across his modest Lahoma town. President of the Lahoma student body, captain of the baseball team, first chair tablet in the Lahoma Electronic Orchestra, and in both of the last two years since he'd become eligible, recipient of the Town Hall Award for Most Distinguished Marked Community Service. Connor was even known for his volunteer work over at the Markless huddles just outside of town, back before all those misers for some reason decided to forfeit any leniency and started causing trouble this past fall.

It didn't matter that Lahoma itself was a small, sleepy stretch of streets, too far out in the middle of the American State to be considered even a suburb of any of the three urban centers. It didn't matter that it was only just slightly too big to be considered a ghost town. And it didn't matter that in the last few months, everything in this measly place had begun to fall apart. The fact was, within his small pond, Connor Goody Two-Shoes was growing up to be a very big fish.

But still none of that had prepared Lahoma for the honor bestowed upon it last September, when the general-in-chief of the then-American Union (now American State, one half of the great G.U.) arrived *himself* to recognize how truly superlative Connor was by awarding him the first-ever General's Award for Marked Excellence, Promise, and the American Dream.

"That award was supposed to make you a *hero*," Sally said sarcastically. "And you think it's 'not that big a deal'? There are kids in this town who'd give anything just to hold it."

Connor didn't turn away from the game board. There was something very much the matter with Sally, that was clear, but it was no excuse for her to take whatever it was out on him. "You know what, Sally? You want it? Go ahead—it's yours. Take it home with you, if you'd like. I'd just as soon never see the cheap thing again." Just talking about it—even in the privacy of his own basement and in the company of his closest friends—made Connor blush with a horrible guilt.

"Well, it's anything but cheap," Sally piled on. She was mad. And she loved the sudden sense that she was making Connor madder. "The whole thing's made of platinum. Marked money can't even buy something as nice as that trophy."

"Your move," Connor said forcefully.

But Sally wouldn't let it go.

"Hey, man, what's your problem? Is Connor Goody Two-Shoes really so wonderfully modest that he'd sooner disrespect a General's Award than admit he's a rising star? I mean, I'm just *so sorry* for you and your inconveniently perfect life . . ."

Connor shook his head. He was hot with shame. But what could he say? He couldn't say anything about his life. He couldn't say that the whole General's Award honor was just a big sham, no more than an elaborate excuse for Lamson to travel to Lahoma and talk with Connor's parents without raising suspicion. He couldn't say that he himself wasn't even worthy of knowing that much; that he'd found it all out only after being held at gunpoint just for looking into it. And he *certainly* couldn't say what Lamson's big meeting with the Goodmans was actually all about.

So instead he just said, "You're right, Sally. I'm sorry. I didn't mean it like that. I was being self-centered. And it was belittling of me to try to help you win our stupid, miserly game of Markopoly, just to cheer you up from this horrible, disgusting, foul mood you so clearly seem to have fallen into." He walked over to the trophy and picked it up. "You happy now? I'll put this in my room the second we're done down here. A moment that I'd welcome, by the way—anytime now."

Sally folded her arms across her chest. "Leave me alone, Connor."

"Just tell us what's wrong!"

There was a long pause. Sally sighed. "My dad was laid off today," she said flatly. "We're gonna have to sell the house."

"Oh *Cylis*," Steve cursed.

"Yeah."

Connor put down the trophy. He turned off the tablescreen. Mark-opoly could wait.

"It just keeps getting worse and worse," she continued. "Without the mill, there just isn't enough work in this town."

"We still have the mill," Connor reassured.

"In what way? Connor, Lahoma hasn't made it rain in months! There's nothing to *do* over there. My dad was in charge of handling shipments. What kind of shipments are there to handle when we haven't launched all winter? Those silver iodide canisters are piling up in a warehouse! They don't need him there for *that*. How long can they possibly pay a guy for twiddling his thumbs?"

Connor was silent. The fact was, Sally's family wasn't the first to be hurt by the technical problems at Lahoma's weather mill this past winter. The whole town's economy had been built around that complex, and without it functioning properly, Lahoma's families were falling out of work right and left. The town had shrunk to three-quarters its former size in just the last six months alone. *Everyone* was hurting.

Steve cleared his throat. "Actually," he said. "I don't know if this'll make you feel better or worse, Sally, but . . . I think I might actually know something about why the mill's been on the fritz so often these last six months."

"Because it's made from cheap, European Union technology?" Sally asked scornfully. Clearly she'd been listening to her father's nightly rants.

"'Fraid not," Steve said. He frowned. "You know how my dad's the head of security over there?"

"Sure—he's one of the lucky few still working. Along with Connor's charmed parents, of course."

Steve sighed. "Well, anyway. Recently, Dad's actually been

saying . . ." He bit his lip. "He's been saying it's starting to look like sabotage."

"*What?*" Sally's jaw nearly dropped to the floor. "*Cylis!* Who in the world would do something like that?"

"I don't know. I'm—hey, look, I probably didn't even hear him right. It's pretty crazy to think about. But if it *is* true . . . and if my dad *can* find the person responsible for it . . . well . . . well, then maybe he can bring the mill back online." Steve shrugged. "I mean, now that he's looking into it—who knows? If the whole thing's over soon, your dad might even be able to get his job back before you have to move."

For a moment, Sally was speechless. "Thank you," she said finally. "Thank you for telling me."

She turned the tablescreen back on and swiped at the random number generator, eagerly taking her turn. Steve smiled.

But Connor didn't very much feel like playing anymore.

2

In Appalachia, half a continent away, the night had already fallen, crisp but pleasant. Its edge had worn from those sharpest points back in January, and Dane Harold walked now along the familiar mountain trail without so much as a shiver. "Spring is coming," he said to Hans, and Hans nodded slowly in the starlight.

"Means it's time to start worrying about crops," Hans said. "Our food stores are low. We'll need a good harvest this year if we plan to survive through another winter."

Dane watched his shoes shuffle against the roots and dirt, and he walked quietly for a moment. "I know I'm a burden to you and

Tabitha," he said finally. "I know you hadn't planned on another mouth to feed."

"You're no burden," Hans said. He stopped and put his hand on Dane's shoulder. "You're a good kid. And we like having you."

In December, nearly two months ago now, Dane Harold, Logan Langly, and Hailey Phoenix had passed through the Village of the Valley on their way between New Chicago and Beacon. The village was an anchor point along the Unmarked River—that secret, nationwide network devoted to helping Markless travel and survive outside the parameters of Union society—and it was village-dwellers Hans and Tabitha who had taken the Dust in and pointed them the rest of the way to Beacon.

For Logan and Hailey, the stay was short-lived. But for Dane, the Village of the Valley had become a new and welcoming home. The Markless radio tower they maintained—and, specifically, Dane's manning of it—had proven to be a key link in the network that made December's Markless uprisings possible. Dane alone bridged the gap between Beacon and New Chicago, and it had been his own broadcasts, in concert with Logan's grandma's and Hailey's mom's out west, that had sparked the Markless protests that continued to this day. Dane was proud of that. To be needed like that. And anyway, after so many years spent cooped up in his parents' mansion back in Spokie's posh Old District, the simple life of the valley suited him.

"I'll pull my weight around here come time for the harvest," Dane said to Hans now. "I'll work more than I'll take—you'll see."

But Hans just smiled. He walked on. And the two of them rounded the bend of the wooded trail.

"This is the first of our farming valleys," he said as the trees opened up into a wide field. "I know you've seen it from above, many times, on your walk to the radio tower. But I need you to see it now as a farmer sees it. I need you to get your hands dirty. I need you to understand how it works.

"Most Markless across the countryside are subsistence farmers. We here in the Village of the Valley are no different. We grow what we need in order to feed ourselves; no more and no less. It's how we survive outside of the Union, without the conveniences of the Mark. It's our entire way of life.

"And it's good work," Hans continued. "It's satisfying to taste for yourself the fruits of your labors. But it's tenuous too. We live year to year. And one bad harvest would kill us."

Dane looked around, noticing the way the land across the valley had been partitioned—this acre for sweet potatoes, that one for corn, a third beyond it for squash . . .

And all up along the ridge too, terraces had been built straight into the steep hillside, maximizing space for planting. In the parts too steep or rugged even for that, the villagers had scattered apple trees for treats.

"Dane," Hans said. "I'm afraid."

Dane swallowed hard. What did that mean? "Afraid of what?"

Hans found a rock resting in the dirt, and he sat on it now, breathing out a long sigh as he did. "You've heard of the Tipping Point, I assume."

"Sure," Dane said. Everyone had. It was the period, pre-Unity, when the weather turned. When it simply got too hot for life to continue as it always had. When the oceans died and the habitable lands dried up. When the food went scarce. When the water stopped flowing. When hurricanes, blizzards, heat waves, and locusts were all that was left, ruining houses and land alike. Historians were quick to note that it was the Tipping Point, in large part, that had led to the Total War. *Hard to keep peace,* the saying went, *when your home is in pieces.*

"Then you know," Hans said, "that the Tipping Point ended agriculture as we once knew it."

"Yeah, but they fixed that," Dane said. Humanity had proven resilient.

It was the chancellor's own scientists who first found a way around the permadrought. One of the things that made him so popular over in Europe, in fact. Just as the Total War was dying down, Cylis used his newfound political capital to build the world's first weather mill smack in the center of what was soon to become the new European Union. At this mill, sophisticated, long-range missile launchers shot canisters of benign chemicals—mostly silver iodide—all over the continent, precisely and strategically, as a way of "seeding" European clouds. Natural rain had become nearly unheard-of throughout the hot spring and summer months, but suddenly, with the introduction of the weather mill's new chemical cocktail, clouds across the sky were able to form rain again. It was a breakthrough that saved millions of lives. And it wasn't long before Lamson adopted Cylis's methods in America too, commissioning from the European Union the world's second great weather mill just ten years ago.

"*We* control the weather now," Dane said. "*We* make it rain. People have been handling it for years." He had learned about this in school, had studied it several times, in history classes and science classes alike, though this was the first time Dane had ever really given it any serious thought. Back in the Old District, rain was little more than an inconvenience.

"That's correct," Hans said. "But with a caveat. Because it isn't really *people* who control the weather, you see. It's *DOME. Theirs* is the technology that makes it rain. And right now, between the Markless protests and the Global merger and the rise of the IMPS and everything else, that department is in the midst of tremendous turmoil. They face discord and unrest from all sides. They *will* react accordingly. And I fear we Markless farmers may be the first to get caught in the crossfire."

Dane stared at him, his eyes widening slowly. "They wouldn't," Dane said. "Inciting a permadrought? It's just too crazy . . ."

"Is it?" Hans asked. "You're talking about a general who spent the last ten years swiping kids to build a secret army whose only possible purpose could be to fight a civil war. *You yourself* are the one who unveiled this truth to America. It is *precisely* this truth that incited the protests in Beacon and New Chicago. And now, privately, you've been telling me that the Department of Marked Emergencies has created a deadly nanovirus just in case we Markless ever get out of hand.

"So are you *really*, now, going to bank on the mercy of the Department's environmental branch?"

"But this is different!" Dane said. "You're talking about the *water cycle*. That's not a *Markless* need—that's a *human* need. Without it, everyone starves!"

Hans smiled, bemused. "Ten years ago Lamson ruptured the dam at the first chance he got. Destroyed the entire east coast in one afternoon."

"Yeah, in order to end a civil war!"

"And where are we now, Dane—if not at the brink of another?"

"He simply wouldn't do it," Dane insisted. "No one would."

"But, Dane," Hans said, lifting his arms to the clear blue sky.

"You don't understand. The clouds haven't been seeded since September. By all evidence . . . General Lamson already has."

∃

It was dinnertime back in Lahoma, and when he entered the dining room, Connor did his best to be polite, as ever. The very first thing he did was comment on how delicious everything smelled. The corn, the mashed potatoes, the soyloaf with ketchup . . . he thanked his parents for their cooking, set the table, and sat down to wait patiently with his napkin on his lap, hands folded, elbows off the table.

Before his family began their meal, Connor even gave a toast to Lamson and to Cylis—to the great Global Union and to his family's fortune for living in it—as he almost always did.

The fact was, Connor wanted to be a gentleman. Even when he was very upset.

"So how'd the 'screen game go?" Father asked. "Any big upsets?"

"Sally won, as usual," Connor said. "Mark-opoly. We didn't get around to playing anything else."

"No G.U. Risk?" Mother teased. "I'm surprised you even let them leave without at least a go of it."

"We got distracted," Connor said. And he waited for them to take the bait.

"Distracted by what?" his father asked.

"Well, first of all, by talking about that stupid General's Award."

Father stopped eating midchew. He swallowed the lump of

food whole and put his fork and knife down onto his plate. "I'm going to assume," he said, "that it was Sally and Steve doing the talking."

"I didn't say anything about the visit, Father, if that's what you're getting at."

"It is."

On Connor's other side, Mother sniffed in that short, curt way of hers; a tic that came out when she was upset. "Then what exactly was there to talk about, Connor?"

"Why—what a great, astonishing, unbelievable honor it is, of course," Connor said caustically.

"It *is* those things, Connor."

"It isn't and you know it. It was a political diversion with me as a prop—and it's left me hated by every kid in Lahoma."

"Jealousy is flattery—" Father began, but Connor wouldn't let him go on.

"Father, stop. I get it. And I don't care. Lamson's entitled to use me any way he wants. That's his choice as general-in-chief, and that's fine.

"But what I *do* care about is that this request of his is *ruining* our town. Do you not see that? It's tearing Lahoma apart!"

"Uh-oh," Mother said sincerely. "Who was it this time?"

"Sally's dad. Fired. They're moving. Who knows where."

"*Cylis,*" Mother cursed.

And for a moment, Father held his tongue. When he did speak, he did so quietly, sympathetically. "Connor. What Lamson asked of us . . . it's bigger than this family. It's bigger than this town. It's for the good of our entire American State."

"It's *killing* our American State!"

"Not yet, it's not."

"It will! When spring rolls around!"

Father sighed. "It's possible . . . ," he said. "It's possible that this will all be over by then."

"Yeah, you got that right," Connor said. "Because guess what—that other distraction this afternoon? It was news from Steve's dad."

Father's eyes went wide.

"Yeah, you guessed it. He's onto you."

Mother dropped her fork. "Us specifically?"

"I don't know. I don't think so. But he knows it's not just some technical malfunction over there anymore. He knows *someone's* sabotaging America's weather mill. And I've gotta believe it's only a matter of time before he figures out who."

Father leaned in closely. "Connor," he said. "You know we can't stop."

Connor wiped his face with his hands. "Why *not*? Because Lamson says so?"

"Because it's what the country needs."

"*Why*? You've never told me why! And it sure isn't making sense all on its own! Tell me how a permadrought, on balance, is the best thing for the American State. Tell me that, and I'll let this whole thing go. But until then, what you're doing is keeping me up at night! I can't live with it! I just can't!"

"Sometimes we do things that *are* hard to live with, Connor. Sometimes that's life."

"Because Lamson *wants* it to be?"

"Because we're at *war*," Father said. "All right? Because the American State is at war."

Silence fell over the dinner table.

Connor leaned forward. "We're a *Global Union*, Father. There's only one country left. *How* are we at war?"

"Civil war," Mother said, speaking up.

But Connor still didn't understand. "*Civil war?* Civil war is *exactly* the thing that this Mark was designed to prevent!"

"Yes," Father said. "And yet here we are. Fighting for our side."

"Then how come no one's talking about it?"

Father shrugged. "Some are."

"Well . . . ," Connor said, the wheels turning quickly in his brain. "If that's the case, then why not just tell everybody about what you're doing? Why not lay it all out for people, so they can at least understand what's happening, in the context of what you just told me?"

"Because, first of all," Mother said, "what we're doing is still technically treason. Lahoma's weather mill is America's only, and DOME's environmental division, as a matter of national security, runs it. Any attack or conspiracy against it is an act of terrorism."

Connor's head spun just thinking about it.

"What Lamson has asked of us . . . it wasn't an order," Father said. "It was a request—far outside the bounds of DOME. And as far as anyone is supposed to know, it is a request that was never made.

"Lamson was here last September to honor you, Connor. That is the only story that anyone besides us can *ever* know. Even *you* weren't supposed to know the truth. The general has given us no official authority to do what we're doing, and he's made no promise that he will pardon us should we ever be caught."

"Well then, watch out," Connor said. "Because whatever computer virus it is that you're feeding that place, whatever wire it is that you've been pulling out here and there over these last six months . . . the jig is very nearly up."

"Okay," Father said. "Duly noted. Thanks." He seemed to mean it.

And Mother cleared the table.

No one was hungry enough to finish the meal.

4

Back at the Sierra Science Center, Logan, Erin, Hailey, and Peck all sat around a sterile aluminum table, with its sterile aluminum floor and the sterile blue tarp wall panels surrounding it. In strange contrast to this was Dr. Arianna Rhyne herself, head scientist of the SSC, balanced on a high stool off to the side, her tie-dye shirt aswirl and her long, thick dreadlocks falling heavy against her fidgeting hands.

"So what's the plan?" Hailey asked aggressively. "You gonna turn us in? Tell DOME you have us?" She looked ready for a fight.

Dr. Rhyne only smiled. "Hailey, dear, you underestimate me! I told DOME I had you hours ago, the moment Sam left to pick you kids up."

A wave of shock washed through the room. Everyone but Erin looked ready to run, and even she *tried* to look ready, fever shakes aside.

But now the doctor laughed, a chuckle at first, and more heartily as everyone else grew increasingly nervous. "Oh, calm down already. You eastern types—always so on edge! It's not healthy at such a young age."

"So you *haven't* alerted DOME?" Logan asked.

"No, I most certainly have!"

Logan and Peck stood defensively at the table, readying themselves for a showdown.

"How else could I have saved you from that corner you backed yourselves into? Do you think DOME's stupid? Do you think they're disorganized? Because they are neither of those things. I assure you, the moment they traced that Markscan of yours, someone over there would have figured you were coming to see me." She shrugged. "The public may not know that you've found out about Project Trumpet—but DOME's head agents sure do."

"Just let us go," Hailey pleaded, adapting rapidly to this new development. "Just let us go. Say we put up a fight. Say . . . say we outnumbered you. We'll just leave and never come back. We can forget this whole thing!"

But Dr. Rhyne just laughed again. Harder this time. "Listen. Children. How else can I put this? *I'm buying us time.* The only reason DOME isn't swarming this place *already* is because they think you're in my custody."

Logan threw up his arms. "We *are* in your custody!"

"Yes! I know! Terrific! And as long as DOME doesn't forget that, they'll take their sweet time getting here. Amazingly good at prioritizing, that department is. The more certain they are that I won't let you get away, the farther you kids fall on their priority list. You do realize," she added, a bit condescendingly, "that you four are not, at all times, their number one concern."

"So you *will* let us go, then?" Hailey asked.

"Not a chance."

Logan looked around the room, confirming that his friends looked every bit as exasperated as he felt.

"Arianna. Maybe, if you could just fill us in on your thinking here . . ."

Arianna tugged at her shirt, its colors shifting and flowing and squishing inside the fabric. "Look. Here's the deal. You're in Sierra now. Just because DOME pays my bills does not mean that I agree with everything they do." She grew more serious now, an abrupt change in tone. "In fact, right now, I'm not sure I'm on board with much of any of it." She eyed them. "Why else would I be helping you? Why else would I have brought you out west?"

"You didn't bring us out west," Erin objected wearily. "We came ourselves. I've been gunning for you for weeks."

Dr. Rhyne raised an eyebrow. "Yes, and why is that, hmm? Is it because your little hacker escapades turned up documents with my name attached? Is it because you—oh, I don't know—caught me red-handed? My dear Erin," she said gently, "if I'd not wanted you to find me—believe me on this—you'd not have found me."

"Well then, how'd you find *us*?" Peck asked, still very much on edge. "Out in the Rockies. Middle of nowhere. That's quite a lucky guess."

Arianna laughed again.

Arianna was full of laughter.

"Ah, Daniel, the Dust's fearless leader. I welcome you humbly to the Sierra Science Center, home to the greatest scientists in the world, of every field. My husband traces SSC hacks like Erin's before breakfast. He had her flagged the moment she poked her nose into my personal files last month, and we haven't lost track of her since." Arianna turned to Erin now, pleasantly. "We knew it was you in that car not because DOME's drone alerted us—though they would have had I asked, I assure you—but rather, because here in the SSC, we scientists hack drones just for the fun of it."

"You work for a department intent on capturing us," Peck said. "You're the engineer of a deadly biological superweapon. You've *already* told DOME we're here. And now you're asking us to just trust that it's all part of some elaborate plan to *help* us?"

Arianna eyed him. "How old are you, Daniel? Sixteen? Seventeen?"

"I'm eighteen," Peck said indignantly.

"Eighteen. That's lovely. In that case I've been working for Cylis since the year you were potty trained."

Peck blushed a little but didn't respond.

"Back then, the Mark, the Global Union, the very concept of the citizen's Pledge itself was just a gleam in young Cylis's eye. My work on Project Trumpet was purely theoretical. A challenge posed to me by the world's greatest minds. I didn't do it in order to kill Markless—Markless didn't even exist yet. I did it because it was a new frontier of biomedical engineering, and because it was waiting to be done."

"Oh yeah?" Peck asked. "Is that how you justify it to yourself? Is that how you sleep at night?"

"I don't have to justify it," Arianna said, suddenly as cold and hard as the stool she sat on. "Least of all to you."

A silence fell over the room.

"But I *am* happy to talk with you," Arianna said. "You came all the way here. Everyone knows it. And they were always going to, with or without my help. But not one of us—not me, not DOME, not the IMPS—not one of us has any clear idea why. So tell me. Tell me what it is you need from me. And *I'll* tell *you* everything I know."

"Why would you do that?" Peck asked suspiciously.

Arianna sneered at him. "Because I *feel* like it, ya piker."

And Peck narrowed his eyes right back. "Don't do it," he told the others. "She's tricking us. Somehow it's a trap."

"I've already *told* you it's a trap! But that doesn't mean I can't help you with enough time left over to get you to safety—*if* we move fast."

Suddenly Erin sat up, waving her arms exhaustedly. "Peck, let it go. I trust her. She's trying to help."

"Thank Cylis," Arianna said. "The redhead's talking sense. All right then, Erin—how much do you know so far?"

"What makes you think I'm the brains of this thing?" Erin asked.

The doctor laughed. "Please."

"Okay," Erin said, clearing her throat. "Well. I know about Project Trumpet."

"Clearly," Arianna agreed.

"I know about it because I hacked into a memo. It revealed that New Chicago's DOME director Michael Cheswick used a group called the Trumpet Task Force to cover up an outbreak six months ago. This task force, I later found out, was part of a larger organization called the International Moderators of Peace. Far as I can tell, the Trumpet cover-up was the first official use of their troops."

The doctor frowned. "First I'm hearing about an outbreak," she said.

"How is that possible?" Peck pressed.

Arianna shrugged. "DOME's always been choosy about who it keeps in the know on these types of things."

"Yeah? And what happened to your expert hacking skills?"

"I didn't say I *couldn't* have found out about it—I said I *hadn't*.

Surely you don't expect me to hack memos that I've no reason to think would exist." She turned back to Erin. "I apologize, Erin. Please, go on."

Erin cleared her throat. "Anyway. Eventually I realized these IMPS were the same people who guarded Acheron. So, with the Dust's help, and with the influence of the A.U.'s Unmarked radio network, I incited the Markless in Beacon and New Chicago to riot. It was my guess that if our protests pulled enough of these IMPS away from their duties in Acheron, then we might be able to drain the prison of its security, leaving the Dust with an opening to sneak in and save Logan." Erin shrugged, a little shy. "Clearly, the plan worked."

"And quite impressively, I might add." Arianna smiled. "That part, I did know. DOME's been feeding its employees updates on the protests for weeks. They aren't—what's the word . . . ah, yes—*happy* with you. No. They aren't too happy at all." Arianna patted down the front of her shirt, and its colors morphed and spread again around her fingertips. "But all *I* care about is your knowledge of Trumpet. I need to find out where that knowledge ends in order to know what you're expecting from me. So will you indulge me?"

Erin took a deep breath. "I know that Project Trumpet is a nanovirus, dreamed up by Cylis to wipe out the Markless if he ever saw a need. I know you were the engineer he asked to create it all those years ago—I've found the documents that point to you. I know Cylis released the dormant virus as soon as you gave it to him, and I know that DOME's been vaccinating the Marked ever since, during the Pledge process.

"I also know that somehow, this vaccine of yours has back-fired, since last August it was a group of Marked who started getting sick, not Markless—"

"Whoa, whoa," Arianna said suddenly. "Hold up. *Backfired?* How in Cylis's name did my vaccine backfire?"

Erin frowned. "I'm not sure," she admitted. "But it's only the vaccinated who have gotten sick. All I can guess is that, somehow, there was a mistake in your design."

"I don't make mistakes," Dr. Rhyne said with a wave of her hand. "Mistakes are ugly, and beneath me, and I don't make them. Period."

Erin shrugged. "Well, Marked have died. So clearly you did——"

"That's impossible——" the doctor interrupted.

"And I'm *betting*," Erin continued, "that you just might be prideful enough to help fix it."

In a sudden burst of anger, Dr. Rhyne bucked her leg back, kicking the stool behind her and sending it skidding across the room. It ricocheted off a distant table, clanging horribly. "Are you *certain*, now, about this? Are you *absolutely sure* that my vaccine has given Marked citizens Trumpet Fever? Do you have *proof?*"

"Show her the Task Force memos," Hailey said, pointing to Erin's tablet.

"I don't need to," Erin said. She turned to the doctor. "I'm your proof—Marked and sick."

"You could be sick with anything," Arianna said. "It's flu season. What makes you think this is Trumpet?" But she leaned in and touched Erin's forehead as she spoke. She jumped visibly upon feeling the temperature of it.

"Apparently I'm one of the early victims," Erin said. "And now that my vaccine is active, I'm here because I'm hoping you might have some way to turn it off."

Arianna looked suddenly as though she knew the tables had turned. No longer was she the one in control. No longer was she the one holding the upper hand of knowledge. She laid a single dreadlock across her mouth and chewed on it for a moment, thinking, perhaps, of her next steps. "You're a good sleuth and a better hacker, Ms. Erin Arbitor. But it appears you have a blind spot for the science behind nanotech. I'm sorry—one cannot simply 'turn it off.' It doesn't work that way."

"Why not?" Erin asked.

"Because a nanomachine is *not* a tiny assembly of metal and gears, and fairy tales, and microchips that flip on like in toasters and tablets. It's not a circuit board at all. It is a molecule, plain and simple, modified ever so slightly to do our bidding. In this case, it is a virus designed to stay dormant without the presence of an activation protein. Tough as it might be for a computer hacker to understand, this isn't simple electronics we're dealing with here. This is chemistry. It's biophysics. It's *messy*. And there is no off switch."

"Well, can't you just remove your activation protein from the environment? Wouldn't that do the trick?"

Arianna shook her head. "It's a binding process. Once my virus comes across its activation protein, it's active for good.

"But here's the thing," Arianna continued. "My virus *hasn't* come across its activation protein. My activation protein hasn't been released at all. If it *had been*, Markless would be dying, not Marked. There's no doubt about that."

Logan stepped forward. "How do you know?"

"I see you're a little slower than your friend," Arianna said. "I've told you already, and I'll tell you once more. But don't make me say it again: I *know* because I don't make *mistakes*."

"Then how do you explain the outbreaks?" Peck asked.

"Out*break*," Arianna corrected. "By the sound of it, there's only been one. And whoever's fault that was, my team had nothing to do with it."

"Are you saying this is someone else's mistake?" Hailey asked Dr. Rhyne.

"That's precisely what I'm saying," Arianna told her. "From what I'm hearing, last summer someone decided to take a test drive with Project Trumpet. But clearly they did so with a *second* activation protein—not the one that I designed. They must have used something else altogether. Something that activated the *vaccine* instead of the nanovirus."

"But . . . why?" Hailey asked. "And who? And how?"

"Well, that's the 98.6-degree question, now isn't it?" Arianna turned to Erin. "So what do those memos of yours say, huh? Any mention of the activation? How it was released? Or who released it?"

"No," Erin said. "Nothing. I found plenty of documents pointing to Trumpet's creation all those years ago. That's what led me to you. And I found several memos between Michael Cheswick and the Trumpet Task Force concerning the effort to contain the outbreak. But nothing ever talked about the activation process itself."

"Well, it sure didn't come out of my Science Center. Nothing so shoddy ever would. This trial run came from somewhere else." Arianna shook her head, devastated. "Someone is butchering my beautiful work."

Erin stared at Dr. Rhyne, confused. "Wait, what do you mean, 'trial run'? Are you're saying this new activation protein *isn't* present nationwide? That the vaccine *isn't* yet active among the wider Marked population?"

"Oh, quite certainly not. The data you've found suggests a very limited area of activation so far."

"But then how did *I* get sick?"

"I don't know," Arianna said simply.

Hailey frowned. "Well, hold on. If the activation protein hasn't yet been released across the country, then we still have time to prevent a national outbreak."

"That's correct." The doctor nodded. "Though by the sound of it, our time is running out. Doesn't take a scientist to know that a trial run is usually the first stage of a wider release. And this trial run happened six full months ago. If someone *is* preparing to release that second activation protein more widely . . . well, just remember—there's no off switch."

Erin cleared her throat, her elbows resting mournfully on the sterile table before her. "In that case," she said, "what about me?"

Arianna looked at her sadly.

"What about a *cure?*" Erin specified.

The doctor sighed deeply. For the first time, all the laughter within her went dead.

"I never developed a cure," Arianna said. "Those nanomeds you risked everything for have bought you a little bit of time. The medical equipment I have here at the SSC will buy you a little bit more. But none of that changes the bottom line: your fever will grow steadily worse . . . and then you will die."

5

It was hard for Connor to focus the next day at school. The morning had passed, and so far he'd missed every last lesson point in meteorology, statistics, chemistry, political relations, and post-Unity history. This was a first for Connor Goody Two-Shoes, and yet he was powerless to snap out of it.

Lahoma High was a small place—a converted house, in fact—no more than sixty students total across all four grades. Ninth and tenth grades were downstairs, each in its own room of about fifteen students, and eleventh and twelfth were up on the second floor, which Connor rarely saw.

Connor's year was a "boom year" with sixteen students, so his classroom had always been crowded, according to his teachers. He'd been attending class with these same fifteen students for his entire academic life. Each year was taught by a new teacher, and he or she covered all possible topics, which varied widely from grade to grade. Now that Connor was getting older, the curriculum was much more practical, and oriented toward a variety of possible careers at the weather mill. Currently, Connor was learning the general stuff, but beginning in eleventh grade, he'd have the opportunity to choose his area of greatest interest and focus personally on that for homework and independent studies. None of it much interested Connor, actually—he'd always been more eager to leave town for one of the great universities in New Chicago or Beacon as soon as he was old enough—but this had never stopped him from paying attention before.

At the moment, he was sitting in the front of the class, center aisle, as always, staring straight ahead at the wallscreen, eyes wide and seeing his teacher's every move. And yet somehow he still hadn't managed to hear a single thing she'd said.

"Isn't that right, Connor?" Mrs. Stokewood asked.

"Uh, yes, ma'am," Connor said, having no idea what he was agreeing to.

"Well then, why don't you tell us about it, if you would."

"Um . . ."

This was a nightmare. Legitimately. For Connor the student, this was a worst-case scenario.

Connor cleared his throat. Good. Okay. That bought him about two seconds.

He cleared it again, harder. Maybe this time he could buy himself another three or even four.

Stop thinking about the stalling part! Connor thought. *Think about the plan for* after *the stalling part!* But this time the clearing of his throat actually managed to bring something up. So now he had to cough. Good! Yes, good! He coughed again. He hit his chest with his fist, eyes watering, his face a little red. That had bought him another six or seven seconds. Okay. Maybe she'd move on to someone else. Maybe, given the pause, she'd even repeat the question. Wishful thinking, perhaps—but possible!

No. Instead, Mrs. Stokewood just waited. Politely.

And Connor could practically see it, the crack forming along the armor of his perfect school record.

Except! What was this? Could it be? Could today be Connor's lucky day?

Suddenly Lahoma's all-school principal poked his head into the ninth-grade classroom. "Connor?" he asked.

It was a miracle. Saved by the bell! Unless . . .

Wait a minute, Connor thought. Could it be? Was he *already* in trouble for zoning out all morning? Had they realized? Did they know? Was that possible?

No, Connor. That's delusional. You're not in trouble with Lahoma's all-school principal just for daydreaming this morning. You're not. That's ridiculous.

And yet, that look on the principal's face . . .

It sure *seemed* like he was in trouble . . . for *something* . . .

"Connor, would you mind gathering your belongings and coming with me, please?"

"Oh." Connor coughed again. "But I was, uh, I was just about to answer Mrs. Stokewood's question," he said reflexively.

Idiot! That was your one, perfect out! "Just about to answer this question I didn't hear"? Is that really what you just said? Who does that?

"It's okay, Connor," Mrs. Stokewood said mercifully. "You can get the lesson notes from Sally at the end of class."

Good. Good old Mrs. Stokewood. Always looking out for her favorite student. Today, Connor's reputation preceded him.

"I'm afraid he won't be coming back, Mrs. Stokewood," the principal said softly.

And a murmur rushed through the class like electricity.

Wow, Connor thought. *Then . . . what if I really am in trouble? Like . . . for something . . . big.*

Connor thought of his permanent record, attached digitally to his Mark and carried on him at all times. He thought of what colleges would think during their admission processes. He thought of job interviews down the line . . .

But out in the hall, the principal's concerned tone quickly broke him from any coherent train of thought. All that was left was the present tense.

"Connor, would you mind taking a walk with me?" the principal asked.

"Not at all," Connor said.

"It will be a rather long walk, I'm afraid."

"May I ask where we're going, sir?" Now Connor was confused. The principal's office was in Lahoma Elementary, sure, but that was hardly a long walk away. Weirder still, the principal didn't seem angry. At all. But he didn't seem happy either. In fact, he seemed . . . nervous.

And that was an odd thing for Lahoma's all-school principal to seem.

"Uh," he said. A pause. Now it was the principal who stood there, clearing his throat, stalling, avoiding the question . . .

Six seconds. Connor counted.

And then it was over. And the principal took a deep breath. And the principal said, "Actually, Connor, we're going to visit the weather mill."

ㅂ

It had taken some time for Charles Arbitor to work up the nerve to do it. But finally he sat, fidgeting on the plush white couch of the Arbitors' apartment next to his wife Olivia, holding the tablet in his sweaty hands, all fired up and ready to go.

"Charles, for *Cylis's* sake, this is one little tablet call we're talking about. If you won't do it, I will——" She went to grab the tablet from him, but he pulled it away quickly and held the screen out of reach.

"I'll do it," he said. "I just wish I didn't have to go behind DOME's back about it. If they'd just agreed to put me on her assignment . . . I mean, was that really so much to ask?"

"What—putting Erin Arbitor's legal fate into the hands of her disgruntled, dysfunctional, beaten-down father?" Olivia laughed. "Yeah, Charles. It was. Now, are we gonna keep moping about it all morning like we did yesterday, or are we gonna *do* this thing before DOME beats us to it?"

"We're doing it, yes—*Cylis*—sheesh. We're doing it," Mr. Arbitor said. And he placed the tablet call.

"Sierra Science Center, this is Arianna," the doctor said from across the video connection.

Mr. Arbitor squirmed on his sofa. His heart beat fast. "Dr. Rhyne, this is Charles Arbitor calling. I'm . . . I'm hoping you might be able to help me in a personal matter—"

Arianna stopped him right there. "Let me guess," she said, deadpan. "You're looking for Erin."

Mr. Arbitor cleared his throat. He nodded.

"Well, you're out of luck," Arianna said. "'Fraid she escaped this morning, while I was distracted, uh . . . calculating statistics . . ."

Mr. Arbitor narrowed his eyes. Out of the video's field of view, Olivia had her hands up in a "Who does she think she's kidding?" sort of way.

"Dr. Rhyne, you can't actually expect me to believe, with the dozens of employees you have on hand over there at all hours, that you actually managed to lose—"

"You listen here, Charles," Dr. Rhyne interrupted. Her face was close and larger than life in the screen of Mr. Arbitor's tablet. "I don't care what you believe. I'm telling you Erin's not here anymore, and that's as far as this conversation goes."

It was hard for Mr. Arbitor to hide his frustration over the cross-country connection. But he did his best to smile.

"Doctor. Please. Try to understand. I'm not calling on behalf of DOME right now. This is personal for me. This is my daughter we're talking about, and I—" Olivia kicked him. He coughed. "My wife and I . . . we just need to know that Erin is safe."

In the video, Dr. Rhyne raised an eyebrow. She had clearly rested her tablet down on one of the SSC's tables because she was looming over the camera now, using both hands to fiddle with her dreadlocks as she let Mr. Arbitor stare up her nose. "You," she said, "are a DOME agent. Doesn't matter what else you are— father, husband, friend—to me, you're just the face of DOME." She shrugged. "This is my official report, Agent Arbitor. If you don't like it, you're welcome to file a complaint."

"But I can help!" Mr. Arbitor pleaded. "I'm trying to help my daughter!"

"Sorry," Arianna said sarcastically. "Connection must be bad. You keep talking, but all I hear is the crackle of DOME's endless red tape."

"I'm not *calling* on behalf of DOME—" Mr. Arbitor insisted.

But Arianna had already ended the call.

For a moment, Charles and Olivia just sat, speechless, on the couch.

And so it was that the Arbitors finally realized—if they really were serious about seeing their daughter Erin again, there was only one place left for them to turn.

⌐

The walk to the weather mill took nearly twenty minutes. Lahoma's all-school principal led the way as quickly as he could, stopping just shy of breaking into an actual jog. He didn't make chitchat. He didn't talk at all. He kept his eyes down, and he stretched his strides far with each step.

But it wasn't until about halfway to the mill, as Connor and the principal passed the sheriff's office at the edge of town, that things really started getting strange. Beside them the screen door opened and slammed shut against the quiet building's front, and in between, the sheriff himself walked out and onto the dirt of the road.

He didn't say anything. He didn't smile at Connor.

He kept his eyes down, and he stretched his strides far with each step.

At this point, Connor thought, *it might be appropriate to worry.*

Outside, Lahoma's weather mill was surrounded by thirty acres of well-guarded ground-to-air missile launchers. By the time Connor came upon them, no less than a dozen Lahoma officials were flanking him. The principal and sheriff, of course, but also the deputy, the judge, the head of the mill, even the mayor himself. What was going on? Connor was beginning to have some ideas, but as the men and women all around him solemnly led the way through the mill's entrance and onto the main factory floor, one single phrase began running through his head:

The sky is falling.

The world as Connor knew it had left him behind.

Inside, Connor and his chaperones were greeted by the weather mill's head of security, Mr. Larkin. Connor knew him well as the happy father of Steve Larkin, his good friend of many years. But nothing about Mr. Larkin seemed happy today. Behind him, the wide-open, industrial weather mill was silent and dead, filled with the haze of an ominous black smoke. Its ceiling stretched fifty feet into the air, and a crosshatched series of steel I beams and corrugated sheet metal lined its surface without any movement underneath. The concrete floor was vacant. The grated metal walkway that lined it twenty feet up, that made a path to the cubical office spaces jutting out from the high walls . . . there was no one on it. The office lights were off. Each one had a little frosted window looking out onto the mill's floor below, but today those frosted windows shed no light. The floor itself had chemical vats and processors of all types, many of them with vents leading up into the ceiling and out into the air through long, aluminum tubes. But none of them churned, none of them whirred . . .

At the floor's edge, looking out onto the missile-launcher field and sectioned off by high walls and even more frosted glass, was the weather mill's control center—a tablescreen that stretched nearly twenty feet across and curved in a giant "C" semicircle around whomever it was who might have stood at its helm. For the last six years, that whomever-it-was had been Connor's parents, the Goodmans.

But right now that control center was empty. And its tablescreen was dark.

Mr. Larkin led Connor past it, through the cavernous space, and over to the mill's supercomputer off in the corner. It was a series of computer racks—tall, refrigerator-sized stacks of hard drives on shelves—and they were laid out all over a wide area across the floor like a high-tech hedge maze.

"All right, Connor," Mr. Larkin said. "Follow me, please."

So Connor wove with him through the mazelike walkways

between the computer racks, left, right, straight, left . . . toward the source of the smoke and into the thickening haze.

"These hard drives are all off-line," Connor said to Mr. Larkin. Their lights were off. Nothing blinked; nothing hummed. By now the air was black and heavy with the smell of cordite.

"What . . . what happened here?" Connor asked, though some screaming, terrified part of him already knew the answer.

At the center of the supercomputer's maze was a crater. The floor was damaged and charred black. The computer racks surrounding it were blown out and knocked down, lying against the denatured concrete like dominos.

"Bomb blast," Mr. Larkin said simply. "Crude. Homemade. Hasty. That's what you're looking at, Connor, in literal terms.

"And yet that doesn't really describe it, does it, Connor?"

Connor shook his head.

"No. I'd have to agree. Because I'm afraid that what you're actually seeing, Connor—what this really is—is the aftermath of a successful conspiracy against our weather mill. Against the very stability of our American State." Mr. Larkin frowned. "A full-fledged terrorist attack. A suicide bombing. This weather mill is now permanently off-line." He led Connor through the dense, dusty air and across the crater of the bomb blast. "I arrived too late to stop them, Connor. I tried . . . I tried to negotiate. I'm sorry. I failed."

And that's when Connor made it to the other side of the smoke.

His parents were there, his father's thumb still pressed against the trigger of the detonator. They rested slumped against the farthest of the blown-out computer racks, together, determined, bloody, and dead.

FOUR

FORECAST

1

A SILVER LINE SLICED LILY'S SKY RIGHT down the middle. She squinted, her eyes following its path all the way out, but it stretched farther—much farther—than she could see: a cable that thinned to a pencil mark against the blue, and then, beyond that, to a razor's edge . . . until it was nothing at all, disappearing completely into the black.

Lily Langly was on an elevator to the stars.

"Few years ago we could've sent you to Europe in a jet plane from Acheron," Cheswick had told her, back on the sonicboat that had taken her all the way to the equator. "But oil's too precious these days, even for official IMP business, and fission planes are much too glaring a target now that these Markless are feeling rebellious. Don't worry about any of that, though." Cheswick laughed. "I hear space gliding's more fun, anyway."

And so the two of them docked at the base of Chancellor Cylis's personal space elevator—which was nothing more than an anchor, really, for a carbon-fiber tether that stretched out twenty-two thousand miles above Earth—and from there Cheswick shuffled Lily alone into that small, winged elevator shuttle, strapping her tightly into its harness. "Last stop on this thing's the geosynchronous space station," he said. "But you won't be going all the way there. End of the line for you is the thermosphere, only about sixty miles up."

"Only," Lily said. She hadn't even known there *was* a geosynchronous space station.

"From there you'll detach automatically, and your shuttle will glide down to Europe from space—like riding a paper airplane tossed from the world's highest cliff! No energy required. A straight shot, all automatically navigated. It'll be just a little under an hour of gliding. Fast!" Cheswick assured her. "You'll be there before breakfast."

"Okay," Lily said as the air lock closed down tightly around her. "Still no idea why the chancellor wants to see me?"

Cheswick shrugged from behind the shuttle's glass. And just like that, Lily's shuttle began to ascend.

Lily thought now of sleeping, tired as she was, while the elevator ride was still smooth. She didn't imagine the glide down would be quite as relaxing. But her eyes just wouldn't close. How could they, with a view like this?

Out the portholes to her sides, she now could see Earth's horizon below, already curving gently off at its ends. To her left was the American State, its Rocky Mountains just bumps in the distance, its whole continent reduced to a little brown place mat on the table of blue seas. At its western side was Sierra, dotting the coast with its sparkling lights. At its eastern side was Beacon, a blinding wash of glow even brighter than the moon above. And between them was New Chicago, far up into the distance, curving out and over the edge of the tabletop horizon.

To her right, the European State just barely crept into view from beyond the edge of the earth, its North African Dark Lands the first to appear, brown and cracked and all dried up. Far to the north, the shimmers of New London promised life across the ocean, while beyond even that, the atmosphere itself was ablaze with the light of Third Rome.

Well, Cylis, Lily thought. *Here I come.* And just as she did, she felt the jerk of her shuttle against its latch on the cable. Two jets of compressed air shot out from below her, condensing and floating off into the black. The elevator cable receded, angling away as the moon and the stars and Earth all somersaulted outside her ship, disappearing below her feet. Lily's stomach lurched into her throat as her shuttle drifted into orbit and began gliding back down toward the world below. A fire engulfed the ship as it reentered the atmosphere. And just like that, Lily was hurtling toward Earth, sailing like a meteor all the way across the sky to the world's new global capital. To ground zero, the heart of Cylis's great empire, Third Rome.

2

The day had already passed into night, and Erin lay on a makeshift medical bed, alone in an alcove beyond the storage shelves of the Sierra Science Center's basement. Wires stuck out in every direction from her arms and legs and chest and head, pinning her down and making her feel more than a little bit like a cyborg in some lost, pre-Unity science fiction novel.

She expected many days like this in the weeks to come. She hoped they wouldn't be her last. The basement of the SSC was far too dark and lonely a place for that.

Beyond the green glow of her medical equipment, the shelves

down here were home to a variety of specimens and experimental waste—preserved giant squids, jars of bacteria, barrels of deadly chemicals, defunct prototype nanotech, skeletons of all kinds, insects on pins . . . Under normal circumstances, Erin would have found it fascinating. But in the spooky quiet of the night, trapped as she was against the rough sheets of her lumpy bed, it was hard to think of any of it as more than just some creepy, discarded side-show . . . with Erin Arbitor as the main event.

And yet, from across the dark, dry, cool basement, Erin did find one small source of company and comfort—the echoes of her friends' muffled argument bouncing down the stairwell from several floors above.

"We need to get *out of here*," Hailey was telling Dr. Rhyne. "You can't tell us in the same breath that DOME's already called looking for us once *and* that we've got nothing to worry about. It's too dangerous here. We have to leave *now*!"

"And what, join your friend Peck downtown at the Sierra Library, wide out in the open? I don't understand—where is it you want to go?" Arianna asked.

"I want us to find the safest-looking ruin in Sierra, and I want us to hide out until DOME comes and does a thorough search of the place. Until that happens, we're sitting ducks!"

"You're better off here," Arianna insisted. "Sweeping the ruins is easy for DOME. But a couple of special ops shoving their way into *my* storage basement, when I don't approve? After I've already *told* one of their agents that you've gone? Now that would be hard." Even down here in the dark, it was easy for Erin to picture the smug expression on Dr. Rhyne's face as she said it.

But Hailey clearly wasn't convinced. "You're asking us to put an *awful* lot of faith in you and your mogul DOME colleagues."

"Well then, it's a necessary risk. You can take your chances with me, or you can run away now and watch Erin slowly boil alive. The only option certain to fail is the latter."

"Do you even actually think you can help her?" Hailey asked. "I mean, *really*?"

The echoing voices stopped for a moment. Erin tried to imagine Arianna's frown filling the silence. "I don't know," the doctor said finally. "But I would like to try."

"*Try*." Hailey laughed. "We didn't come three thousand miles to watch you *try*. You were supposed to have a cure *ready* for us. What kind of person designs a bioweapon without making some sort of contingency to begin with?"

"The *contingency* was the *vaccine*, you dimwit! I can't help it that someone went and turned that vaccine against us!"

And so the argument continued, though by now Erin was doing her best to tune out the rest of it. She already knew how slim her chances were; hearing Hailey throw blame around at this point was hardly going to help.

So instead, Erin rested back on the bed, closing her eyes and absorbing another bout of fever pain. She thought of Iggy. She thought of her parents back in Beacon. She thought of Spokie and the good times she'd had chasing the Dust with Logan out by Slog Row . . . and she stayed in that daydream, happily, all the way until the heavy door clicked and clanged at the edge of the basement, far past the veil of darkness before her.

She heard the rush of air against an insulated seal, the sound of the metal sliding open, the squeak of sneakers against the concrete floor. Together, the commotion pulled her quickly back to reality.

"Arianna?" Erin called, a little nervous.

"No. It's me."

"Logan!" Her voice lifted with surprise.

"Mind if I join you down here? I can't take much more of the arguing upstairs."

"Sure—yeah," Erin said, trying to sit up a little. "I'm not exactly busy."

Logan entered the glow of the medical equipment and frowned when he saw Erin's face.

"That bad, huh?" Erin asked.

"You've looked better."

Erin tried to laugh, but the pressure against her temples pounded hard and quieted her fast.

"So am I hearing things right?" she asked after a minute. "Did Peck really run off to the Sierra Library?"

"Of course he did." Logan laughed. "You kidding? After all the times he talked about it on our drive out west? The biggest collection in the country, every banned pre-Unity classic you can think of? Peck can't turn down the chance to pick up a book even under normal circumstances. Now that we're fighting a 'real war,' according to him, his reading list is about a mile long."

"What war? We're not fighting any war."

"Yeah, well, you know Peck." Logan shrugged. "He can be . . . dramatic. I think really the poor guy's just been starved for literature ever since the Spokie warehouse was burned down back on the night of—"

"'Was burned down'?" Erin laughed. "The passive tense, Logan? Really? That's very generous of you." She closed her eyes, but her amusement didn't fade.

"Okay, fine—ever since you burned the warehouse down and chased us all out of Spokie. That better? You happy now?"

"Anytime you show a little backbone, I'm happy," Erin teased.

"Yeah, great, thanks. Nice to see you're feeling like your charming old self again," Logan said, gesturing to the medical equipment and whatever fancy ways it had of making her feel better.

"Don't worry—I'm not," Erin assured him, and that quieted things down a bit.

It'd been months since the two of them had spent any real time together. Between Logan's escape to Acheron and Erin's delirium all throughout the road trip here, Logan realized now that this was the first real conversation he'd had with her since his birthday— the same night Logan dodged his Pledge and went Markless and watched his whole life come crashing down all around him—many eventful months ago. Looking at Erin now, he wondered briefly if he'd forgotten how to talk to her.

It used to be so easy, back in Spokie, last fall. Down here, things had changed. The dim basement air was still for a long time.

"Kinda cool, these artifacts, at least," Logan said, pointing to the storage shelves.

But behind Erin, Logan caught a glimpse of a tank full of spiders, each spinning tangles of deformed webs under the influence of what could only have been some strange series of drugs. He wondered how tight the tank's lid was. He wondered about all the things he *wasn't* seeing, in the dark, all around him. His skin started to crawl. And he quickly dropped that line of conversation.

"You know . . . Logan . . . for what it's worth . . . I really am sorry I chased you out of Spokie," Erin said. Her eyes were still closed, but any amusement in her face was gone now. "I shouldn't have done that, I think, looking back on it. I'd take that night back, if I could."

The sudden sense of contrition caught Logan off guard. Apologies weren't exactly in Erin's wheelhouse, and this particular one had the distinctive, rancid scent of deathbed air about it. "Stop it," Logan said. "We don't need to talk like that."

But Erin laughed at him. "Like what? Earnestly?"

Yeah, Logan realized. That was the word for it.

Erin sighed and lay there thinking for some time. "I don't wanna die, Logan."

"You won't! We're here now. We made it. Dr. Rhyne's gonna fix this. It's just a matter of time—"

"Yeah, great," Erin laughed. "Time. The one thing I don't have too much of."

"True," Logan joked. "Too bad it's not just a matter of sarcasm."

"I'd be all set."

"Or recklessness—"

"I think you mean bravery—"

"Or—"

"Okay, okay! I get it." They were both laughing now.

"You know . . . Erin," Logan started. "If it makes you feel any better, I actually think you and I might be in this thing together. More than you think . . ."

"What do you mean? You have nothing to worry about. You aren't Marked."

"Well. Actually . . . ," Logan said.

"You aren't. I may be barely lucid, but I can still see that you aren't. You're the Markless flag bearer, for crying out loud. I watched you dodge your Pledge. You're, like, the *last* person who's gonna catch Trumpet. Quit whining."

Logan laughed. He couldn't help but smile at her, even in the face of all this. "You're right," he said. "There's no nanoink on my wrist." He paused and turned it over, rubbing at the skin. "But I *did* get the vaccine. The nurse does all that before the Marker comes into the room. And as I'm sure you remember, I managed to get that far before I defected.

"Erin, as far as this virus is concerned—I'm as Marked as you are."

"Aw, Logan! Terrific. Now I have to be worried about *that* too? Come on—why would you tell me that?"

Logan shrugged. "Solidarity?"

"You're an idiot," Erin told him.

"Yeah." But Logan pulled a small book out of his pocket. "You know," he said. "There've been a lot of times these past few months when I'd just about lost hope."

"Tell me about it," Erin said.

He handed the book to her. "A friend gave this to me," he said. "Down in an underpass in New Chicago's ruins."

Erin flipped through the book's whisper-thin pages.

"It helped," Logan said. "Especially the last half."

Erin nodded.

"So now it's my turn," Logan said. "That whole warehouse debacle you feel so sorry about? It was my fault. I put you in an impossible position. I should never have dragged you into it before-hand. The Pledge escape, I mean. It was wrong of me to do that. Really wrong."

"Are you kidding?" Erin said, sitting up with a jolt of renewed energy. "You'd be an IMP right now!"

Logan frowned.

"Besides," she added. "I don't accept your apology. That night beforehand is a nice memory for me. The ice cream, I mean, when we went out for it. You can't just take that away from me now because things didn't work out as perfectly as you'd hoped."

"Stop *talking* like that," Logan said.

"Like *what?*"

"Like you're already taking stock or something. Like your best days are behind you. Just stop it, all right? You're not going to die!"

Erin closed her eyes again. She wasn't so sure. But it wasn't worth an argument.

"Besides," Logan continued, "your memory sucks. That wasn't a happy occasion *at all*. We argued the whole time, we each made promises that we immediately broke . . . I mean, you didn't even say *good-bye* to me at the end of it."

"You remember that?" Erin asked.

"Of course I remember it!"

Erin laughed. "It's funny," she said "which memories end up being the nicest. That whole fall we had in Spokie . . . I mean, it wasn't exactly fun, going through it at the time."

"It was terrifying," Logan specified.

"And yet . . ." Erin stopped herself.

The basement was quiet for a while. Slowly, Logan moved to sit at the foot of Erin's bed. A tension rose. Erin ignored it. But neither of them breathed.

"You know, when I found you back at the farm, in December," Erin began. She pulled the covers up to her chin. "I really was trying to help you. I know you don't believe me. And that's okay, I guess. But I just thought, maybe, you know, if I could talk to you . . . just negotiate the situation, you know? Between you and DOME? I just figured . . ."

"Sure," Logan said, once it was clear Erin wasn't going to finish.

"I mean, seriously, Logan! Why'd you have to be such a jerk about it?" Erin raised her voice to the limits of her energy, legitimately working herself up now. "You just about scared me to death, jumping into the river like that!" She hit him hard on the arm, and Logan laughed.

"Yeah, well . . . that almost killed me too, so . . ." He thought back to his hypothermia in the woods. He thought of Hailey pulling him out of the water, staying with him until he was better. He put his hand on Erin's foot now, and suddenly he had no idea what he was feeling anymore. His heart was beating fast. Erin didn't pull away. But she didn't move or say anything either. Her foot felt hot through the blanket. The medical equipment beeped in the background.

"Logan!" Peck yelled, barging in through the stairwell door and flipping the lights on unceremoniously. "Logan, you need to see this!"

"What?" Logan asked, standing quickly from the bed and frustrated to feel all the weight of the moment before just fall away from him. "What is it? You manage to find something worthwhile at the library downtown?"

"Uh—yeah," Peck said. "*You could say that.*"

He walked quickly between the storage shelves, followed closely by Hailey, who was every bit as worked up as he was.

"Okay, try me," Logan pressed, still irked at the interruption. "Sun Tzu's *The Art of War*? A copy of the Old Testament? I mean, what's so important—"

"*This.*"

Peck arrived at Erin's alcove and held out a printed copy of a book. Logan turned it over in his hands. He read the cover.

Swipe. By Evan Angler.

"What is it?" Logan asked.

Peck laughed. "It's us. Seems we're more famous than we thought."

∃

Lily's final descent was fast and smooth. At ten miles' altitude, she soared over New London, over its sprawling, industrial cityscape that stretched from coast to coast of what Lily knew had once been called Great Britain. At five miles' altitude, she glided over the first traces of Third Rome, Cylis's continent-spanning global capital that put even Beacon's reach to shame. And at two thousand feet, she swooped in on Central Circle, its city streets swelling up, each rooftop seeming practically to skim the bottom of her incoming shuttle.

Everything below her was a blur, but from Lily's bird's-eye view, it was clear that Third Rome was not like other urban centers. Its buildings were pre-Unity style, either spared during the Total War or else restored once the fighting had stopped. Even the newer construction had been designed and built clearly to match the historical aesthetic. Structures were low, no more than a few stories high, and each was made with stone sidings, their roofs an orange terra-cotta clay. Bigger buildings were gothic or baroque in style, made of marble; streets themselves were mostly cobblestone or brick. The city was laid out thoughtfully around its pre-Unity neighborhoods, with wide sidewalks for rollersticks, plenty of room for parks and fountains and monuments, and not a single Total War ruin to be found.

There was a history to Third Rome, and the implication was clear: Cylis's rise to power was no fluke, his leadership no temporary reign. The chancellor's European Union was—Third Rome seemed to insist—the ultimate conclusion of thousands of years of human civilization. His capital built itself upon the shoulders of humanity's greatest empires, and it had done so on Cylis's terms. Under him, Third Rome confirmed, even the cataclysmic toll of the Total War could be swept clean, forgotten—*erased*—in just ten years' time. War was no threat to him. Uprisings were no threat to him. His Marked society was the end of the road.

Lily's shuttle slowed as it approached the chancellor's palace at the heart of Central Circle, landing gracefully on the flat roof of the building's visitor wing, and its air lock opened automatically.

A lone man was waiting for her when she stepped over the shuttle's side and out onto the roof's landing tarmac. The man's short, wavy hair was brushed back neatly, white strands here and there but an oaky brown overall. He had a wide smile that carved deep, happy wrinkles into his cheeks and under his eyes, themselves a pale blue. He was even handsomer in person than he'd always been in pictures and video, and he walked toward Lily now with his arms outstretched and welcoming. He wore a crisp blue suit with a bright red tie, and Lily was struck by the energy she felt in his presence. In that moment, it was if she were the only person in the world that mattered to him.

"Welcome," he said. "Welcome to your country. And welcome to my home."

Immediately, Lily went rigid, holding her breath, standing up straight, and responding with a crisp salute.

"Oh, enough with that! There's no need for formalities here. Come, come! Join me! I imagine you're starving."

Lily paused. "Yes, sir."

"No 'sirs' here—please. We are hardly in Acheron anymore."

"Yes, Chancellor Cy—"

"Bah! You'll call me Dominic, and there'll be no more discussion about it. Friends speak to one another by name. And friendship is the sincerest form of respect. Isn't that right—Ms. Langly?"

"Lily," she corrected, recognizing the gesture.

"Yes." The chancellor smiled. "Yes, I had hoped so. Come, Lily. Let us eat."

And in the white warmth of the new morning sun hitting Cylis's palace, Lily Langly followed the chancellor through his rooftop's grand, private, double-door entrance—and into the Capitol of Third Rome.

4

Back across the Atlantic, the day in Beacon was clear and dry and bright, and for his part, Tyler was ready.

"All right. Time to make hay while the sun is shining," Blake said, but Tyler just laughed at him, slapping his knee and waving a fake lasso above his head.

"We aren't making hay, skinflint. We're wreaking havoc."

"Okay, yeah, I *know* that, ya tightwad. It's called an *expression*."

And Tyler *would* have said something about them not being at the Hayes's farm any longer . . . but already Tyler wasn't paying attention. Instead, he was several feet ahead, practically running the final stretch along the third tier of Beacon's sidewalk system, eager to ring the bell and dying to get started.

"Hello?" the voice said over the apartment building's intercom.

"It's me," Tyler said. He looked over at Blake, who'd just caught up. "Well, me and some lame skinflint I can't seem to shake." Blake punched him on the arm and Tyler laughed silently, making a face. And the entrance before them buzzed open.

Prior to joining them, the Dust's newest member, Shawn, had spent years building up a vast network of Markless sympathizers by working as what he called "the Tech Wiz." Under the Mark system in Lamson's America, everything from shopping to hospital visits to travel to opening doors was done digitally, with a scan of the Mark. This was, of course, an incredible convenience. But it also meant that somewhere in its database, DOME had a log of every single thing that each of its citizens had done over the past ten years. This made surveillance easy, and it made prosecution cases open-and-shut.

It also put Shawn in exceedingly high demand. Because the fact was, Shawn's was a rare skill set, and in Lamson's America, his services had become an invaluable commodity.

For a price, Shawn could hack into DOME's ultrasecure Marked database network, delete any logged Markscan he wanted, and exit without a trace. Shawn could take a person's actions and, in the eyes of the law, erase them for good. For Marked Beaconers the city over, Shawn could rewrite history.

Among a certain crowd, this made him a popular guy.

Of course, not being Marked himself, Shawn couldn't ever be paid for his services in credits, even under the table. His own personal economy, instead, was a barter system, a complex arrangement of IOUs and favors and goodwill, all of which Shawn was happy to leverage at any time.

For the Dust's newest prank, Shawn had called upon the Sweeneys, a middle-aged couple with a taste for breaking and entering and getting away with it, and so it was that the Sweeneys' home became the staging ground for the Dust's newest stunt.

"Think it's fancy?" Tyler said to Blake on the elevator ride up.

"A third-tier City Center apartment?" Blake asked. "Yeah, I'm gonna guess it's fancy."

"Good timing," Shawn said as he opened the Sweeneys' door a minute later. Tyler and Blake walked in, and Mr. and Mrs. Sweeney waved a friendly hello from their couch in the living room across the way. "Just finished readying the ropes and pulleys. Meg's at her perch across the street with Rusty. Jo's down below, too nervous to watch. You sure about this, Tyler?" Shawn asked.

Blake looked around the lavish room, soaking in, for just a moment, the perks of living with a Mark. But Tyler was all business. He'd already walked to the Sweeney's open window, and he was leaning out over its edge, looking down now. "I'm sure," he told Shawn. "You have the spray paint?"

Shawn handed him the can.

"We're likely to hit a big swath of IMP squads with this one, guys, so be ready. We should be talking a whole lot more than our usual ten or twelve guys." Blake said it to the room, though for all anyone was concerned, he might as well have been talking to himself.

"Let's hope you're right," Tyler said after he'd made his way out of the window and tied himself onto Shawn's dangling rope. "I'm getting pretty tired of this." And with that, he lowered himself down and out of sight.

Skyscrapers in Beacon were more than just glass and concrete and steel. Famously, their walls were made almost exclusively of ground-to-sky wallscreens. Every last building in City Center, private or public, in addition to anything else, was a skyscraper-sized television that hawked endless advertisements for products, brand names, food chains, and entertainment. Walking through Beacon City's sidewalks, one's peripheral vision was on constant sensory overload with colorful commercials and breaking news flashes, stretching as high as the eye could see.

This citywide projection system also provided Lamson and Cylis with a quick, reliable way to communicate with Beacon denizens. Frequently, one or the other of them could be seen walking from building to building, their colossal projections strolling across each successive skyscraper wall, supcrimposed on each advertisement, taking precedence above everything else.

And *in addition* to this, ever since the Markless protests had begun several weeks ago, one entire skyscraper had been commandeered for the use of a dedicated Chancellor Cylis video feed, a short looping projection of him just standing there, arms crossed, watching over all, as if generously listening to everyone's concerns, as though ready to sympathize and ponder them and respond at any moment, even if so far, he never had.

As it happened, the Sweeneys lived in this commandeered building. And right now, dangling from the ropes that Shawn had hung from their window, Tyler was staring that enormous projection of the chancellor right in the face.

He shook his can of black spray paint giddily. And he began to give Cylis the mustache Tyler always thought he deserved.

The IMPS descended fast, rappelling down from the building's rooftop with slick tactical cables and lining the city sidewalks at ground level over a hundred stories down.

For blocks all around him, Tyler could see Markless protesters gathering below, laughing and pointing and cheering at the sight of Cylis's projection as it more or less stayed remarkably well-aligned with the gigantic, black mustache Tyler had so crudely given it. For a moment, he sat, basking in the glory and the attention. But the speed and force of the IMPS' response was hardly surprising, and Tyler figured he had about thirty seconds to get back inside before one of these rappelling Moderators started shooting at him.

"Move, Tyler, *move!*" Blake shouted from the Sweeneys' window two stories above, and Tyler began climbing fast, hand over hand.

From inside the Sweeneys' apartment, Shawn stood, feet braced against the base of the kitchen counter, turning the pulley of Tyler's harness as fast as he could. It wouldn't be long, he knew, before the IMPS isolated the apartment and ambushed from inside as well. Through the movement and the shouts, he thought he could hear the elevators ascending already.

"You're gonna wanna vacate," Blake yelled to the Sweeneys, who, it seemed increasingly clear, were more than a little unprepared for the magnitude of the response this little act of vandalism would bring.

Soon, Tyler made it to the open window, but not before an electrobullet grazed his shoulder. It shorted and sparked blue, leaving Tyler just one good hand with which to pull himself up. More and more cables dropped into view all around him, and

Blake sprang into action, leaning out the window and dragging Tyler in before the IMPS slid all the way down from the rooftop above.

Tyler lay on the floor now, clutching his shoulder and laughing hysterically as Blake slammed the window shut on the Moderators who'd just now made it down to their level, dangling outside.

"Time to run," Blake said, turning from the window and dragging Tyler up to his feet.

"Gotta make hay, right, Blake?" Tyler joked as he followed him and Shawn out the apartment's main door.

In the hallway, IMPS had already begun streaming in through the main elevator to the Dust's right, arms drawn and shouting commands. But the stairwell on Shawn's left looked open, its door left slightly ajar by the Sweeneys, who'd snuck out just moments before.

"This way!" Shawn yelled, as behind them, IMPS smashed in through the apartment windows one by one.

The boys were one hundred and thirty stories up. "There's no way we'll get all the way down," Blake said. "They'll corner us before we've even made it halfway."

"We don't have to make it halfway," Shawn said. "All we have to do is lose them."

So Blake and Tyler followed as Shawn ducked almost immediately back out of the emergency stairwell, and into the apartment building's 127th floor hallway. Sure enough, for the moment, this floor was empty. The coast was clear.

"From here, we might be able to make it onto an empty elevator before the IMPS figure out which floor we're on," Blake said, and the three of them ran full sprint toward the elevator doors at the hallway's end.

Tyler hit the down button and laughed at the excruciating wait that followed. Blake tapped his foot nervously. Shawn had his head in his hands.

Finally, the doors slid open, an elevator waiting for them. They dashed inside without looking twice.

Except the elevator wasn't empty. Tucked in the corner and hidden from the hallway, a man was waiting inside. He was smiling.

"It was a good run, boys," Mr. Arbitor said after the doors had closed behind them. "But the show's over now."

5

Shawn was confused. "Who is this guy?" he whispered, hands magnecuffed behind his back. He was still reeling from the speed and efficiency with which Mr. Arbitor had subdued and cuffed all three boys. He'd been aided by the element of surprise, no doubt, but even so, Shawn could hardly believe it—the scuffle was over practically before it'd begun.

"Erin's dad," Blake told him. "From DOME. He's been after us for months."

Mr. Arbitor looked down at the boys as the elevator descended smoothly, beeping with each passing floor.

"Hey, Mr. Arbitor, I'm not so sure this magnecuff's good for my shoulder," Tyler said, still laughing a little at the blood seeping through his shirt. "The way it's pulling my arms back? I don't know if you know this, but I was shot, like, two minutes ago. With a gun."

"You weren't shot," Shawn said. "Quit being such a baby—the bullet barely grazed you."

"It grazed me. That *counts*," Tyler said. "Admit it. Tyler one, Blake and Shawn zero."

Mr. Arbitor watched the boys argue, his mouth slack, momentarily dumbfounded.

"I'm winning," Tyler said to him. "Mr. Arbitor, tell Shawn I'm winning."

But the ride was over. The elevator stopped. And Mr. Arbitor pulled the Dust out and through the building's side, second-tier exit.

"Where're all the IMPS?" Tyler asked, as though he were just casually curious about it.

"I'm not *with* the IMPS," Mr. Arbitor said. "Today, I'm not even with DOME."

"Yeah, well, either way, we're headed to Acheron," Blake said, resigned. "Whether we stop at DOME's headquarters first or not makes very little difference to me."

Mr. Arbitor dragged the three boys down the sidewalk tier away from the crowds and the Moderators still flooding the building. "We aren't going to DOME," he said quietly.

Shawn looked at him, suddenly frightened. "Then where are we going?"

Just then, Joanne rounded the corner, Meg and Rusty trailing close behind her.

"You see Eddie anywhere among the troops?" Tyler asked Meg.

But Meg shook her head, frowning.

Tyler hadn't been fazed by the shooting. He didn't even care that Mr. Arbitor had caught him. But hearing Meg's news, Tyler finally hung his head, and the laughter inside him died out.

He'd pulled *so many* IMPS out of their underground stations. He'd brought *so many* of them right to within Meg's field of view from across the street. For Eddie not to be among that kind of crowd, not anywhere . . . that was one defeat Tyler hadn't been counting on. He was out of ideas now. Eddie was gone.

But there wasn't much time to mourn. Joanne got one good look at Mr. Arbitor holding him and Shawn and Blake like that, and she prepared the lot of them for a fight.

"Rusty," she said. "Flank 'em." And she reached into her pocket for something sharp.

"I know what you're thinking," Mr. Arbitor said, hands out and heading her off at the pass. "But I wouldn't do that if I were you."

"Why?" Jo asked. "DOME got reinforcements on the way? 'Cause I got news for you, Mr. Arbitor. There's a new threat in town. These IMPS are scarier and better at this than DOME ever was—and we've outrun *them* a dozen times now. So if you think we can't fight off a couple of overweight has-been DOME agents, then you've got another think coming."

Mr. Arbitor's grip on the boys only tightened. "You don't understand," he told her. "I'm not threatening you. There *are no* reinforcements. We *aren't* going to DOME. And we *aren't* going to Acheron."

And then, as if to drive the point home, Mr. Arbitor took a tablet out of his pocket and made a call to his wife right in front of the Dust's very eyes. "Olivia," he said. "I have them. They're safe."

"Thank Cylis," Olivia said. "I'll make sure we've got something ready to eat by the time you all arrive."

Just two blocks away, a whole new round of IMP reinforcements ran through Tier Two, closing in on the group and announcing formations over some type of megaphone.

"Thanks, Liv," Mr. Arbitor said, ending the tablet call and holding eye contact with the Dust. "Now we *have* to move. Please. Those IMPS aren't far behind."

And with that, Mr. Arbitor, the man who just six months ago

tore his own life apart trying to lock these kids up, found himself deliberately sneaking the Dust all the way across town, away from DOME, away from the IMPS, to his own private apartment.

To apologize.

And to ask the Dust for help.

ㅂ

Inside the chancellor's palace, Cylis led Lily through a maze of ornate hallways and rooms, each one decorated in a style reminiscent of one of the many historical cultures that had been subsumed by his own under the Mark. This particular hallway was adorned with Picassos and Dalís and Goyas and El Grecos, the artwork of pre-Unity Spain; that one with the portraits of kings and queens and royalty of pre-Unity England; and on and on, like a graveyard of culture, a memorial to ethnicity and divergent ways of life. Cylis's palace was the greatest museum the world had ever known, available only to him.

Finally, Lily and the chancellor made their way to the palace's grand dining hall. Lily estimated it at around the size of a soccer field, and while she'd only ever actually seen one of those matches via television frame, the estimation wasn't far off.

Lining the dining room's walls were the remains of sculptures from all over the world, from all throughout history. Michelangelo's *David*, intact except for its right arm; the ancient Greek Discus Thrower, missing its head but still holding its discus; a bust of Julius Caesar; Rodin's *Thinker*, still pondering some great mystery; the Venus de Milo; and, breathtakingly, at the far end of the hall, the head of the Statue of Liberty itself, long thought lost in Lamson's great Rupturing of the Dam toward the end of the Total War, but preserved here and forever for Cylis to see.

"Please," he said with a warm smile. "Sit."

And Lily did.

On cue, a team of Head-Marked servants arrived and laid out a series of dishes across the long table before her. Lily leaned forward, examining them wide-eyed. On one of the plates was a pile of lightly fried and salted grasshoppers. Next to it was a dish of grub sausage, and beside that, hash browns sprinkled with scarab beetle bits.

Lily had heard talk of this, and yet still it surprised her to see it. Ever since the agricultural collapse that followed in the wake of the Tipping Point, the world had dealt with its meat shortage in two very different ways. Americans, slightly more squeamish about such things, transitioned mostly into a vegetarian diet. Europe, on the other hand, began eating bugs.

"This looks delicious," Lily insisted, and she took a scoop of cockroach porridge for herself.

For a moment, there was quiet while Lily ate. Her chewing echoed across the dining hall. She swallowed, and it felt to her like the whole world must have been able to hear. Eventually, the chancellor sat down beside her, and he said, "Lily. It would not be insubordinate of you to ask me why you're here. It was a difficult trip. You had no notice. I've ripped you from your duties out west . . ."

Lily looked up at Cylis, her mouth still full. She swallowed too quickly and choked a bit on the food as it went down just slightly wrong. "Sir?" she asked.

"Dominic," the chancellor corrected. And then he waited . . . and he laughed. "Well, if you won't ask, then I will volunteer it: I need your help.

Lily sat still. She held her breath. Indeed, Cylis said, lifting his eyebrows a bit and looking down in humility. "You? Helping me?" He laughed. "You don't have to say it—the thought alone gives you pause. And why shouldn't it? You and I have never met. You're not the highest-ranking IMP I could have found. You aren't even from my own European State. You're foreign, young, inexperienced, and unfamiliar. It does not, as one might say, add up."

Cylis smiled. "Except that it does, Lily Langly. For I know precisely how exceptional you are. And I have not gotten to where I am today without being an exceptional judge of character myself."

Lily looked uncomfortably around the dining hall, from one Head-Marked servant to the next. They lined the halls, standing at attention between the sculptures.

The chancellor leaned in.

"I know about your brother, Lily. I know he went Markless. I know that he questions the Department and my government and the IMPS and everything I do. I know, full well, the trouble he has caused.

"It is not generally my concern, of course, the day-to-day of DOME's cases and findings and troubles. But when your brother found Acheron in December . . . when he ran in, headfirst, to pull you out of there . . . well . . . a thing like that will get a man's attention.

"And, Lily. I must say. What I saw in you on that day did not disappoint. The character you showed . . . the patience and the prudence you demonstrated in the way that you captured him. Marvelous! Where others might have acted in haste, you waited, biding your time, allowing *him* to come to *you*, instructing sub-servients to do the same . . . where others might have seen their brother and doubted, you remained steadfast, resolved. You put country above family that day. You put country above yourself.

"You are, truly, Lily, the model of patriotism and excellence among the IMPS. And that is why I've chosen you. That is why I want you by my side.

"And so, humbly, I ask that today you give me your loyalty once more. I ask, Lily, that you work with me, now, to stop a threat far greater than your brother could ever be or even imagine."

The chancellor sat back in his chair, assembling his thoughts. Lily was speechless and could do nothing but wait.

"I hope you'll forgive me for being quite blunt about it, since there's no nice way to say this sort of thing. My own most trusted ally . . . has betrayed me." Cylis allowed the shock of it to sink in before he continued. "General Lamson is, I am quite certain now, a partner of mine no more."

Lily couldn't help stealing glances at the servants lining the room, seeking even some small confirmation or hint as to how she ought to react. "Dominic," she said, somewhat clumsily. "How . . . how is that possible? The G.U. Treaty isn't even a month old."

"A last-ditch effort," Cylis said. "My final attempt to bring America's general back onto my side." He shook his head sadly, thinking of it. "It failed some time back, our partnership, I suspect. But only as of yesterday has it officially collapsed."

"But . . . what about Unity?" Lily asked. "What about living together, and all the talk of harmony and global community?"

"None of that changes," Cylis said. "So long as I can help it, the public will never know of any of this. We remain, Lamson and I, a symbol of those ideals. Regardless of the truth."

"So then the rumors were true," Lily said to herself. "The IMPS' greatest fears . . ."

"There's talk of this?" Cylis asked. "Controllers are aware, among the ranks?"

"It's being denied," Lily said. "There'll be no talk of it anymore. But yes, there was some speculation."

The chancellor nodded. He plucked a cricket from the dish in front of him and ate it in one distracted bite. "Then allow me, Lily, to get right to the point:

"There is a weather mill in America. European technology, loaned ten years ago to the general, as part of our peace accord following the Total War. Surely you know of it."

"I know of it," Lily said.

"Then I don't need to tell you how important it is for that weather mill to function, should we hope to continue fighting Earth's permadrought . . ."

Lily nodded slowly.

"Lily, the mill has not operated since September. America has now gone six months without state-controlled weather." He shook his head. "It's been bearable, so far. The cooler winter months still rain or snow frequently enough, and the water reserves have been tapped effectively to shield against any negative effects. But come springtime . . . Lily . . . there is no bigger threat to your American State."

"All right . . . ," Lily said. "Okay. But—forgive me, Dominic—this sounds like a technical problem. It hardly has the signs of a political standoff."

"And so I thought too," Cylis said. "So I thought for quite a long time. The outages were worrisome, of course. But they were a mechanical concern. One that would be addressed, surely, with plenty of time left to avoid the worst of the consequences . . ." The chancellor stood now and paced back and forth along the dining hall's heavy table. "Until this week when Lahoma security began to suspect sabotage. I called you here to help me root out any traitor . . . but I called too late. Two have already revealed themselves—they blew up the mill while you were en route."

Lily frowned, uncertain. "And, Dominic . . . you think the *general* put them up to this?"

Cylis stopped pacing and pivoted quickly to face her. "There can be no doubt. For months, I've sensed his distance . . . seen sign after telltale sign of his ongoing betrayal. I denied it. For too long, I denied it. And finally, now, it fits. All of it fits, in light of this."

"But why?" Lily asked. "What does Lamson have to gain by starving his own people?"

"Political instability!" Cylis exclaimed. "It's not just the suffering Marked and dead Markless at stake here, Lily. A plot like this will destroy our already fragile global economy. It will shut down America's power plants. There will be food shortages, mass extinctions, even fewer acres of habitable land . . . Marked citizens across the *globe* would feel its awful effects. And if we learned one thing from the Total War, it's that cataclysms of the magnitude we're talking about lead to one thing and one thing only: revolution. With the right timing and finesse, a person could swoop in under such circumstances. Could save the day. Could get the whole world on his side . . ."

"So you think this drought is a *power play*?" Lily asked.

Cylis frowned. "Hey, what do I know, right? But at the end of the day, the motives here hardly even matter. In time, a permadrought like this will destroy the lives of the very Marked citizens I am sworn to serve. That alone is my concern. You Americans are my responsibility too, remember, under the umbrella of this great new Global Union. I cannot allow this drought of his to continue."

Lily tried very hard to be respectful of the claims.

She coughed nervously.

"Sir—"

"Dominic."

"Dominic." Lily paused. She looked for the right way to say it. "If this is true, why not just confront Lamson yourself? Have you tried reasoning with him? Negotiation?"

"Lily—this is a man who has betrayed me repeatedly over the last six months! He's been working behind my back, off the record, this whole time, in ways that I can't trace, *specifically* to rob me of the chance to negotiate. If I confront him, he'll simply deny it. At best, he'll admit to something small—and then proceed to work twice as hard to shut me out of whatever else he has planned down the line. I cannot risk pushing him away. I cannot risk losing what little trust of his I still have left. Not now. Not with this new G.U. as fragile as it is.

"Outright accusation is out of the question too," Cylis added. "I can't accuse him, and he knows it. I can't prove anything at all. He's been far too careful. Whatever meddling he did over in Lahoma, it was contained . . . and I am left merely to speculate. None of the surviving workers appears to know about Lamson's involvement. Even now, they're working tirelessly to get the mill up and running again. At the moment, they're aiming to have it back online in time for planting season."

Immediately, Lily's face lit up. "Well then, that's great! Problem solved!"

Cylis sighed. "I have my doubts," he said. "Where there were two traitors, there could easily be more. If *any* other Lahoma citizens are still working under General Lamson's request, then this reopening remains a pipe dream.

"I *need* to know that our mill is secure, Lily. I need to know there aren't any ongoing plots to destroy it. This first attack was devastating enough. If anyone out there is planning a second . . . Lily—the American Marked way of life could be destroyed by the time a new mill is built."

"Okay," Lily said. "Well . . . well, what if we send a few squads of IMPS to Lahoma for security? We could set up a detail to guard the weather mill day and night."

"I've tried," Cylis said. "Probably where those infighting rumors came from, in fact. Lamson simply vetoed the order. The IMPS won't act without agreement from both of us—and it is clear to me, now, that he and I will never agree on the issue of Lahoma's security. I can't afford to risk further unrest among the IMPS by straining that already delicate balance of power. The last thing this G.U. needs is to think that its joint leaders are feuding."

Lily frowned. It was clear that Cylis had thought through his options already. It was clear, now, that calling upon Lily already *was* Cylis's last resort. This was where things stood. Whatever his request of her was now, it was how things had to be.

"All right," Lily said. "Then what do you need from me?"

Cylis sighed. "I've pulled some strings within the inner workings of Beacon's Capitol. You'll be positioned there, effective upon your return, as General Lamson's personal assistant. He doesn't know I have anything to do with your reassignment. He doesn't even know you've been gone. No one does, Michael Cheswick aside."

Lily gulped.

"Lily, I need you to find out if there is anyone left who might take measures to destroy Lahoma's weather mill. The fate of your country depends on its reopening."

Lily nodded, slowly at first, but increasingly resolved. "Of course, Dominic. Of course I will."

Cylis sat down and reached into his pocket. He pulled out a small Markscan, and he took Lily's head in his hands. "I brought you here in person because I could not risk the possibility of a hacked tablet call. But once your duties to Lamson begin, you will not be able to leave Beacon.

"Thus, with the most incriminating of our discussions already behind us, what I am giving you now is access to my personal line of communication." He waved the Markscan in front of Lily's face, coding the Mark on her forehead into its system. "You alone now have the authority to reach me in this palace, day or night. Any tablet or computer system will know to grant you access. But you must be extremely careful with this power," Cylis added. "In the event that Lamson should discover what you are doing . . ." He trailed off, shaking his head and sighing a slow sigh.

Lily understood.

"Excellent," the chancellor said, standing now, abruptly. "I knew I could count on you. You're a good soldier, Lily. A loyal Marked. And you will do great things for the Global Union."

"Thank you, Dominic," Lily said.

The chancellor smiled and gestured grandly toward the hall. "Your shuttle awaits."

FIVE

GHOST TOWN

1

IT WAS NOT A BAD DAY FOR A FUNERAL.

The sun was out. It wasn't raining. The air was cool and blue.

And yet Connor alone was there. The only one. An hour into the service, and without a single other guest from all of Lahoma.

Connor stood by his parents, so still that he might've looked lifeless himself.

He wasn't. But it would have been hard to say for sure.

He wasn't thinking about much, in fact. The wide range of emotions he'd felt up to this point had been largely whittled down into one fine point. Guilt. By now, that was more or less all that remained, lodging itself in his throat, sinking its tentacles deep down into the pit of his stomach, grabbing hold and not letting go, squeezing with a sickness that made the world spin.

Was Connor responsible? Was his parents' death as much his fault as it seemed? He told them, two days ago, that the jig was very nearly up. He told them to work fast, or risk losing everything. And it seemed clear to him now—they had taken that to heart.

They had done both.

In the aftermath of his dinner with them, Connor's parents had quickly realized that their sporadic, stopgap measures couldn't continue for long. In these past months since September, they'd skillfully kept Lahoma's weather mill running more or less smoothly, while at the same time maintaining an unbroken chain of inconvenient system failures serving to perpetually delay any successful canister launch. In this way, they'd kept hope among mill workers alive that the next cloud seeding could happen "any day now," while continually ensuring that it would not.

But that phase of the plan was over. The Goodmans were suddenly sure to be caught any day now, and the only solution they could find was to bring the whole place down in one fell swoop.

This was all Connor's speculation, of course. But there was little room for doubt. The one option his parents would not have entertained was a cloud seeding. The one thing they would not abide was a mill-induced storm.

They knew the stakes. The stakes were worth this to them.

"Hey," Sally said, walking up behind Connor and startling him a little.

He was happy to see her. And he wanted to say so . . . but somehow, he just couldn't find the words.

"They're cold," he told her instead, nodding at the bodies in front of him. "I touched them. Touched my mom's hand." He swallowed. His parents were covered now by the white sheet wrapped around them. Sally guessed that Connor must have pulled the sheet off, momentarily, to say good-bye. "They felt cold."

For some reason, this made Sally burst into tears.

In another hour, DOME would take Mr. and Mrs. Goodman away from Lahoma in order to dispose of them. There wouldn't be a burial, of course. Burials were for pre-Unity deaths—and Markless.

No, these days, DOME's Ends and Beginnings Bureau took Marked bodies and cremated them. Those ashes were then taken and purified, and the carbon within them was compressed into graphite, and then again, into diamonds, and each was set onto a ring and delivered generously back to the departed's closest surviving relative.

Originally, this tradition began as a way to discourage any end-of-life religious practices that Marked citizens might have been accustomed to pre-Unity. But over time, DOME realized the system had a secondary benefit as well—by destroying Marked bodies, it seriously limited the supply chain of black market hands.

So Connor had *that* to look forward to, he guessed. Two diamond rings, coming his way.

Connor mentioned this to Sally.

She cried harder.

For what it was worth, the Ends and Beginnings Bureau had done a nice job, Connor thought now. Merciful of them, given his parents' ultimate "traitor" status. Unheard of, in fact. In post-Unity history, no traitor had ever been given a state-sanctioned funeral. Not once. And yet Connor's parents had been dressed nicely and laid carefully onto a small wooden stage at the grassiest spot of the browning Lahoma public park. A single flower adorned the stage. And deep down, Connor knew he had General Lamson to thank for all that. But it was small consolation. This past hour, what Connor had mostly thought of the funeral was that the Ends and Beginnings Bureau had combed his father's hair wrong. It didn't look like that. It wasn't supposed to look like that. The minutes had passed, the guilt had flared and subsided and flared again, and through most of it, Connor was lost in some great, computer-rack rat-maze of thoughts about hair, parted all wrong and bizarre, as the tentacles of guilt gripped harder . . .

Connor couldn't see it for himself, of course, the shock he was in. But Sally sure did.

"It's okay to be upset," she told him finally. She put her arm around her friend's shoulder and brushed a stream of tears from her own blotchy face. "It's *better* to be upset. You *should* be upset."

So Connor nodded at Sally, as if that might adequately cover the whole "emotion" thing she was looking for.

"Where are you going to stay?" Sally asked. "Do you know?"

Connor shrugged.

"I'd say you're welcome to stay with us, at my house . . ." Sally trailed off.

"But I'm not."

Sally nodded at her feet. "Not just yet, I think . . ."

"So where is everyone?" Connor asked. A town this size, there wasn't a single family that hadn't been friends with the Goodmans. In fact, given Connor's General Award, from six months ago until yesterday, the Goodmans might have been the most beloved family in all of Lahoma. "Not that I expected them, I guess, given the circumstances, but . . ."

"Central Square," Sally said. "The mayor's holding a town hall, in conjunction with the head of the weather mill, to discuss next steps."

"He couldn't have waited an hour?" Connor asked.

"Could've," Sally apologized. "Didn't."

Connor nodded. "Come on, then," he said, waving his arm.

"Where?"

"Central Square." He nodded to his parents. "They can't take me with them. I'm still as much a part of this town as anyone else."

"Sure you are," Sally said, trying hard to mean it.

Connor didn't look back at the stage when they left.

2

The Arbitor family apartment had always been a tidy home: the type where the countertops shined and the white floors were waxed; with rows in the carpets where the vacuum had rolled; where shoes stayed outside in the building's hallway, and junk drawers had filing systems; where the windows sparkled with nanosolvent . . .

But just a few short hours into the Dust's visit, the Arbitor family apartment already looked a bit more like the impact zone of a minor bomb blast.

Immediately after lunch, Tyler had found the packing boxes left over from Charles and Erin's recent move from Spokie. He'd torn them open, of course, as was Tyler's way, and he'd scattered them across each room, creating long tunnels and forts for him and Rusty to play in. Meg, meanwhile, amused herself by strewing the boxes' contents about in piles, making a series of things not unlike nests for mice. She slept now in one of them, snoring loudly.

Already the floors were so cluttered, Charles Arbitor and his wife Olivia were more or less stranded on their own couch. They needed to shout just to be heard. And everywhere they turned, there was Dust.

"What do you mean, you lost him?" Jo asked.

"I mean I *lost* him, what do you think? How was I supposed to know he'd run off the first chance he got?"

"Because he's an *iguana*, Tyler. They have legs and brains and—amazingly—they move on their own!"

"Okay, look, let's everybody just stop for a second, and we'll all just stare out and glaze our eyes over a little bit, and in a few minutes time, one of us should see which of these mounds starts moving on its own. Good plan, guys? Good plan."

Such was the state of Charles and Olivia Arbitor's best hope. Olivia had her head in her hands. Charles watched with his jaw slightly slack. But it was worth it, he knew. Anything to get these six kids to stay awhile. Anything to get Erin back.

"Hey, Tyler, maybe let's forget about the iguana," Mr. Arbitor said. "The iguana will be fine."

"It's just that it'd be so easy to step on him given that we can't really see the floor right now—"

"He'll be fine!" Charles yelled. "Now, could we all *please* just sit down for five minutes so we can talk about Erin?"

Meg was still sound asleep. But Blake, Joanne, Tyler, and Rusty all obediently sat down where they were.

"Found Iggy!" Shawn yelled, immediately bouncing back up and reaching down into the pile he very nearly squashed.

"Careful," Tyler warned. "He moves all on his own."

"Mr. Arbitor," Blake said, cutting through the nonsense. "We appreciate you giving us shelter like this—we really do. But I'm just not sure what exactly we can do to help you find your daughter. We don't know where she is. We have no way of contacting her. She *deliberately* kept us in the dark in case any of us were ever captured and interrogated—"

"Hey!" Tyler said. "Just like what really happened!"

"Yeah, Tyler." Jo nodded. "Just like that."

"It's all right," Mr. Arbitor said, laughing a little. "I don't need your help with any of that. I already know where Erin is. Or—at least, I think I do."

"Well, in that case, why are we here?" Blake pressed.

"You're here because I've hit a wall. I believe Erin's found sanctuary at the Sierra Science Center out west, but the scientists there won't put me through to her on account of my affiliation with DOME. They think I'm just trying to apprehend her."

"Aren't you?" Shawn asked.

"No. *DOME's* trying to apprehend her. *I'm* looking to protect her."

Olivia sighed. "Right now, the head scientist at the SSC is insisting that Erin and the rest of your friends have already escaped for the northwest. Personally, we don't believe it. But DOME does. And we'd like to keep it that way."

"If we could just *confirm* that Erin's there . . . if we could just *talk* to her," Charles said. "Then I just know that Olivia and I could figure out a way to help. There must be something we can do from here."

Olivia sat forward on the couch, begging the Dust now. "But the SSC's scientists don't trust Charles and me enough to tell us what's really going on. We can't get through to Erin on our own."

"And that's where you kids come in," Charles said. "You're Erin's closest allies. A call from you is totally different than a call from Olivia or me. She trusts you. She'll talk to you."

"Please," Olivia begged. "We just want to know our daughter's safe."

"Could be a trick," Blake said to the others. "He *does* still work for DOME."

Mr. Arbitor sighed. "Think about it, Blake. If I were working with the Department on this, I'd have just ordered a raid on the place by now. The whole point here is to *prevent* DOME from figuring out what I'm up to. The whole point is to do this without them."

Olivia smiled hopefully. "And you kids are the key."

"I'm sure I don't need to remind you," Mr. Arbitor added, "that right now, a plan to help Erin is a plan to help Peck."

Blake looked like he was about to speak up. But Jo stopped him. "They're right," she said. And she turned to the Arbitors. "We'll do it."

∃

The town hall meeting in Lahoma was in full swing now, and Sally held Connor's hand supportively as the two of them entered and watched the end of the mayor's speech from the back of the riled crowd.

"Lahoma! The Goodmans' psychotic, reckless, and systematic sabotage of our great weather mill these last few months is unthinkable, unbelievable, unconscionable . . . and, indeed, their final, heinous act of destruction has only cemented the legacy of hardship, suffering, and hatred these traitors leave behind. For the foreseeable future, it would appear as though these two terrorists have succeeded. The mill is down. Its computer system has sustained irreparable damage and will need to be fully replaced. Now, unfortunately, DOME's Meteorology Bureau, so far, seems somehow to be tied up in enough red tape that we cannot rely squarely on them for the funds and support necessary to repair this damage in a timely way—"

An uproar of anger filled the town hall, but the mayor spoke on.

"That said, Lahoma has dug deep into its own pockets, and,

with the help of a flood of generosity from fellow Marked across the country, we believe we have the foundation necessary to begin repairing and rebuilding within the immediate future.

"Let me be clear. This damage has no easy fix. Programming and calibrating a new supercomputer system from scratch, without the Goodmans' unique expertise in the field, will take time to get right. Of course, with thirty acres of missile launchers at our command, it is our duty not only to get Lahoma's weather mill back online but to do it in a safe and responsible manner. We therefore ask for everyone's patience as we embark upon this long and arduous recovery.

"However, hear me today, and mark my words—this mill *will* be up and running by the end of business day on April 1. America's rainy season will *not* be missed."

The crowd cheered and hollered its approval.

"Our great town of Lahoma *will* make up for lost time—not with a drizzle, not with a sprinkle, not with a shower, but with the biggest man-made rainstorm this continent has ever seen!"

The town roared, and the mayor of Lahoma reached his crescendo. "And with Cylis as my witness, this long, national drought will be over. Our public health, our economy—our very *ecosystem*—will be restored. We will not go hungry, we will not go thirsty, we will not go powerless. We *will* storm into this new year, we *will* give this great Union the weather it deserves, and the fruits of our hard and honest work *will* rain down on our fellow Marked—stronger, better, and safer than ever before!"

Connor stood silently at the back of the hall as the applause drowned out the end of the speech. He let go of Sally's hand. He knew what he had to do.

He ducked out of Lahoma's town hall without anyone else noticing he'd come or gone.

4

Logan, Hailey, and Peck had spent the day hiding among the storage shelves of the SSC's basement, keeping Erin company, reading *Swipe* aloud, and trying their best to dissect all the stuff they found in there.

"So what do you guys think?" Peck asked once they'd finished.

Logan shrugged. "I'm not sure. He gets a lot of stuff wrong. A lot of the details, you know?"

"He made up a good bit of it," Erin agreed.

Peck nodded. "In my chapters too. And yet . . . the big stuff's all there."

"He got your iguana right," Logan said to Erin. "When you lost him in Spokie's park that one time, with Hailey?"

Erin nodded, looking a little creeped out.

And Peck said, "Somehow he knew about Tyler's card game too. King's Punch-Out. Little stuff like that is spot-on, all throughout. How would a stranger know about any of that?"

"Are we really this famous?" Logan asked. "That some guy was able to write a book about us in just these last few months? I mean, where'd he learn all this stuff? How's he have any idea what kinds of things we were up to back in Spokie?"

Peck shook his head. "I don't know," he said. "But he keeps a low profile and he calls himself an 'Angler.' By the sound of it, I'd guess he's a fisherman along the Unmarked River. If so, he'd meet plenty of Markless passing through. Guess one day he just started piecing together the rumors he'd been hearing and—"

"That's a lot of rumors," Logan said.

Peck nodded. "His author's bio says he lives in Beacon. So who knows . . . It's possible he was there back with the Markless huddle under City Center, in the fission reactor, watching us, listening . . ."

Logan shuddered. The thought of it, of being observed like that . . . it sent a chill down his spine. "I don't want to be famous," he said.

Peck laughed. "Then you shouldn't have done something so remarkable."

"I didn't even know they still *published* paper books," Erin said, as if that somehow made the artifact less real.

"They don't. I have no idea how this one was printed. Or where they found the equipment. Even the library downtown, lawless as it is, is mostly electronic. What you're holding there is highly illegal. Someone risked quite a lot carrying that copy all the way out to Sierra."

"You think many people have read it?" Logan asked.

But before anyone could hazard a guess, Arianna was bounding down the basement steps with a tablet in hand.

"Erin," she said. "Tablet call for you."

Erin sat up slightly in her bed. "Who . . . who is it?" she asked tentatively. Already, Logan, Peck, and Hailey were tense, ready to run or fight in case the doctor was handing them a trap.

"Hey, relax," Arianna said. "You think I wouldn't vet these guys first?"

"'These guys?'" Peck asked.

"Yeah! The whole group of 'em!" Arianna smiled. "Seems they call themselves 'the Dust'?"

The reunion among the friends was chaotic and warm.

Immediately, Logan, Peck, and Hailey flew from their circle on the floor and into a small huddle around Arianna and her tablet.

"Blake!"

"Joanne!"

"Peck!"

"Hailey!"

On both ends of the video connection, the Dust spoke too fast on top of one another for any of them to be heard.

Arianna laughed at the warm welcome, watching it unfold.

Of all of them, only Erin held back. "How'd they get through to us?" she asked suspiciously, still resting in her medical bed. "They didn't know where we were headed, they couldn't have guessed Arianna's identity . . . they don't even have a tablet that can make calls."

"I know!" Tyler yelled. "But listen—now that we're all here, I have this brand-new game we can play—"

"Now, wait a minute!" Erin said, raining on everyone's parade. "I'm not saying one more word to these guys until we figure out how they found us. Something's not right." She leaned forward and stared into the video screen at the foot of her bed. "So what exactly is going on here?"

There was a brief silence on the other end. Several of the Dust even slinked sheepishly outside the view of the screen.

"I'm what's going on here," Mr. Arbitor said, entering the video feed. "Well—your mom and I, both."

Right away, Erin was dumbstruck. She held a hand to her mouth and teared up just a little, though no one else was quite sure whether it was over fear of being caught, or joy at being found.

"We're here to help," Dr. Arbitor said, waving inside the tablet. "The Dust too." And behind her, Tyler stuck a finger in his mouth and made a gagging motion.

"Arianna," Erin said. "You *know* my dad works for DOME, don't you?"

"Yeah," Dr. Rhyne said. "But if he's working with 'em right now, then he sure has a strange way of apprehending DOME's number-one group of rebels."

The next few minutes of conversation were filled with ups and downs: Erin's apology for running out, the Arbitors' forgiveness, Tyler's account of being caught in the elevator, Dr. Arbitor's stories of how worried Mac had been back on Barrier Street . . .

But ultimately, the joys of reconnecting were snuffed out once and for all by the Arbitors' realization that Erin's trip to the Sierra Science Center wasn't for pleasure.

"*Sick*? What do you mean, Erin's sick?" Dr. Arbitor said quickly.

"You guys didn't tell them?" Erin asked.

Mr. Arbitor turned his head. "You *knew*?"

"Well, of course," Tyler said. "With Trumpet. Obviously."

"*Obviously*? What in Cylis's name is 'Trumpet'?" Dr. Arbitor asked.

For the first time since the Dust had arrived, a heavy silence fell over the room. Mr. Arbitor hung his head in his hands, slowly remembering the rumors he'd heard over the years.

"Olivia," Dr. Rhyne said. "You might want to sit down for this." And she proceeded to tell the group everything.

"I'm afraid right now there's not a whole lot we can do for her," Arianna said by the end of it. "Somehow, Erin must have come in contact with a second activation protein. Something I had nothing to do with. And one that . . . well, that activated her vaccine.

But right now we haven't the slightest idea what that protein is or where it came from. Without it, we're looking at a bit of a dead end. Sorry," she added quickly. "Pun not intended."

Each of them stood somberly, hearing the reality of it.

After a moment, Erin broke the ice. "I've been thinking a lot about it," she began. "About where I might have been exposed. Whether I breathed it, or drank it, or touched it, or smelled it . . ."

"There's no way you would remember," Dr. Rhyne said. "I don't blame you for—"

"No, that's just it," Erin interrupted. "I think I do."

Dr. Rhyne raised an eyebrow.

"Before we made it out here, I'd just assumed it was just from . . . I don't know . . . from whatever. But since you're sure the protein hasn't been released nationwide yet . . . well, it's clear that I must have been exposed through something specific to me."

"That's right," the doctor said. "But as for what that specific thing is . . ."

Erin frowned and tugged a little at the wires in her arms, trying hard—and failing—to get comfortable. "Back in Spokie, I did a lot of snooping around DOME's headquarters at the Umbrella." She looked at her dad now in the tablet, apologetically. "I stole things. More things than I could count, really. Lined my pockets with tactical equipment, filled my backpack with spy tech I couldn't even recognize . . .

"We all know Trumpet originally came from within the ranks of DOME, and I certainly got my hands on enough top secret stuff over there—powders, gels, vials . . . Who's to say some of it wasn't carrying this new activation protein?" Erin laughed. "I gave the stupid fever to myself."

Her words hung in the stale basement air. Erin could almost

picture them swirling around everyone's heads, like birds around a dazed character from some old, pre-Unity cartoon.

Soon, Mr. Arbitor's mind was racing. Trumpet. *Trumpet* . . .

If it had been inside the Spokie headquarters, then it stood to reason it'd be at Beacon's too.

"Erin," he said. "If we were to find traces of that activation protein ourselves . . . is there any way that could help you all with your research out there at the Science Center?"

"Are you kidding?" Dr. Rhyne chimed in. "Having the info on that protein would make all the difference in the world!"

Already, a big smile was stretching across his face. It was exactly what Mr. Arbitor needed to hear. "Dust," he said, turning back to them. "Start planning. We're going on a field trip."

5

It was late afternoon in Lahoma. The sun was low and golden on Main Street, though not much of it seemed to make its way inside.

"Sheriff, thanks for meeting with me," Connor said, walking into the room. The sheriff's office was dim and cool, its dirt floors and wooden walls brightened only by a single, large wallscreen that hung oddly against the rest of the room's out-of-era simplicity.

Connor found a seat. The sheriff raised an eyebrow and leaned forward at his desk. "You've come here, I assume, with some sort of confession?"

"Well, maybe yes and maybe no," Connor said.

The sheriff nodded. "Before you speak, son, I feel obligated to tell you—my investigation into your parents' crimes is ongoing, and it's only a matter of time before I'm going to need you to testify in the town's hearings against their conspiracy. You're a Marked man now, and that makes you fully adult in the eyes of the law. Anything you say to me today can and will be used against you. You understand me, Mr. Goodman?"

Connor sat still for quite some time. *Why must this be so much harder than it needs to be?* "In that case," he said finally, "I'll only say this: whatever it is my parents may or may not have been guilty of . . . whatever their plan and actions may or may not have entailed . . . I need you to know—they were acting at the request of General Lamson."

The sheriff stared at Connor for a moment. And then he couldn't help but laugh.

"Connor. You're a good kid. You're a smart kid, a hard worker, and a selfless volunteer for your community. You're our country's first General's Award recipient and you should be very proud of it. But just because you've been honored by our general does *not* mean that your parents had carte blanche to commit whatever treasonous acts they fancied. Surely you understand the wide leap in logic between these two things."

"It's not a leap!" Connor pressed. "Forget the award—the award itself meant nothing. It was a setup! Lamson came here to talk to my parents. The night after the ceremonies, he stayed, he asked me to leave. He talked with my parents himself . . . nearly an hour, he was in there . . ."

"And I'm sure he had many complimentary things to say about you, but—"

"No! He didn't! That's what I'm trying to tell you! That meeting—it had nothing to do with me at all! Lamson came here *for my parents*. Not for me. I was just the distraction. The rabbit he used to pull off his magic trick. I happened to be a believable candidate for the award that he gave me, sure, but that's only because he *designed* the award to fit my profile. He could have made something up for anyone! If he'd wanted to conspire with the Jeffersons, then he would have given Patrick a General's Award for swimming. Had it been the Wolfes he needed, then right now Katherine would have a General's Honorary Medal for best actor. It's all just nonsense! The trophy as it was went to me because *my* parents were in charge of the weather mill's launch systems. *My* parents were the ones best positioned to do Lamson's bidding. And his bidding—was to shut down America's cloud seeding for as long as humanly possible!"

"Connor. At this point I feel I must tell you—slandering the general-in-chief of the American State is, in and of itself, its own form of treason—"

"But it isn't slander! It's the truth!"

"Mr. Goodman, *why*? Why in *Cylis's name* would the leader of the American State, one half of our great, new Global Union, *conspire to starve Americans*? Why would the general ask his own citizens to wreak havoc and hardship upon their fellow patriots—and his biggest supporters? Connor, I admire your familial devotion, but this fiction you're spinning doesn't stand to reason. It's only out of compassion for your obvious state of shock that I'm not arresting you for it as we speak."

Connor sat back against his chair with his head in his hands. "Sheriff, what I'm telling you is *serious*. Lamson's guards pointed *guns* at me just for prying into this!"

"Well, you'll forgive me for taking the general's word over yours."

"You haven't heard the general's word! That's exactly what I want you to do—ask him about it! He'll tell you! He'll tell you my parents weren't traitors. They died for him! They died for their country!"

The sheriff stood up and walked to the front of his desk. He leaned back on it, trying, perhaps, to look calm and cool, for Connor's sake. "Connor. You're not hearing me. If I were to call DOME and inquire about this . . . were I even to *suggest* that what you're saying to me might possibly be true—something I do not believe, by the way—then you and I *both* would face charges for treason."

"Sheriff, I know. Trusting me on this—even entertaining the idea of it—is most definitely a risk. I grant you that. And I'm aware of what this ongoing drought could mean.

"But try, Sheriff—for me, please, just for a second—to see things from my perspective. The fact is, I don't *know* why the general asked my parents to sabotage Lahoma's weather mill. My father did say something two nights ago about a civil war, and he seemed to know what he was talking about, but do I have any idea what that meant? No. You got me. I can't tell you.

"But I *can* tell you that whatever precise reason Lamson had for his request, it was convincing enough that my own mother and father—two Marked citizens who never wronged a single person once in their entire lives—were willing to pay the ultimate sacrifice just to see it through. Doesn't that mean anything to you?"

The sheriff didn't look doubtful anymore. But he didn't look convinced either. He just looked . . . concerned.

"Oh, Connor," he said. "It's natural, you know, to defend the ones you've loved —"

But Connor had heard enough. He knew a dead end when he saw one.

And so it was that Connor Goody Two-Shoes stormed out of a sheriff's office midlecture.

He was on his own now—truly on his own. He walked fast along the dirt road of Main Street.

April 1, he thought.

That's my deadline.

Six weeks.

He would have to begin now.

SIX

HAIL TO THE CHIEF

1

THREE WEEKS HAD PASSED.

Lily Langly pushed through the Markless protesters that crowded Beacon's ground level streets, and she thought about how much the demonstrations had grown.

In the beginning, her commute from Acheron to Lamson's Capitol Building had been relatively easy. On a normal day, it was hardly more than a fifteen-minute walk, and as long as Lily could stick to the moving sidewalk treads, it was easy to avoid the worst of the crowds that had been mobbing City Center for weeks. Barricades along each road had, up until that point, done a good job of keeping the Markless protesters on the streets and off the sidewalks, so that IMPS and stand-up Marked citizens could shop and travel and go to work without too much of an inconvenience.

But as the days passed, these barriers slowly eroded, one block at a time, until City Center became just one single mass of wall-to-wall protests. IMPS stood shoulder to shoulder with the Markless now, magnecuffing them, tasing them, taking them away . . . any excuse was good enough. Marked Beaconers, meanwhile, had given up traveling at ground level. It wasn't just inconvenient any longer—it was dangerous. And yet still the Markless kept coming. By now, everyone knew that Lahoma's weather mill was down, and rumors spread wildly about why and how and what it meant for Americans and for the Markless in particular. More than a few protesters had started to cry foul, and the anxiety and fervor of the demonstrations had only grown from there. *Was it endless?* Lily wondered. Her commute wasn't so easy any longer.

Finally, Lily reached the steps of Lamson's Capitol building, climbed to the top, and passed by the two heavily armed IMP guards stationed at its entrance.

There'd been a time, Lily knew, when these steps had been welcoming, inviting even, to all of Beacon's citizens. The Marked could walk up, sit leisurely at the top, enjoy a snack or pose for a picture . . . the Marked could even go inside, could take a tour of the Capitol's outer rooms, could walk through those hallways just one hundred yards away from the general-in-chief himself.

That time had passed.

Lily entered the general's oval office now, approaching his desk and reporting for duty as she did every morning. As usual, Lamson was sitting behind his desk, facing away from the door, and confiding in Michael Cheswick about his schedule for the day and about his current list of priorities and concerns. He hadn't much use for Lily this morning, he said, which was hardly a change in the status quo. Sometimes, Lamson even wondered why Cheswick had stationed an extra IMP assistant in his office at all, though he usually backed down once Cheswick reminded him of all the day-to-day tasks Lily had taken over. Juggling the general's calendar, arranging both standard and emergency meetings with Parliament members, coordinating triangulations during legislation negotiation . . . all meaningful stuff.

"My apologies," the general would say upon hearing the reminder. "Carry on then, Advocate. For now."

Personally, Lily concluded, Lamson was more or less everything that Chancellor Cylis was not. Where Cylis was young and handsome, Lamson was old and decrepit. Where Cylis was strong and charismatic, Lamson was weak and disagreeable. Where Cylis was confident and empathetic, Lamson was nervous and dismissive.

Cylis was a politician, fresh and eager and ready to lead. Lamson was a general, war-battered, tired, and quickly losing patience for the situations that surrounded him.

"You can speak, you know," he said one morning to Lily when she handed him his daily news screen. Lily had nodded when he said so, but at the same time, she couldn't help but wonder, *What would be the point?*

The one thing Lily *hadn't* heard about was anything regarding Lahoma. No talk of the drought, no talk of the mill being offline, no talk of the effort to get it running again by April 1, now just five weeks away . . . as far as Lamson's office was concerned, Lahoma would take care of itself. The country needn't worry about *them*, thank-you-very-much.

But all that changed this morning, when Lily went to deliver Lamson his messages.

Mostly, it was just the standard stuff. Updates on the movement of a variety of bills and proposals that had reached or would soon reach the Parliament floor, communications with Cylis and with the European branch of the new Global Union, financial news from Barrier Street (almost always bad these days) . . .

But then, too, there were the personal messages. Thank you letters from Marked students for visits the general had made to their schools, requests from hospital patients for a dying-wish visit . . .

that sort of thing. And finally, there was *this* one. Addressed personally. From a certain recipient of this past year's General's Award for Marked Excellence, Promise, and the American Dream.

Protocol stated, of course, that Lily not open any messages of the first sort—those regarding politics or national security or sensitive matters of any kind.

But the personal messages—the standard fan-mail type stuff—well, now that was at Lily's discretion. Once in a while, if something seemed particularly heart wrenching or funny or interesting or inspiring, she might slip it in with the rest of the important stuff and pass it along its way. But for the most part, the general couldn't be bothered (or expected, he insisted) to read every single message that came his way. *Someone* had to respond to them, but it sure wasn't going to be him, and so this was a task that most commonly fell to Lily.

A message from a General's Award recipient sounded very much like standard thank-you fare, so Lily opened it without giving it a second thought. She even had the standard response already planned out, regardless of what the note actually said.

Except this message, it turned out, was no ordinary piece of fan mail. This was no "Thank you for the award." This was no "I want to grow up to be you one day."

Instead, this message was *exactly* what Lily had been waiting all these weeks to find.

2

For Tyler, it was a dream come true. It had certainly taken long enough for them to coordinate everything with Arianna out west, but finally, today, the plan was in place. The Dust was making its way into Beacon City's top secret DOME headquarters. And they had explicit orders to let loose.

Back in the early stages of planning, of course, the team realized that Mr. Arbitor himself couldn't be the one to look within DOME for Trumpet's new activation protein. Having been Marked and vaccinated himself, to come in contact with the stuff even just briefly enough to get a sample would put him at a tremendous risk.

But not so with the Markless Dust.

It took a few days for Mr. Arbitor to get his hands on all the materials and cloth Detection Swabs they'd need to take their protein samples, and another few days on top of that for Arianna to explain properly how to use them. But the real holdup was caution. It had been an excruciating two weeks before Mr. Arbitor finally found the right opportunity for an office break-in—the window between busy work hours and the souped-up automated surveillance of off-hours was short to begin with, and on most days, some office event or meeting or crisis closed the gap altogether. But the time was finally upon them. The perfect window had opened. And the Dust was called quickly into action.

So while Mr. Arbitor distracted Head Agent Tate in her office down the hall, Tyler, Joanne, Blake, and Shawn were given free rein to snoop, pry, open, hack, and swipe their filthy Markless hands along every last DOME office, trinket, and surface they could find. "The more swabs you can take, the better," Mr. Arbitor said. "As long as you don't get caught."

It was a game Tyler understood all too well.

"Do you think we're doing it right?" Tyler said, slinking out of a hall closet and already on his fifty-third Detection Swab.

"I think it's hard to go wrong," Blake said, while behind him,

Shawn "the Tech Wiz" hacked into the floor's filing system on one of DOME's many state-of-the-art plastiscreens.

"I can't find a single thing in here that actually mentions the word 'Trumpet,'" he told the others as they rummaged through yet another supply closet. "Nada. Zip. Closest thing I've found so far is some annexed note from home about one of these mogul agent's kids forgetting his musical instrument at school."

"It's not going to be advertised," Jo said. "This thing's clearly top secret, even among DOME officers. And if this protein were hiding anywhere obvious, everyone here would already be sick—Tyler? Hey, where'd he go?" Jo spun around a few times and eventually found him poking his head out of a heating grate.

"I am getting *all sorts* of bonus points," he said.

And the four of them continued like this until the earliest hours of the morning.

"You wanna know the funniest part?" Tyler said, a few hours in. "I don't even really *like* Erin."

But a favor was a favor, and the Dust was happy to do it.

Plus, Tyler left with a brand-new pair of prototype hover boots.

"It's complimentary," he told Mr. Arbitor on the way out.

And Charles didn't even put up a fight.

⊐

"General Lamson?" Lily asked. She stood at the threshold of his office, waiting to be invited in.

"Yes, Advocate, come in already. What is it now?"

Lily took a deep breath. For weeks, she'd promised herself that if it came to this moment, she would not allow herself to do what she was about to do. But Lily couldn't help it. Connor's letter had said too much for her to leave the matter alone. Lily knew she was supposed to act without question. To do anything else would be to question Cylis's orders. And yet in the moment, three thousand miles away from the chancellor and all his charm . . . she simply had to ask. She *had* to give Lamson at least the opportunity to explain himself, and to explain what he was thinking. She owed him his side of the story, at least. She was still an American, after all. She could give her general that much.

"Sir," she began. "There's a message here that I'd like to ask you about."

"You know I don't have time for the personal ones, Advocate. Read the thing over and answer it yourself. You don't need my permission for such trivial—"

"This isn't personal, General, despite coming from a citizen.

"You must forgive me," she added, clearing her throat. "I never would have opened it, had I known—

"Sir," she said, interrupting herself and getting right to the point. "This letter is from Connor Goodman of Lahoma. It is a matter of national security."

4

Back in Acheron at the end of the morning, a world away from her position at the Capitol, Lily rode the elevator down to Level Six. She squeezed her eyes tight. She made sure to compose herself before stepping out into the array of desks and helmets and IMPS. What the general had told her that afternoon had left her feeling sick, nervous, betrayed by her own country . . . but it also gave her resolve.

She knew, now, that she had to do it. She had to stop Connor Goodman. She would betray her general for the chancellor, after all. It was her only choice.

And she had the perfect idea as to how to do it.

But first things first, Lily thought. This was the fourth time in as many weeks that Moderator Eddie Blackall had been sent down for Revision. It was time to pull him out. She hoped this would be the end of it.

It was a game to him, Lily realized. It must be. How many times can he beat the system? How many times can he shake loose from his Pledge? It was the one act of defiance he could still manage to make. And he was milking it for all it was worth.

This infuriated Lily.

His was a game with only one end.

And it was torture for Lily to watch it unfold.

She approached Eddie's desk and was surprised to find him sitting outside of his BCI helmet already. That meant the punishment was over, right on schedule. These helmets only ever unlatched once their Revisions were complete.

It was the first time since his initial Pledge that Lily hadn't needed to coax him out of it. And that meant one of two things: either these BCI stints were wearing Eddie down . . . or Eddie was getting better at fooling them.

"Are you with us, Moderator Blackall? Have you returned?" Lily sat halfway on Eddie's desk, looking down at him sympathetically.

Eddie opened his eyes, still groggy from his time in the interface.

"How much do you remember?" Lily asked. "How much can you recall of the world before your Pledge?"

Eddie frowned. "All of it, I should think."

So far so good. Step one of a successful Revision was the illusion of a complete memory bank.

"Do you remember a Markless named Peck? Do you remember his friends in the Dust?"

"Of course I do," Eddie said.

Lily held her breath. It was the moment of truth.

And Eddie continued, "That's the miser who kidnapped me two years ago. Kept me hostage with all his skinflint friends, used me to lure even more innocent kids into his crime ring as he flouted laws, broke rules, slandered DOME and Lamson and the great Global Union, and even as they rejected Cylis, again and again, along with all of Cylis's great ideals. Yes," Eddie said. "I remember Peck and his Dust all too well."

Lily nodded. This was exactly as it should be. Time in Revision didn't serve to wipe memories; it served to *mold* them. To, quite literally, revise them into a narrative that fit with the Moderator's new allegiance to the great Global Union. For the moment, it appeared as though Moderator Eddie Blackall was fit for service.

"Then you're ready to resume training," Lily said, and she put Eddie's taser rifle back in his hands.

Eddie looked at it, feeling its weight. Then he glanced back up at Lily. He tried to look very serious. But a smile cracked a thin line across his face.

"Something funny, Moderator?"

And now Eddie couldn't help himself. The second she suggested it, he burst into hysterical laughter. "I can't!" he revealed.

"I'm sorry, I just can't. It's just too stupid, even for me. This whole miserly charade."

Defeated, Lily hung her head into her hands.

"Do you have any idea how easy it is to trick these stupid things?" He slapped the helmet in front of him. It *clanged* with the thick, deep sound of expensive equipment. "I mean, it took me a few tries to get the hang of it, I'll grant you that, but come on! Where's the challenge?"

Lily looked at Eddie, and somehow, seeing the smug look on his face brought years of pent-up frustration boiling to the surface. In her own quiet, restrained, undetectable-from-afar way, Lily snapped, right then and there. She leaned into Eddie, her face so close to his that their noses almost touched. And she grabbed Eddie's uniform to keep him there, under her tight control.

"*You*," Lily told him, "*are an abject fool*. Do you know that, Moderator Blackall?"

Eddie stared at her, mere centimeters away. Eyes wide and out of focus.

"Right now you are being so stupid that I don't even know what to say to you. You are going to blow the cover *off this whole. Miserable. Thing. Do you hear me?*

"What do you think happens when the Controllers realize that this Revision process is fallible, hm? What do you think happens then?

"Has it honestly *never* occurred to you to think that maybe, *just maybe*, you weren't the *very first person* to figure out how to beat the Revision process?

"The only thing you're the first person to be, Moderator Blackall, is *stupid enough not to know how to quit while you're ahead*."

"You knew," Eddie said, slowly realizing. "You knew before you put me away. That first time last month—you told me then that the fire wasn't as bad as the frozen lake. That Level Six was easier than Nine. You knew. You're a backslider too. You aren't under their spell after all. And you weren't really assigned to my training, were you? You volunteered for it. So you could watch over me. So that you could look out for me . . ."

Lily stared at him blank-faced. "Eddie, listen to me. This game you're playing—it's going to end. The IMPS will not stop until you are one of them—one way or another. Now, that's either going to happen on *your* terms . . . or it's going to happen on theirs. That choice is yours. But if you want to have even a hope of keeping your own mind intact, you're going to have to learn to play by the rules, and give the right answers, and make the right faces. You're going to have to become a false positive. You're going to have to *learn* to do the things that this helmet was designed to make automatic . . . or else the IMPS *will* wear you down to a stub—until they really *are* automatic.

"Do you understand that choice, Eddie? I mean—do you *really* understand it?"

Eddie nodded slowly.

"Now, I'm partly saying this for your sake, because it sure would be nice not to watch my brother's friend slowly burn alive inside an interface over the next few months."

Eddie nodded again.

"But I'm *really* saying this for my sake. A case like you, backsliding again and again . . . it's going to turn heads. Suddenly, the Council will start wondering—what about all the other backsliders? How can we be certain all those extra Revisions worked on *them*, when they won't work on *you*—the invincible Eddie Blackall.

"And *that*, Eddie. That would be very bad. For me."

Eddie gulped visibly.

"What is it you're planning, Lily? What's your long game? I can . . . I can help you with it, if you'll let me. I know I'm a screw-up. But I *am* good at helping."

Lily thought about this for some time.

"There's a way," she said finally. "There's a way you can help. But it'll be pretty boring," she said. "Mostly, it just involves walking up and down a bunch of steps all day long."

"'Mostly'?" Eddie asked. "So what else does it involve."

"Standing." Lily laughed. "Though this job will come with one distinct perk . . ." She cracked a sly smile.

"Okay . . . ," Eddie said.

"I don't know," Lily told him. "You gonna be able to keep up the act long enough to make it work?"

Eddie laughed. "I promise I'll try . . ."

5

There was a *flip-flop* of sandals coming from the SSC stairwell, and Erin perked up at the sound of it. "How do I look?" she asked as Arianna entered. "Any better?"

Dr. Rhyne examined the monitors arrayed all around Erin's alcove in the storage shelves, and she sighed. "Not yet, Erin. I'm sorry."

In the weeks that had passed, Logan, Hailey, and Peck had each made their own use of the time they had in Sierra. With DOME having long moved on, the three of them felt freer now to explore a bit. Logan had been visiting huddles throughout the city, learning about each one's way of life, listening to their individual woes and concerns and triumphs, and telling them about what he'd learned from the little Bible he'd been given outside of New Chicago.

They'd all heard of him, of course. Logan Langly, the boy from *Swipe*.

He still didn't know how he felt about that.

Hailey, meanwhile, had spent most of her time at the SSC, listening to the radio and catching glimpses of her mom's and Logan's grandmother's amateur news hour, which the two of them started broadcasting last December in an effort to keep in touch with Logan and Hailey while the two of them were on the run.

"That cough," Hailey would say, each time she listened in. "That cough sure isn't getting any better . . ."

Hailey's mom, Mrs. Phoenix, had been unhealthy for years, suffering a terrible chronic cough due to the dust she breathed at the nanomaterials plant where she worked just outside of Spokie.

"It's just the nanodust," Mrs. Phoenix would say on air whenever she launched into another one of her coughing fits. "It sounds worse than it is."

But Hailey couldn't help worrying, even so. She was eager to get back to Spokie, to take care of her mother, as soon as her ordeal in Sierra was over.

Of the three of them, Peck's time in the city had been, perhaps, the most illuminating. Between the books he'd been reading at the Sierra Library and the discussions he'd been having every day with Sierra's intellectuals, historians, philosophers, political scientists, anthropologists, and theologians, he'd been talking nonstop about the war he saw coming just over the horizon. It was getting to the point that even Logan and Hailey and Erin were sick of hearing about it, but still he talked on every night before bed.

"All of us," he said. "*All* of us are missing the forest for the trees. All this time we've been fighting these little battles, waging these little acts of defiance. But a tidal wave is about to hit. And when it does, you, me—everyone—will be woefully unprepared."

Logan would ask Peck what he proposed any of them do about it. He asked Peck what, in all his research, he'd discovered in the way of solutions to this impending Armageddon—the one that made even Project Trumpet look like a frivolous concern.

"I don't know," Peck would say, again and again. "I just don't know."

But of all of them, it had been Erin's time that was the most valuable these last three weeks. In her days with Dr. Rhyne, she'd become more than just a test subject for Trumpet cures. She'd become a partner, learning the science behind the medicine, learning the theories behind the research, suggesting her own solutions, fiddling with her own ideas for treatments during Arianna's off hours, experimenting a little here and there.

In all of this, the doctor had grown quite fond of Erin. She hated herself for it—how stupid, Arianna knew, to grow attached to a science experiment—but it was a hatred that pushed her forward.

"I just don't understand it," Arianna said to Erin now, examining her vital signs. "What kind of scientists with knowledge of Trumpet and access to its materials could have been so careless as to manufacture an activation protein that targets Trumpet's *vaccine*? I mean, who is responsible for this? Their PhDs should be revoked!"

Erin rested back on the bed, closing her eyes.

"Another headache?"

"Yeah," Erin said. "It's fine."

"Are you sure you saw nothing in all your hacked Trumpet

memos about who might have been responsible for this protein release? Or its manufacture? *Nothing?*"

"Nothing," Erin said. "You?"

"No," Arianna sighed. "Not a thing. If it's DOME, there's no trace of it. And if it's someone else . . . well, where would one even begin?"

"It's a mystery," Erin said.

"Bad at science, but good at hiding." Dr. Rhyne clucked her tongue. "A strange, baffling combination."

"And we're sure we can't blame this on a fault in the vaccine? You're sure we've ruled that out?"

"*I'm sure*," the doctor said, putting a quick end to that discussion. "Hey, speaking of which—your father called again, while you were sleeping."

"Oh yeah?"

Dr. Rhyne nodded. "The Dust made it through DOME. They got the samples. You're dad's already mailed them our way."

"That's good," Erin said. "Really good."

"Really good is an understatement," Arianna said. "If those friends of yours found anything . . ." She shook her head excitedly. "You know, you're pretty lucky to have parents like you do," Arianna said.

Erin laughed. "Just a few weeks ago I would have said the only reason Dad was doing any of this was to get me back in DOME custody. For years, I was sure the only thing he cared about was his career."

Arianna nodded. "Well, whatever loyalty he does have to that department of his . . . apparently it doesn't much compare to what he has for you." Arianna leaned over and fixed the IV in Erin's arm, swapping out one clear plastic bag's substance for another.

"I miss them," Erin said of her parents. "I never thought I would."

Arianna didn't look up from her notes and charts. "That's probably for the best. I'd be more worried if you didn't." Then she peeked up and smiled. "I have a son of my own, remember." She sighed and rolled her eyes. "*Family.*"

Erin laughed. "Yeah," she said. "I know."

⊢

That night after curfew, Lily Langly snuck off into the farthest corner she could find of Acheron's vast, underground labyrinth, and she placed a private call on one of the many Markscans that lined the prison walls.

"Hello?" Lily whispered, leaning down toward the computer terminal.

Normally, a Markscan call automatically brought up a video on its small screen. But not with this call. This call's video was only static. And Cylis's voice on the other end was masked with a deep filter.

"It's me," Lily said. "You were right. Lahoma's weather mill remains in jeopardy." She looked nervously over her shoulder as she spoke. The coast was still clear.

"But I have a plan," Lily continued. "I know how to handle it. And all I need from you is a quick look at DOME's database."

In deep, nearly alien tones, Cylis asked what for.

"I need to trace the last-known whereabouts of a fugitive," Lily said. "My brother. Logan Langly."

7

Off on their own and sitting between the storage shelves in the Sierra Science Center basement, Hailey, Logan, and Peck were tuned in to the old radio Hailey had been listening to for weeks, found buried in one of the mounds of equipment strewn about the place. This wasn't a foxhole radio either, Logan and Peck noticed, but an actual, nice, pre-Unity model, complete with Sierra-style batteries (that is to say, experimental technology Hailey didn't recognize, but which worked like a charm), and an antenna that managed to pick up shortwave signals even down here underground.

Hailey had the radio tuned to 3900 kHz, as usual—the universal Markless frequency—and she and the others had kept silent for some time as they tried together to listen through tonight's static.

"*Shh!*" Hailey said, a little ways into the exercise. "I think I hear it." And sure enough, the voice breaking through was Sonya's, Logan's grandmother's, speaking to every foxhole radio in the Union. "And there's my mother's cough," Hailey said after two short bursts of crackling.

"Markless Today," Grandma said, announcing the program that, ever since the protests, had become a certifiable Markless phenomenon. "More bad news, I'm afraid, as if any of you heroes needed it." And Grandma went on to talk about the latest relay of news from Dane Harold out east and from her cohort of Markless broadcasters all along the many Unmarked River routes. "Across our country, it is confirmed, the great American permadrought continues. Ration your food, folks. Save your water. Because this thing's bound to get worse before it gets any better." Grandma sighed into the micro-phone. "And should any one of us be surprised?" She paused for effect. "Of course not! No! Every day, no! After all, I'm merely saying what you enlightened Markless out there already know to be true: that these are the end of days." She whistled softly into the mic. "One-world government, an enforced Mark of loyalty . . . war-fare, famine, scorching heat . . . a west coast already destroyed by massive earthquakes, nearly a hundred and fifty thousand Markless rising up and fighting back, an IMP army attacking, a charismatic chancellor leading it all from across the sea, a beastly General Lamson supporting him from here . . . it hardly takes much to con-nect the dots here, friends. These are the signs we've been waiting for—the unmistakable fingerprints of the Tribulation."

Logan listened intently. Peck nodded along in agreement. Hailey sat perfectly still.

"And what's next?" Sonya asked. "There certainly shouldn't be any mystery about it. Plague, darkness, pain . . . life will get worse," Grandma warned. "Things will get much worse." And she told her Markless listeners to keep their heads down, and she asked them all to pray.

"Oh *Cylis*, you're not listening to that Markless radio program down here, are you?" Dr. Rhyne asked, walking over from her check-up on Erin and rolling her eyes dramatically.

Logan turned to her, startled. "You know about it?"

"Sure I do. They spend half their airtime trash-talking my initiatives. Why?"

"I don't know," Logan said. "Somehow, I thought they'd man-aged to stay under DOME's radar."

"Oh, I'm sure they have," Dr. Rhyne said. "DOME's very bad at thinking outside the box of their own systems and technologies."

"*You're* DOME," Hailey reminded her.

Dr. Rhyne shrugged. "I guess that's true."

"Wait, what's wrong with Markless radio?" Logan pressed.

Dr. Rhyne raised an eyebrow. "Well, it's all a load of bunk, for one thing. Bunch of talking heads thinking we're living in end times, scaring one another with conspiracy theories and ghost stories."

"Well, what if they're right?" Logan asked, tallying the details in his head. "Some of their predictions seem pretty accurate."

"So I've heard," Arianna said. "How flattering, to think that someone was writing about my accomplishments thousands of years ago." She laughed at the thought of it.

"Then what about all the other stuff? It certainly lines up . . ."

"Anything lines up if you look at it long enough," Arianna said. "The fact is, *countless* stories have been written over the years, saying *all kinds* of things. We cannot just pick and choose which data to look at based on what fits with the results we already wanted to find. Even a broken clock is right twice a day."

But upon hearing this, Peck spoke up. "Arianna, I'm not sure we can refute it any longer. Even going back years now, when it all began. Four billion people disappearing without a trace . . . hasn't that alone ever made you wonder—"

"It was the *Total War,* Daniel. People died. People defected. Of *course* many of them disappeared."

"Four billion?" Peck asked. "Poof? Leaving everything behind?"

Arianna shook her head. "*Total. War.* Don't know how else to spell it out for you. And anyway, four billion is the government's number. We don't even know what's going on outside the G.U.'s borders. The Dark Lands? Eastern Europe? Africa? South America? There's plenty of space for those four billion to have gone. That number could mean anything."

"Well, what about Israel?" Peck asked. "In the Total War—and ever since, for that matter—what about the Middle East—"

Dr. Rhyne stopped him. She held a hand out and began counting on her fingers. "Islam—the Day of Judgment, Allah's final assessment of humanity. Judaism—the end of days and the coming of the Messiah that will usher in peace and unity for all mankind. Buddhism—doomsday scenarios where the teachings of Dharma disappear after five thousand years, following a period of turmoil and strife. Hinduism—time is cyclic, the Kalpa comes to its end.

"Don't you see, kids? *All* religions have end-times scenarios. And their followers have all been on the lookout for them, ever since as far back as these religions go. Of *course* every few years someone is sure that they've finally seen the signs. That's how pattern recognition *works*. It's like finding shapes in the clouds—you look long enough, and you're going to start to see something. That doesn't mean there's suddenly a sheep floating around up in the sky!" She shook her head. "This is precisely why Cylis's Religious Inclusion was necessary—to get people like these radio hosts to stop wasting their time thinking this way. It's counterproductive! Spending all this energy just wondering how current events may or may not fit into some prediction written thousands of years ago . . . I mean, how about we focus our attention on real solutions to actual problems—"

"Like the Mark?" Peck asked. "Like solving loyalty problems by Marking every citizen on his hand or forehead? *That* kind of solution?"

"Yes!" Arianna exclaimed. "*That* kind of solution! My colleagues here *designed* that Mark. Just five floors above your head! It didn't just come down from on high. We *worked* on it. And yes, it *did* bring people together. And I'm sorry if that happens to fit with some terrifying conclusion this disc jockey made about a bunch of two-thousand-some-odd-plus-year-old text or whatever, but—"

"It's my grandma," Logan interrupted, uncomfortably. "It's . . . it's my grandmother you're talking about. The disc jockey. On the radio."

"And my mom," Hailey added, clearing her throat.

"And they're both Marked, even. They're not some set of out-there radicals. They're citizens." Logan shrugged. "They've formed their beliefs on their own terms. We're all entitled to that. So maybe let's just keep this whole thing civil before someone gets offended, all right?"

"Yeah, *before*," Peck scoffed. He turned to Dr. Rhyne. "I'll pray for you, Arianna."

"And I appreciate that, Peck. In the meantime, I'll keep looking for the actual cure to the disease we actually have to deal with right now."

"Oh, you mean the one that's unfolding exactly as it was prophesied in the book of Revelation?"

"Sure, Daniel. If you want it to be."

"Good."

"Good." Arianna turned to Logan. She sighed. "You say this person is your grandmother, huh?"

"Yeah . . . ," Logan said.

"Because if what you're interested in is keeping in touch with her, then you don't have to use several-hundred-year-old technology to do it."

"What do you mean?" Logan asked.

"I mean that if you'd like to actually *speak* with your grandma—and your mother, Hailey—instead of just listening to them idly through this awful static . . . well, I'd be happy to set up a connection for you. So long as your grandma has a computer I can hack . . ."

"She does in my mom's office," Logan said. "Mom was a meteorologist, back before Lily disappeared and she, uh . . . retired. But she's been dabbling with it again recently, Grandma tells me. She has all sorts of computers up there, tracking various weather patterns and such. And that office is where my grandma and Mrs. Phoenix broadcast their radio show. They commandeered an antenna my mom used to use to track thunderstorms."

"Well then, they're there right now," Arianna said. "I can have that computer hacked inside of five minutes."

"You think that'll really work?" Logan asked.

"Everything I do works, Logan. *Cylis*, how many times do I have to tell you kids that?"

But no sooner had Arianna made it to the staircase than her son Sam came barreling down it. Preoccupied by his news and blinded by the dark of the basement, Sam slammed into his mother's stomach with a full-sprint force, doubling her over and knocking himself back with a hard bounce onto the concrete floor.

"What's up?" Arianna said, waiting for her breath to come back, but otherwise just pleasantly curious.

"An IMP breach," Sam said. "Dad read it in his computer alerts. Something about a hack coming from Acheron in Beacon. There's an IMP spying on us."

"*What?*"

Sam nodded.

"I might have expected DOME, but *IMPS* now too?" Arianna was fuming. "This is ridiculous! I already *told* these moguls—the fugitives aren't *here*. They left for the north! How much more clearly could I have said that?"

"But we *didn't* leave for the north," Logan said. "We *are* here."

"Yes, I *know* that!" Arianna snapped. "But why in the world would anyone authorize IMP jurisdiction against my orders?"

"They aren't," Sam said, still winded. "Not according to the logs, at least. No one authorized anything. One of them's just . . . hacking."

"Hacking?"

"Yeah," Sam said. "Just spying."

"We need to get you kids out of here," Arianna said to Logan and Hailey and Peck. "I can have this hack shut down within the hour, but until then—I'm not taking any chances. I'll call a few PODs— one for each of you, so you can scatter. They'll meet you out front."

Already, Logan, Peck, and Hailey were scrambling. "What about Erin?" Logan asked.

"What about her? She can't move."

"But—"

"Go. Run!"

The three of them did. And sure enough, within moments, the first POD did appear in the distance.

"Logan, you first," Peck said.

"Why me first?"

"Because you need to get out of here. This IMP'll want *you* the most."

"No—they'll want *you* most, Peck! You're the leader. The Dust is yours. You've always been the priority."

"I *was* the leader. I *was* the priority. This is your show now."

"Peck, seriously—"

"We don't have time to argue. Go!"

The POD came down with a blast of air and a *thud*, landing precariously on a pile of rubble in front of the SSC building. The junk shifted under it, kicking up a cloud of dirt and dust, and the POD rolled slightly off, down from the mound and onto a more level concrete chunk of street. It sat still there and waited with its glowing blue anticipation.

"Go. Go!" Peck said. He pushed Logan hard toward the POD, and Logan tapped at the door button furiously. He looked back and gave a final, short wave to Peck and Hailey. They nodded.

And Logan nodded too, turning just as the POD door opened, hopping quickly into the front seat of it and pressing the wallscreen input to close the door behind him. The glass of the POD unfogged as whatever previous advertisement ended, and Logan could see out, through the fishbowl sides, to the group sending him off.

They were horrified.

For the life of him, he couldn't understand why.

"Hi again, Logan," a voice said from the POD's advertisement speakers.

And Logan's heart froze in his chest.

Immediately, Peck rushed to the glass casing, banging hard with his fists and yelling something that was too muffled for Logan to hear. The door wouldn't open. The POD's next coordinates had already been set. It prepped itself for launch, and a blast of air shot out from all sides beneath it, knocking Peck down against the debris along the sidewalk. Hailey fell too, pushed to her back from the force of it. The POD launched with breakneck speed into the dark night air.

Her projection had been waiting on the POD's hacked advertisement wallscreen behind him, translucent against the clear glass, but just visible enough for Peck to see. Her image now walked around to the front.

"What have you done to this POD?" Logan demanded. "Where

is it taking me?" The glass fogged up as he said it. And suddenly it was very easy to see. All around her, a prescheduled video played of kids scrimmaging with the newest model of TechPlay Hoverdisk and all its unbelievable fake-out features. But superimposed on top of there, stone-faced, arms crossed, cool as could be, was Lily.

"We're going to go where we can talk," her projection said.

Around her, the advertisement kids laughed.

The POD hurtled through the air.

SEVEN

SIBLING RIVALRY

1

IT WAS A DARK NIGHT OFF THE SHORE AT Sierra's edge. Under a gray sky, the bay rocked gently, its surface capping here and there with the foamy white crests of its turbulence. In the distance, the ocean grabbed feebly at the city's junkyard coast, hoping, perhaps, to claim some ruin's shard or brick or slab for itself.

There were no fish below the water. There were no birds below the clouds. It was a dead view of a broken city, and even the few lights still shining did little to promise otherwise.

"Well, that's the end of that," Logan said, sitting in the dark as the propulsion system sparked and shut itself off underneath him. All paid advertisements had stopped at this point, and as it was, the only image left on the POD's wallscreen was the dim, ghostly vestige of Lily on the glass, fuzzy around the edges, and broken and wavy like a bad TV signal. When she moved, the projection jumped and jittered crazily.

Outside of the glass, the lip of the water's surface danced and bobbed at eye level. Ripples from the POD's ocean crash still stretched into the black.

"Nice job hacking the landing," Logan said sarcastically. "I think the salt water just shorted the POD."

"I should hope so," Lily said. "DOME will certainly be tracking it otherwise."

"They don't think I'm here," Logan said. "They think I'm headed up north. There's a doctor in Sierra. She told them—"

"I know what she told them," Lily said. "I didn't say they'd be tracking *you*. By now, my fingerprints are all over this POD hack. And they'll have started showing up in networks somewhere. The worse shape this shuttle's in by the time I'm done with it, the harder it'll be for them to trace the hack back to me."

Logan was quiet for a moment. "DOME doesn't know about this?"

Lily laughed. "No, Logan. This little virtual visit's between you, me, and the Dust. And I intend to keep it that way."

Logan leaned forward in his POD seat, trying hard to read the expression on Lily's broken-up, translucent face. "The others don't believe you're on our side," he said. "Even now, they'll be thinking you tracked us down so that you could kidnap me for DOME."

"Indeed. The look on Daniel's face left little room for doubt."

"Did you?" Logan asked.

"No."

Logan smiled. He reached over his seat and touched the glass where his sister was projected. "I knew I'd see you again," he said. "I was sure of it."

But Lily didn't return the gesture. "You shouldn't have come for me in Acheron," she said scornfully. "That was stupid, and rash, and selfish." The projection of her batted uselessly at his hand. "Making me choose between you and everything I've worked for these last five years . . . I mean, what were you *thinking*?"

Logan's head spun with the accusations. "I was thinking I could save you."

"I didn't ask for that!" Lily said.

"You didn't have to. You're family."

Lily looked at him, astonished. "Do you have *any* idea what your actions have done to this country?"

"They've started the uprisings," Logan said. "People are fighting now. Even some of the Marked. Is that such a bad thing?"

"*Yes!*" Lily yelled. "People will *die!*"

Logan was silent.

"There was a way to do this without sacrificing lives. That moment's passed now, thanks to you."

"I didn't *know*," Logan said. "How could I *possibly* have known?"

"Well, maybe if you'd had even the tiniest amount of *faith* in your big sister—"

"I was *eight* when you disappeared. You didn't say *one word* to me before you left. Even now I haven't the slightest idea what your actual intentions are. You haven't told me. I'm sorry for doing the best I could with zero information."

"You weren't supposed to do anything," Lily said. "You were supposed to get Marked and lead a happy life."

"And what were *you* supposed to do?"

Lily stared at him with a look Logan barely recognized. "I was supposed to overthrow the Union. When the time was right."

"Well," Logan said. "Sorry for incorrectly assuming that my sister wasn't an insane renegade double-agent revolutionary. What, you intend to kill me for it?" Logan looked at the water lapping against the POD's fishbowl glass. "I've certainly made that easy for you, it seems."

"Oh, give me a break," Lily said. "I'm not trying to drown you. You're barely out from shore. That POD'll wash up any minute now."

"And then what?" Logan asked.

Lily frowned. "And then we play defense."

"Defense against who?"

Off a ways on the shore, two shadows closed in. Lily couldn't have seen them, of course. But she didn't imagine they were very far away either.

She smiled over the video. "Our own best friends."

2

When Logan's POD reached the shore, Peck and Hailey waded out and grabbed at it, rolling it onto the junkyard beach and tugging hard at the emergency latch by the door.

Logan braced himself. Hailey climbed into the POD and glared at Lily's projection. She looked ready for a fight; sad, even, that there was no one physically there to push around.

"What's your game?" Peck demanded as he poked his own head into the broken POD's door.

"No game," Lily said. "I'm here to warn you—that's all."

Peck narrowed his eyes. "Then how'd you find us? How much do you know?"

"I know last DOME could tell, you guys were out here. I know you bought nanomeds at a corner store a while back. So I figure most likely you're looking to cure Trumpet."

"Smart," Peck said.

"Well," Lily said somberly. "You are looking at America's expert in stopping Trumpet outbreaks so far. Guess you could say I still have it on my mind."

And a cold shiver went down Logan's back.

"Anyway," Lily continued. "DOME figures they lost you. But I thought either way this was as good a place to start looking as any."

Hailey glanced nervously between Peck and Logan. "But you aren't with DOME," she told Lily. "So how'd you get DOME's records?"

"I'm well connected," Lily said simply.

"Okay, fine," Peck said. "So what, then? You trying to stop us?"

"It wouldn't be worth my time to stop you, Daniel. Looking for a cure to Project Trumpet . . . it's a fool's errand. Wasted effort."

"The doctor thinks it's possible."

"I didn't say it wasn't possible. I said it was a waste of time."

For a moment, Peck listened without disputing.

"Come on, Peck. You're not uninformed. You're no idiot. Project Trumpet is over. I erased it myself, last summer! You know as well as I do that there hasn't been an outbreak ever since. So spending your time out here, with everything else that's going on, with all the other good you could be doing . . . it isn't helping anyone."

"It's helping Erin," Hailey said. "It could save her life."

"Fine." Lily waved her hand dismissively. "Save Erin's life, what do I care? But you don't all need to be in Sierra for that, and deep down, I think you all know it. Right now, we have bigger problems to solve."

"Even if that's true," Peck said, "we can't work with you. I don't trust you enough for that."

Now Logan chimed in. "It's okay, Peck. She's on our side."

"Was she on our side when she betrayed us three months ago? Was she on our side when she left you for dead? Eddie's an *IMP* because of her!"

Lily rolled her eyes. "Oh, give me a break—Eddie's fine."

"Fine? *Fine?* You've *Revised* him! He's your *prisoner!*"

Lily shrugged. "I'd say he's better off than you are, actually."

Peck shook his head. "What *happened* to you? What did they *do* to you?"

"It's not what *they've* done, it's what *I've* done. You aren't see-ing the bigger picture here, Peck. This isn't Slog Row anymore. These aren't simple street cleanings. You need to start thinking more broadly."

"Okay, that's enough," Logan said. "Peck, calm down and give Lily a chance. She didn't *want* to set us up back in Acheron. She didn't *want* to turn us in. She had no choice. It was that or blow her cover."

"*What cover?*" Peck demanded. "*Look at her forehead—she's an IMP, plain and simple!*"

"She is an IMP, yes. She's an IMP so that she can be in a posi-tion to do what it takes to stop Lamson and Cylis. She's *fighting* them, Peck. She's fighting them from the inside."

"If she's an IMP, she's been brainwashed."

"People backslide," Lily said.

"Okay, then they've reprogrammed you *again!*"

"That's true," Lily confirmed. "Many times. But it didn't con-tinue until it worked. It continued until I figured out how to trick the IMPS into *thinking* it had."

"She's a double agent, Peck. She told me she's trying to over-throw the Union."

"Of course she said that," Peck said. "She has to say that. It's easy to say that. What, you think IMPS can't lie? She'd tell you the sky was green if she thought it'd get you to do her bidding."

"She's not lying," Logan insisted. "I could tell if she were lying."

"Oh yeah? Because you're just *such* a good judge of indoctrination? You're just the expert around here? Know all the signs? Know all the tells?" Peck laughed. "Remind me not to play poker with this guy," he said sarcastically to the group.

"She's my *sister*," Logan said. "I'd *know* if she were *lying*."

"She's not your sister! She's an IMP! A person can't be both!"

"Oh yeah, and what do you know about it?" Logan yelled back.

"Guys. That's enough." Lily didn't even raise her voice, but at once both boys went still.

"I dropped everything for you," Peck said to Lily, a deep pain showing through him. "I gave up my friends. I gave up my life. I gave up my future. All for even a *guess* at what they did to you.

"I braced myself for anything. I waited to learn of your death, of your torture, of your wasted years in some dark cell. I gathered my strength . . . and I braced myself.

"And now I see you, projected on this miserly POD screen— and I realize I wasn't prepared at all.

"I learned how to lose you, Lily. It took time, and it hurt. But I learned how to do it."

Peck laughed a sad, defeated laugh. "And now I realize. What I never learned was how to see you again. Not like this. Not like how you are." Peck's face went red. "I want *Lily* back. Not some rising star IMP Advocate. Not some Head-Marked Lamson loyalist—"

"I'm no Lamson loyalist," Lily said calmly, just loud enough for him still to hear. "That's the truth, plain and simple. But I am not asking you to take me at my word.

"I'm asking you to help me. I'm trying to *stop* Lamson, you fool, not honor him. And I'm close now. Turning you all in, proving my allegiance to country—it worked. I know the general's plan now. And it's not too late to end it."

"Go on," Peck said.

"Thank you. Because like me or not, you're the only friends and family I have left in this world. You're the only ones I can trust." And Lily took a deep breath. "This spring General Lamson either solidifies his stranglehold on the American State, condemning this great continent to a generation of tyranny—or General Lamson falls. It's going to be one or the other. And I came to you because I thought you'd want some say in that outcome."

"We're listening," Logan said.

"Good. So do you know about the current permadrought?"

Peck scoffed. "Everyone knows about the drought."

"All right," Lily said. "Then tell me—what do you three know about the state of our weather mill?"

Ǝ

Logan, Hailey, and Peck were still sitting in the busted POD on Sierra's beach, circled around Lily's shaky projection, a tentative alliance forming. She'd told them everything—about Lahoma, about the offline weather mill, about Lamson's involvement, about the tactical brilliance of strategically stirred political instability . . .

"It's retaliation," Peck concluded. "For the uprisings. This hits the Markless hardest, and Lamson knows it."

Lily shrugged. "It's more than that. But sure, that's a part of it."

Logan shook his head. "The Marked—they'd never stand for

this. Even now, the Markless are gaining sympathy. And that's just over all the new martial laws. There's no *way* they'd sit back and let Lamson get away with this. They'd seed the clouds themselves if they had to!"

"They won't be able to," Lily said. "Lamson isn't just holding up the cloud seeding—he's destroying America's weather mill itself. Once he's done with this next attack . . . well, let's just say the drought will have done its damage by the time anyone will be able to fix it. But you're right," Lily added. "Marked wouldn't stand for it. Which is why Lamson has stayed as far away from the execution of this plan as possible. His IMPS aren't involved. DOME's not involved. He's found a loyal patsy to pin it on. A fourteen-year-old kid, in fact. A real go-getter by the name of Connor Goodman. Lamson asked Connor's parents to start sabotaging the mill last September, shortly after the Marked outbreak of Project Trumpet— and no doubt as a result of it. For months, the Goodmans delayed launches and created one temporary malfunction after another. But just a few weeks ago, the Goodmans got scared—and they got hasty. They blew the place up—destroyed all the computer servers that run the place, along with a good bit of the rest of it.

"The whole town of Lahoma's come together since then to bring the plant back online—and they're succeeding. First launch of the new and improved mill is set for three weeks from now— April 1 at 5:00 p.m.

"But now it seems Connor's taken up the mantel of his parents' responsibility. He's set out to complete what they started. And this time, he's going to destroy the mill for good.

"It'll be billed as domestic terrorism, carried out by a lone, crazed individual. He's likely to die in the act. Not the prettiest plan, perhaps . . . but Lamson's hands stay clean."

"How do you know all this?" Hailey asked. "And why does it need to be us who stops it?"

"I've been working as Lamson's personal assistant in the Capitol for weeks now. At this point, he's told me everything.

"Needless to say, I myself am powerless to stop it. I can't even leave town, let alone find a way to get to Lahoma. Even this call is putting me at enormous risk.

"DOME won't stop it, because they don't see it coming. Same goes for the IMPS. And anyway, Lamson would never give the order for them to interfere."

"So it falls to us," Logan said. "That's what you're saying."

Lily paused. Her connection flickered. "That's right."

Logan, Peck, and Hailey were quiet for a minute. Waves crashed behind them. The salt air mixed strangely with the sweet, rancid smell of the junkyard beach.

"Okay," Hailey said finally. "So where do we begin?"

"Lahoma's about a thousand miles from Sierra," Lily said. "Just a few hundred miles south of Spokie, in fact. It won't be an easy trip."

"Getting there's not necessarily the hard part," Logan said. "We have the River for that."

"The hard part," Hailey added, "is that even if we make it there in time, none of us has the slightest clue how to actually run a weather mill. Depending on what that Connor kid is planning, the reboot process could easily end up falling to us—and what then, huh? We'd be screwed."

"So we'll have to learn the basics before we head out," Logan said. "We'll cram for it ahead of time."

"How?"

"The SSC must know how weather mills work," Logan said. "Arianna can explain it to us."

"Well, yeah, she can explain the science of it," Hailey said. "But she won't have any idea how to man the control panel—that's all European proprietary technology. It didn't come from the SSC. There's no way she has a schematic of the controls themselves. What we need is a technician. And unless you just happen to know someone who's actually been hands-on with a weather mill before—"

Logan's eyes lit up. "Hailey, that's it—you're a genius!"

"Why?" Hailey asked. "What'd I say?"

But already, Logan was climbing out of the POD. He kissed the glass projection of his sister on the way out. And just like that, he was off and running along the Sierra junkyard beach, fast as he could back to the SSC.

4

The evening in Spokie was calm and hushed, as almost every evening was these days in Logan's old home. His parents, Mr. and Mrs. Langly, sat on the fifth floor of their Wright Street residence, stretched out on the couch and watching the television frame with the sound on low. It was turned to the news, quietly spilling out useless facts about the Markless protests in New Chicago and Beacon. Some of these facts were more factual than others; this new Global Union media left something to be desired.

It did speak of middling protests here and there, of the loyal men and women in uniform who were containing it—the word "IMPS" was never officially used—and of the occasional statement made by Lamson or Parliament addressing both the sanctity of democratic dissent, and also the importance of keeping the peace across city streets. But to date, the mainstream press had said nothing of Logan or Lily or the Dust or Acheron or any of that, and the Langlys didn't know what they were missing.

They had an inkling, perhaps, that there was more to the story than they knew. But it was no more than that.

Ironically, had the Langlys spent even one night listening to the radio program that Charlotte's mom was broadcasting in secret just six floors above, they'd have long ago learned everything they were so eager to learn. But once again, the Langlys didn't know what they were missing. And Grandma Sonya couldn't risk telling.

"Dianne still here?" David asked when Sonya entered a few minutes later.

"She left," Sonya said.

"Good game of gin rummy?" Charlotte asked.

"Yes, quite fun," Sonya lied. As far as her daughter and son-in-law knew, Dianne Phoenix's nightly visits had nothing at all to do with a nationally broadcast, illegal talk show. And they *certainly* didn't know that tonight, their own missing son Logan had placed a hacked computer call to talk frantically with Grandma afterward.

"Actually," Sonya said, "tonight Dianne and I got to talking about . . . *ahem* . . . weather mills, in fact—your area of expertise!"

"That's interesting," Charlotte said, clearly uninterested.

"It's funny, really—she and I got into the most bitter argument over how Lahoma's weather mill was run."

"Oh?" Charlotte asked, more out of manners than anything else.

"Yes, you see . . . Dianne thinks that the cloud seeding is done by plane. But *I* told her, 'No—it's all automatic now, dozens of ground-to-air missile launchers, controlled from a single, central hub.' She didn't believe me, but I'm just sure I'm right!"

"Yes, you're right." Charlotte yawned.

"Oh, so it *is* all by control panel these days?"

Charlotte nodded.

"My! Well, isn't that something—I *knew* Dianne had her facts wrong! You know, Char, I would just *love* it if you would show me how that whole system works!"

Charlotte looked at her, one eyebrow raised. "You thinking of picking up a part-time job?" she asked.

"Oh, no, no." Sonya laughed. "It's only . . . well, if I knew how these weather mills were run—how their control panels worked, and so on and so forth—oh, well, then I could *really* rub Dianne's nose in it, so to speak, during our game tomorrow. You wouldn't happen to mind bringing me up to that office of yours and explaining it to me, would you, dear?"

Charlotte shrugged, still flipping through pages of useless news sites online. "Sure," she said. "In fact, I even have a copy of the electronic manual for Lahoma's technicians. Got it years ago from a colleague. I could just give you that, if you're interested."

"*Could* you?" Sonya asked, delighted. "Oh, that would be marvelous!"

David rolled his eyes on the couch and stayed glued to the news. How anyone could be so concerned over gin rummy small talk with all these important things going on, he would honestly never know.

5

That night, Logan, Hailey, and Peck sat down in a corner of the Sierra Science Center's third floor, and they discussed next steps. They'd gotten the weather mill control manual from Logan's grandma, they had the full story and marching orders from Lily, and the only thing left to do now was chart a course along the River and push off.

"We agree?" Logan asked.

Hailey nodded quickly. But Peck sat quietly, deep in thought.

"Yes," he said finally. "It's the right thing for you to do, I think."

Logan looked at him, leaning in. "But . . . ?"

"But I have a feeling . . . ," Peck said. He held his breath for a moment before letting it out in a big, frustrated burst. "I don't know. I can't explain it. But all this research I've been doing out here, all these talks I've been having . . . I just feel . . . unprepared. And suddenly it feels very urgent that I begin taking steps to fix that."

"What are you talking about?" Logan asked. "What's urgent is making sure this weather mill is safe."

"I know that," Peck said. "But for me, it seems . . . well, it seems like I'm needed somewhere *else*."

"Like a pilgrimage?" Logan asked. "You're talking about a pilgrimage?"

Peck shrugged.

"A pilgrimage to where?"

Peck was quiet for a moment, staring, unfocused, at the table in front of them. "I don't know yet," he said. "Europe? The Dark Lands? There's still too much about this world that I don't understand. I grasp at it, I try . . . and yet . . ."

Logan nodded, trying to follow along. But Hailey just laughed.

"Look at this guy. One little cameo in some Markless paperback book, and he thinks the world's calling him, all of a sudden."

Peck smiled distantly.

"So you're abandoning us?" Logan asked. "Is that what I'm hearing?"

"That's not what this is," Peck said, getting out in front of whatever it was Logan was about to suggest. "This, now . . . it's about a broader struggle." He sighed. "You and I are fighters. But these battles we're waging—I just can't help but feel as though . . . I don't know. As though it's all still small-time stuff." He looked around at the bustle of the Sierra Science Center and sighed.

"Five and a half years ago—six, almost—your sister disappeared. And I can't explain it, but I knew then, at that moment, that I needed to follow a different path. So I dropped out. I went Markless. I found Jesus. Became a Christian. And I spent months—*years*—by myself, just reading. Just listening. Just learning what I could.

"And it's *because* of that," Peck said, "that the Dust exists today. It's because of that research that we knew Lily was alive. It's because of that introspection that we're here right now.

"Five years ago, I looked out at Spokie, and I realized there was something to it I was missing. Some truth I could feel but couldn't see.

"And I found that now. And it's brought us here. As though we've finally reached . . . I don't know . . . the mountaintop."

"The mountaintop," Hailey repeated.

"Yeah. The mountaintop. And so now here I am, looking out at the view. And I'm seeing so much more than I used to, down below. But I'm seeing above the clouds now too, for the first time. And suddenly I realize there are peaks that I didn't even know were *there* before.

"And now that I *do*, it's time to start the climb all over again." He laughed. "Does that make any sense?"

"Not much," Hailey said.

Peck sighed. "I've been seeing signs," he said finally. "In my research at the library. Every electronic book I read, every page I browse on the Internet . . . it's like Someone, or some*thing*, is dropping hints. Telling me to keep my head up. Pointing me in some new direction . . .

"I can't explain it better than that," Peck said. "But somehow, I need to follow it."

"Are you talking about *visions*?" Logan asked. "Like, *prophetic visions*?"

"Sort of," Peck said. "Yeah. Ever since I started exploring Sierra."

Hailey gave Peck a look, some mix between intrigue and pity. "Well," she said. "Do what you gotta do then . . ."

"Try to understand," Peck said. "If these really are end times . . . then *none* of us are prepared. We need you guys to keep fighting the battles today. But all I'm saying is, it may be time to brace ourselves for what's coming around the corner too."

Logan nodded. Peck hugged him and Hailey both. He said, "Have faith." But neither of them found any comfort in it.

And that night Peck went off in search of something even he couldn't yet comprehend.

ᛒ

The basement of the SSC was dark, and the harsh formaldehyde smell rising from the storage shelves struck Logan more now than it had in the past. Perhaps he was eager for distractions. Perhaps he was simply on high alert.

"Logan!" Erin called when she heard his footsteps coming down the stairs. "Are you okay? Did the IMPS find you?"

"There was only one, but yeah. She found me," Logan said. "It wasn't a raid, though. It was a message. I'm fine." He rounded the corner of the last storage shelf, and he frowned when he saw Erin there. Whatever cocktail of medicine she was on, its effects were starting to wear off. And without any real Trumpet cure in sight, Erin was looking worse these days than ever.

"They're probably monitoring the entrance of this place. You shouldn't be here. You can't stay."

"It wasn't official IMP business," Logan said. "It was just someone going rogue. But you're right. And I won't be staying long." Logan swallowed. "Hailey and I have already made the arrangements, in fact; I came to say good-bye."

Erin looked down. She pulled her blanket up past her shoulders, tucking it in around her neck. "Oh."

"There's been a, uh . . . development."

Erin looked at him. "What kind of development?"

Logan scanned the various monitors, all beeping and flashing above Erin's bed. He still didn't know what any of it meant. It made him nervous to look at them. Were any recording sound? What about video? Was the room bugged? Who was listening?

Logan leaned in, taking every precaution, pretending to give Erin a hug. He whispered into her ear, "The IMP that found me . . . it was my sister."

"*Lily?*" Erin sat up now, just a little.

"*Shh!* Act like you're hugging me."

"Why?"

"Just in case," Logan whispered.

"Logan, the room's not bugged."

"*Yeah, but just in case.*"

After a moment, Erin put her arms around him, reluctantly at first. But soon they just rested there. Comfortably. They felt natural there, somehow, clasped around the back of Logan's neck.

For a moment, the two of them were quiet, perhaps pretending the hug was real.

But that's silly, Logan thought. *Of course it's not.*

"Lily, uh . . . she had no intention of turning me in," Logan whispered. "She was trying to help me. Or, more accurately, to see if *I* might help *her.*"

Erin didn't speak for a few long breaths, her arms still draped around him.

"You gonna tell me not to trust her?" Logan asked. "Everyone else is. Peck's not even coming," he added, somewhat bitterly.

Erin frowned. "Lily's not out to hurt you, I don't think."

Logan nodded. "That's a relief, hearing you say so."

"Doesn't mean you can trust her, though; don't get me wrong. Not too long ago, you and I were enemies. I wasn't out to hurt you either. But we were enemies all the same."

"We were never enemies," Logan said. "Your intentions were too good for us to be enemies."

"Oh yeah? Well, look what good *that* did us."

"It *did* do us good," Logan insisted, breaking away from their pretend hug. "You got me out of Acheron. You saved my life." He sat down at the side of Erin's bed, and Erin laughed.

"Yeah. Great. Out of the frying pan and into the fire." Erin sighed and wrapped an IV cord a couple of times around her finger. "So where are you off to now?"

And Logan told her everything. About Lahoma, about the weather mill, about the drought, about Connor Goodman's plans and the need to stop them at all costs . . .

"Don't go," Erin said suddenly.

"*What?* Why?"

"I don't know," Erin said. "Something's fishy about it."

"How is it 'fishy'? There *has* been a drought. Grandma's been saying that for weeks. She's been getting her reports straight from Dane out in the Village. It's bad out there for them, Erin. Scary bad."

"Well, sure, I believe the drought's *happening*," Erin said. "I believe the mill is down. I even believe there'd be someone out there crazy enough to make sure it never came back up. But, Logan, why you? Last time we saw Lily, she was throwing you into a BCI helmet. And now here we are, doing actual good work to stop an impending plague, and we're expected just to trust that her intentions are good when she comes to pull you away from all that? To deal with another threat entirely? One that just came up out of nowhere? Just all of a sudden?"

"It isn't sudden," Logan said. "This has been going on since September. And she came to me because who in the world else is she supposed to go to?"

"So how'd Lily hear about this weather threat?" Erin asked. "How'd she get so lucky?"

"She's been assisting Lamson personally these last few weeks. She found out from one of his letters."

"So how'd she get that position then? That's a pretty remarkable promotion for her to have gotten, so quickly like that."

Logan shrugged. "Well, she did just throw her own brother into Acheron's ninth level. I mean, if *that* didn't get people thinking she's loyal . . ."

"So Lamson requested her assistance then? She told you that specifically?"

"Well, no," Logan said. "But who cares who promoted her? Look—the story checks out, all right? She's on our side. And even if it is taking me away from the SSC, what Lily's asking me to do is *good*. It's the *weather*, Erin. It's *important*."

"I believe it's important!" Erin said. "I just don't want you walking into a trap. She's lured you into one before—you can't say she hasn't!"

"That was because she had to," Logan said.

"Oh yeah? And what if she thinks she has to this time as well?"

"She's on our side, Erin—I'm telling you! She did all that back in Acheron precisely so that she could be in a better position to fight the bigger battles later on. And this is one of those battles, Erin! She's *betraying* Lamson for us."

"Yes, Logan, because that's what she does. She *betrays* the people who trust her. She's good at it. And you're fooling yourself if you don't believe she could betray you again too."

"It's not that I don't believe it," Logan said. "It's that I don't see how she possibly could, in the context of this mission right here. It's not to say I won't tread lightly with her in the future. But in the meantime, this threat is real. Lily's *confirming* it, not making it up. And she's risking everything just to give me a way to fix it. I'm sorry. But I don't see any red flags with this."

Erin laughed for a while, like a loud manifestation of the fight leaving her body. She wasn't going to convince Logan to stay, and she knew it. So instead she gave Logan the book he'd lent her a few long weeks ago. She flipped through its thin pages one last time, letting the wind of them tickle her face. "Take it," she said. "I've been reading it. And I think I understand now what it means to you and what it means for me. And you may need it." She laughed. "For a dweeb, you sure do know how to find trouble for yourself."

"Yeah." Logan laughed too. "I guess so."

Then they both fell quiet for a moment.

Twice, Erin started to say something else. She stopped herself both times.

"I missed you, the last time we were apart," Logan said. He felt his face go hot the moment he did.

"Okay," Erin said simply, stepping on Logan's exposed and vulnerable heart. But only just a little.

Logan stood up to leave, not saying anything else.

Erin watched sadly as he did. "I won't be able to save you this time!" she called. "So try not to be as big of an idiot out in Lahoma as you were back in Beacon, you hear me? I'll blame you first, if you get yourself killed."

"Whatever," Logan said.

And he left the basement, his heart still beating fast. And he walked up the stairs like the idiot he was.

And he went off to embark on his idiot's quest.

⌐

That night, Erin ripped the medical equipment clear off of her. She tore out the IV drips and pulled off the heart monitors. She stood up from her bed. And she left the SSC altogether.

It wasn't long, it seemed, before she made it to the base of the mountain. And when she arrived, she looked up at it, and she wondered about the peak beyond the clouds. Was there blue sky above? Were there people up there? She felt certain she could speak with someone, if only she could make it to the top. And they would know what she was feeling, up there. They could help, she was sure. In a way no one down here could.

At its base, the mountain was an easy climb. The hike began with a wide trail, and it turned and followed the contours of the slope generously, never too steep, never too narrow.

So Erin climbed that tall mountain all by herself. She climbed for hours. She climbed all night. It was effortless, this climb, and that surprised her, but it was terrifying too. With each step, Erin grew increasingly fearful. By the time she was halfway up, it was nearly too much to bear. Was it the height that was getting to her? Was it the loneliness? She wasn't sure. But she screamed now, loud. Louder than she'd been in weeks. And still no one seemed to hear.

It occurred to Erin in this moment that she was helpless. Helpless and stranded and alone on a mountain that terrified her.

So she spoke, pleading aloud with the people at the peak. "Please," she called out. "Please help me. I can't do this alone. Please! I'm not ready to be alone. I'm not ready, please!"

No one called back, and at once she was shivering. But in this moment, the cloud covering above her went dark, and a heavy rain fell and made the mountain slope slick. And Erin began running up, up in the rain, and the rain cleansed her. She wasn't fearful anymore, and she wasn't cold. She was wet and her clothes stuck to her skin, but it didn't bother her. She was comfortable and she was clean. And as she ran through the rain, she tripped and slipped on the slope and she fell, down, down, fell all the way back. Into the SSC. Into her bed. Into her covers and the tangle of medical wires.

And Arianna was by her side, sitting with her, her hand on Erin's arm. "Bad dream, huh?"

"Is it raining?" Erin asked.

"No."

"But I'm soaking wet."

"You're sweating," Arianna said, swiping a finger across Erin's arm. "Your fever's the highest I've seen it. You've been dreaming about it."

But Erin didn't think so. "It didn't feel like a dream," she said, sinking back into the pillow behind her. "The rain, the way it hit me, the storm . . . I'm sure I was there. But who was it at the top?"

"The top of what, Erin?"

"The mountain. Who was it at the top of the mountain?"

"There is no mountain, Erin. You've been dreaming." Arianna smiled encouragingly.

But for once, Erin knew, Arianna was wrong. The mountain was real.

The rains were coming.

Erin closed her eyes. This time, all she saw was black.

EIGHT

ON THE ROAD AGAIN

1

NIGHTTIME FELL ACROSS LAHOMA LIKE A blanket. The moon was low in the sky, hanging red like some great lantern, and it lit the weather mill with an eerie, ominous, dying-ember glow.

The electrotrucks idled on the dirt path to the loading dock. Men and women rolled crates bigger than they were through the cargo door. Others swept the field of missile launchers, inspecting the electronics and the mechanics of each, jotting notes on tablets, ensuring that everything was up to code and ready to go.

March 15, Connor thought. *Two more weeks.*

It had been days since he'd sent his message to General Lamson, pleading for help, for backup, for even so much as an explanation—*something* for Connor to go on.

The general had not responded.

But it is *the right thing*, Connor reassured himself. It had to be, confirmation or not. His parents weren't fools. And they certainly weren't traitors.

Connor really was on his own. But that was no reason to give up. Since when did Connor Goodman ever back down from a challenge? When the general-in-chief makes a request, you do what it takes to follow through. And if anyone could figure out how to destroy this mill for good, he could.

He lay prone on the ground outside the mill now, observing, strategizing, and planning.

No way to sneak in, Connor noticed, looking at the place now. There were too many workers at the entrances, too much security on site. By the looks of it, he was facing video feed, laser trips— the works. The best cat burglar in the world couldn't get in there.

Well then, that's step one, Connor thought. *You can't hide in the shadows on this. You're going to have to walk in with your head held high.*

So that was step one, he supposed. But what about the rest of it? What about the destruction itself? Connor was no arms dealer. He didn't have demolition equipment, he didn't have bombs . . . *You don't even own a slingshot*, Connor thought, laughing a little at himself. So what options were there?

He could set fire to the place. Except that his parents already did that. It shut the mill down for a couple of months, sure— but it hardly destroyed it. What Connor needed now was to level the place. So that it couldn't be rebuilt. So that his job—so that Lamson's wish—could be complete, permanently.

And that's when the missile inspectors caught his eye. The way they handled the launchers, the way they double- and triple-checked so carefully the calibration of each . . .

"The launcher angles," Connor whispered aloud. Of course! How could he not have seen it sooner? Connor didn't need bombs or ballistics of his own—he was staring at a whole *field* of them! And the day of the mill's reopening, that field would be fully loaded with thirty supersonic ground-to-air missiles *just waiting* to be fired.

If he could get out there onto that field between load-up and launch . . . if he could manually throw off those launch angles, could just manage to set their sights for the weather mill itself . . . then Connor Goodman could turn America's seeding canisters into the missiles of their own mill's destruction.

2

It took Logan and Hailey the day to find the carved waves that announced the Unmarked River, several hours longer than either of them would have liked. But the Unmarked River didn't exactly get its name by advertising itself with all too many signs.

They'd been walking in circles all night by the time the little scrawled boat revealed itself on the stump of a fallen maple tree.

"Should be a captain this way," Hailey said. She pointed in the direction of the trunk, as if the tree itself were their compass.

"Straight as we can walk?" Logan asked.

"Straight as we can walk."

Logan nodded. Hailey took the lead. And yet somehow, Logan's feet didn't follow.

"You all right?" Hailey asked, stopping short.

Logan paused. "No," he said, bemused. And all at once, he crumpled to the dirt.

"*Hey*," Hailey said, rushing over to him. "What's the matter? Are you sick? Are you exhausted?"

"I can't," Logan told her. His eyes glinted in the starlight. "I just can't. It's too much."

Hailey frowned. She sat down beside him.

"How can we possibly make it?" Logan asked. "It's too far to walk. Peck was right to abandon us—"

"Peck didn't abandon us!" Hailey said. "Peck just . . . I don't know . . . Peck just sorta lost it, if you ask me. But he'll be all right. We'll see him again."

"Yeah?" Logan asked. "And what about Erin?"

"Erin too!"

Logan closed his eyes. "She's dying, Hailey. No one's saying it. But everyone knows it. They aren't close to a cure for this thing. And she's already dragged her own fever out longer than any of us thought it could go."

"Well, Erin's tough!" Hailey said. "She's not your average *anything*—fever victim included."

Logan laughed. "Maybe," he said. "And what about us?"

"Not average," Hailey said again. And for a while, she watched the stars sing.

"It was easier last time," Logan said. "On the River."

"We had Dane with us last time," Hailey told him.

"And a purpose. A mission we were sure about. Friends to support us . . ."

Hailey laughed. "I don't think I'm sure about *anything* anymore. But we still do have friends, though." And now she glanced at Logan, hunched over in the starlight. What was he holding? She smiled. It was his old Bible.

Hailey smiled. "You're really still carrying that thing around with you," she said.

"I lent it to Erin these past few weeks," Logan said. "But yeah. Ever since the underpass." He flipped through the book's whisper-thin pages. "Peck always told me there was strength in this book. That you could pray with it and that it makes you strong."

Hailey frowned. "That'd be nice," she said.

In the distance, crickets chirped.

"Pray with me," Logan said, out of nowhere.

Hailey looked at him. "Really?"

"Yeah. Come on, pray with me. Please."

It was dim under the night sky. There was no moon. There was only a soft blue glow. And yet somehow, the reading was easy.

"'For truly, I say to you,'" Logan began, "'if you have faith like a grain of mustard seed, you will say to this mountain, "'Move from here to there,'" and it will move, and nothing will be impossible for you.'" Logan stared at Hailey as the breeze washed over them. "That's what we need, Hailey," he said. "Faith."

"Yeah, well . . ." Hailey laughed. "A miracle wouldn't hurt, either."

And Logan took Hailey's hand. And he closed his eyes. And the two of them prayed under the singing stars and the gentle breeze.

"This is nice," Hailey said.

The crickets chirped louder.

Logan lowered his head.

He wept.

The sun came up not too much later. Logan wasn't sure whether he'd slept or not. But there was light on the fields now.

And in the distance, two horses appeared on the horizon, quickly galloping into view.

Logan didn't believe it.

"Is that . . . ?" Hailey asked.

And he rubbed his eyes as if to make the vision go away. Except it didn't.

Charging, charging. White. Speckled gray.

"Horses," Hailey said.

The path before them was bright.

∃

It was morning in Beacon, too early still to call Erin out west, given the time difference.

The Arbitors *should* have been at work. But they weren't. It had become the unspoken rule between them since reconnecting with Erin: no one leaves the house for the day until contact with their daughter was made.

"Bet you never thought you'd be spending the busiest days of the G.U. merger babysitting a bunch of Markless, huh?" Charles joked.

"No," Dr. Arbitor said. "And I can't imagine you ever pictured yourself harboring fugitive traitors in your off-hours from DOME."

"Disgraced," Charles agreed. "While the Markless overrun this whole miserly country."

Olivia laughed. "Well, at least you finally caught the Dust," she said.

Behind her, the kids were all taking turns leaping around with Tyler's prototype DOME hover boots.

"Hey, Meg can hit the ceiling!" Shawn yelled encouragingly, as with each bounding step Meg launched up and cracked her head, sending little flakes of white plaster floating down to the floor.

Charles buried his face in his hands. "And somehow our daughter's behind all of it."

Olivia laughed.

"I mean, did we do right by Erin?" Charles asked, bemused and unsure. "Or wrong? Are we proud of her? Ashamed? I'm honestly asking you."

"Right now I'm not anything but worried," Olivia said.

"Look. I know . . . I know you and I have had our differences these last few years. It's not exactly been an easy, uh . . ."

"Yeah," Olivia said.

"And I'm sorry for . . . you know, I really am sorry . . ."

"I know," Olivia said.

Charles closed his eyes. "All this time, you and I have worked to make the world a safer place for our daughter. Because the world she was born into was . . ."

"Unfair," Olivia said. "It was unfair, growing up in a place like that."

"I mean, the *sounds*, you know? Just the sounds alone were horrible. The explosions. The gunfire. *Pop, pop, pop,* all through the night. Remember . . . you remember how we'd have our groceries delivered to us?"

"Because we were too afraid to go outside. I remember," Olivia said.

"Until our delivery boy was shot right on our doorstep. I was holding Erin when it happened. She must have been ten months old. I was reaching for my wallet."

Outside the apartment, it was sunny. The sky was blue.

"We swore that night that we'd do anything if it meant Erin could grow up without all that."

"We were happily Marked."

"Happy to Pledge to Lamson."

"The guy was a hero," Charles said. "I'd have Pledged again and again to the man who ended that war."

Olivia was silent for a moment. "And now it's all happening again. No matter what we did. Another war is already upon us. And somehow, our daughter snuck her way onto the front lines."

Charles and Olivia both shook their heads, disbelieving. But just moments later, the tablet between them rang. Dr. Arbitor practically jumped on it. "How are you feeling, honey? Are you feeling any better?"

"Much," Erin said.

"Really?" Dr. Arbitor asked. "Erin, that's great! Has your fever gone down?"

For a moment, Erin was confused. "Oh," she said quickly. "No. No, I'm still sick as ever. Worse, even, I think." And yet Erin looked more energetic than she had in weeks.

"So then what's the news?" Mr. Arbitor asked.

Erin smiled. "The news," she said, "is that those Detection Swabs you sent us?"

"Yeah?" Dr. Arbitor asked, sitting on the edge of her seat.

"One of them came up positive. Dr. Rhyne thinks we might have a match. Now it's just a matter of running that protein through a series of tests and—"

"Erin, that's amazing!" Mr. Arbitor said. "So you're going to find a cure?"

Immediately, Erin's shoulders slumped. She sank down a bit in her bed. "I, uh, let's not get too far ahead of ourselves, right, Dad?"

Mr. Arbitor nodded.

"The question right now is just—where did this new protein

come from, what was its purpose . . . you know, that sort of thing."

"Sure," Dr. Arbitor said. "Sure."

Over the video feed, the Arbitors could see Dr. Rhyne step into the frame. She felt Erin's forehead and shook her head somberly. "No more talking today," she said to Erin. "Rest. Doctor's orders."

The Arbitors could just barely hear her over the connection.

When they hung up, moments later, Charles and Olivia hugged for the first time in years. Behind them, the Dust bounded around the apartment, breaking things.

And the two of them just sat, holding each other.

4

Nearly a week had passed. It was late on a Thursday. The stars were out once again and bright enough to read under. Logan and Hailey had spent the day on horseback, as they had each day since Saturday, and they lay now sprawled in the dusty grass, aching and tired and hopeful.

But Logan couldn't sleep. His mind raced groggily from one worry to the next. He flipped the pages of his Bible and skimmed its contents distractedly. "You awake?" he whispered finally. He turned to face Hailey, and his cheek brushed a few scratchy, brown blades of grass.

"Reading, like you," Hailey said, and she waved her copy of *Swipe*. "Or rereading, I suppose. Hey, when you went through this thing, did you happen to notice how much of a *weirdo* Evan Angler makes me out to be?"

Logan thought about it. "You are a weirdo," he said finally.

And Hailey threw the book at him.

For a few minutes, they both lay in the field quietly, just counting the stars.

"You know, it doesn't . . ." Hailey stopped, considering her words. "It doesn't make sense to me," she said. "Why Lamson would destroy the country he fought so hard to save. Why he'd ruin the land that's already his . . ."

Logan shrugged. "We're on the brink of Markless civil war. Last time around, he blew up the dam and flooded the whole east coast. This time around, he'll dry us all out. It's not so unbelievable, when you look at his past."

"I guess," Hailey said. "But why'd Lamson go to Lily about it? Why *her*, of all people?"

"She's his personal assistant," Logan said. "Makes sense that he'd confide in her."

"Okay, but how'd she get to be in that position? Who put her there? And why?"

"Like I said back in Beacon, months ago—of all of us, Lily was the one best positioned for the fight. She's spent the last five years getting close to Lamson. She even betrayed me as proof." Logan shrugged. "Now we're finally seeing the payoff."

"I guess so," Hailey said. "I'm just . . . worrying, I suppose."

"I know," Logan said. "Me too."

There was a pause.

"You see that?" Hailey asked, pointing up at the sky.

"What?"

"A shooting star. Supposed to be good luck, I think."

Logan smiled, though he hadn't seen it.

5

It was late, and Connor was sitting in Steve's room with the lights off, just thinking, when Steve opened the door and got such a shock that he nearly fell backward with surprise.

"*Cylis*, you just about scared the life out of me!" Steve said, clutching at his chest. "Man, what are you *doing* in here?"

"Homework," Connor said flatly.

"In the dark?"

Connor shrugged. "The sun just sort of went down."

"Yeah, but we have lights . . . ," Steve said, flipping the switch next to the door.

"Okay," Connor said. He was squinting now, but other than that he hadn't moved.

"Also, your homework's not out," Steve said. "All the tablets in here are off."

Connor looked around slowly and acknowledged this was true. "I was getting to that," he said.

And for a minute, Steve just stood there, taking in the gloomy scene. It'd been a week since Connor started staying with the Larkins, sleeping on a blow-up mattress on the floor of Steve's room. In the beginning, Steve was glad to have him. He enjoyed helping out as Connor transitioned into his new life, whatever that ended up being, and anyway, he liked spending time with the guy. Those first few nights, the two of them stayed up late reminiscing, joking around, and talking about girls. The one thing Connor never mentioned was his parents, or the scandal they'd been swept up underneath. And Steve was fine with that, of course. He imagined that in Connor's shoes, he might not want to talk about any of that either.

It was later in the week that things had started to deteriorate. First, it got harder and harder to drag Connor out of bed each morning. By Wednesday, Steve wasn't even able to get him up in time for school.

Second, what started off as nice Larkin family meals with Connor as the gracious and well-mannered guest had quickly turned into morbid affairs with little eating and even less talking. Eventually, Connor just stopped showing up for meals at all, even when called. Today, he'd spent the whole day in Steve's room, just sitting in Steve's desk chair. Not really doing much of anything.

"I'm worried about you," Steve said finally. "I think you're depressed. I think you need help."

Connor nodded. "That's probably true."

"I, uh . . . I invited Sally over for Mark-opoly tonight. Do you . . . would you mind if she joined us?"

Connor shrugged. "Nah."

Sally poked her head out from around the door frame. She waved a little. "Hey, Connor," she said.

"Hi, Sally."

The tablescreen was on and the game was ready to go, but it'd been nearly an hour and nobody had made a move. Instead, they just chatted, about nothing in particular.

"You know," Sally said. "Steve and I . . . Connor, we're worried about you."

"Thanks." Connor smiled.

"No, man," Steve said. "You can't just shrug it off anymore. We're here to help you, one way or another."

Sally leaned in and laid her hand on Connor's wrist. "We couldn't help but notice that your grades are slipping," she said. "Steve saw the tests you've been bringing home this week."

"They were just lying around the room," Steve apologized. "I didn't mean to pry . . ."

Connor shrugged.

"We thought," Sally said gently. "We thought tonight we could, you know . . . help you with your homework, maybe? I've already taken a look at it . . . and Steve too . . . and we thought, you know, maybe we could walk you through it. Make sure you don't fall too far behind . . ."

Connor chuckled softly. "Sally," he said. "There's no point."

"No—there is!" Sally said encouragingly. "There is, there is! That's the whole thing here, Connor. That's what we're trying to tell you—it does still matter! Your life still matters—very, very much!"

Inside, Connor was screaming. This was a nightmare, being treated this way. Pitifully. Like he was a child.

It had been like this ever since his parents' funeral. And not just Sally and Steve either. *Everyone* in Lahoma was walking on eggshells around him. They all *hated* his parents, he knew. But they were also all hyperaware of Connor's great-big-awful tragedy, and the sympathy and attention they were giving him as a result was suffocating. Insulting. Like he was some stray dog just barely cute enough to be worth Lahoma's table scraps.

Exploiting it now was necessary, Connor knew. It was part of the plan. And as difficult as it was not to lash out about it, the fact was, right now, he had these two right where he needed them. *Suck up your pride, Connor.* It was time to make his move.

"I just feel . . . ," he said, trying to cry a little. "Ever since they died . . . ever since the truth came out . . . about what they were doing . . . about how awful it was . . . I just feel . . ." He paused for effect. Sally squeezed his wrist comfortingly. Steve leaned in and turned his head, as if to display more prominently the ear that was so dutifully listening.

"It's okay," he said. "You can tell us."

"I just feel like I have nothing to look forward to," Connor blurted out. "I have no family. I have no future. I have no place in this town . . ."

"Of course you do!" Sally said. "Don't be silly! The weather mill is reopening in just a week—that's a *huge* thing to look forward to! Everyone will forget all about this stuff with your parents after that."

"But no one's talking about it," Connor said. "Around me, everyone just pretends like it's not even happening." Connor sniffled and took a moment to catch his breath. "Hey, you know, what if . . . ," he began. Sally and Steve hung off his every word. "What if we found some way to honor the mill's reopening?"

"Like a celebration?" Sally asked. "Like a big party?"

"Yeah . . . ," Connor said. "Like, if only there were some way to get the town all together. So we can appreciate the mill's reopening. So we could move on . . ." He sniffled.

"We could have a big picnic!" Sally said. "We could have food, and games, and raffles, and . . . and we could get the whole town to come!"

"A last-day-of-sunshine picnic!" Steve added. "One last hurrah before the rains come. Something to celebrate the first cloud seeding of the season—in style."

"In *style*," Sally said.

"That might be good," Connor said. "That might be just the

thing to make me finally feel forgiven, you know? Proof that we've moved on from this episode, as a town."

"As a *community*," Steve said. "A community with you in it."

"At the center of it!"

"The winner of the General's Award!"

"Prize of Lahoma!"

"Connor Goodman!"

Connor was smiling now, big and toothy and wet from all the crying. "You'd do that?" he asked. "You'd really set that up . . . for me?"

"Of course we would!" Sally said. "We'd love to!"

"We'll have it on April 1," Steve said. "The day of the seeding. Sally and I will invite the whole town!"

"Everyone will want to be there," Sally said. "I'm just sure of it."

Connor smiled.

He'd like that very much.

⊔

Another week, and the Sierra Science Center was buzzing. No longer the stuffy place it had been upon Erin's arrival, it seemed every level of the SSC was now in fully motivated, lockstep crunch mode. Erin herself had migrated up to the main levels, where she could be watched 24-7 by Dr. Rhyne and her associates, and where Erin could maintain an open video call with the Arbitors and the Dust out east at all times. Right now, everyone's priority within the SSC was to get Erin well again. She was their focus.

And the key to that lay in the Dust's DOME samples.

They scoured that data, day and night.

Erin had not been feeling better. In fact, over these last few days, her fever had only gotten worse.

101 degrees, 102 degrees, 103 degrees . . .

But for the moment, she was medicated heavily enough to keep the worst of her symptoms at bay, and with her parents' video feed streaming by her side, Erin even caught herself feeling, once or twice—dare she think it?—*optimistic.*

Was that possible? Certainly, it was an outlook she'd not expected to have again.

And yet, it was a pleasant thing, this optimism. She decided to hold on to it for as long as she could.

The Arbitor reunion, it turned out, continued to be the unexpected bright spot on Erin's otherwise rotten winter. If she ever did see them again, she'd always figured, it would be in magnecuffs, through glass, on the wrong end of a lineup.

That's the one, they'd say, pointing shamefully at their daughter. *That's the traitor you were looking for, no doubt about it.* Her father might even have been in on the hunt.

But instead, to Erin's utter surprise, her parents were *smiling*—every time that video feed went live. Sometimes they'd cry—happy tears! Not from shame!—when they saw her. They didn't yell at her for running off, they didn't suggest that her fever served her right—even if it did, as far as Erin was concerned—and they hadn't even guilted her for what she'd clearly done to their careers.

For the first time in as long as Erin could remember, the Arbitors were simply happy to be connected again, regardless of the circumstances.

It was in the midst of this optimism that Dr. Rhyne spoke up from her lab bench across the floor. Erin couldn't see her. But she could hear her voice fill the room.

"The data's complete," Arianna said. "Everything's done compiling."

All around her, doctors rushed back and forth across the floor, reviewing their latest results in the context of Dr. Rhyne's.

Erin nodded. "And?"

"It's not a mistake," the doctor said, practically disbelieving her own words. "The second activating protein, targeting the vaccine. It wasn't an error. It wasn't a fluke. It was deliberate."

Arianna walked over to Erin now, showing her the graphics and the characteristics of the protein that had made her so sick.

"The trial run last summer," she said. "It was no failure—it was a success. Erin . . ." Dr. Rhyne gulped—actually gulped—at the thought of it. "This whole thing's just getting started."

٦

From where he sat atop his horse, Logan could see Lahoma all at once.

The land was flat around it, stretching out in all directions, uninhabited and vast. To his left, the sun rose red and vibrant over the plains, and streaks of morning rays shot triumphantly through the air, glowing at the edges.

Ahead of him, tall shadows stretched out from Lahoma's houses and shacks, casting their limits far to his right, nearly again the width of the town itself.

Indeed, from out here, Lahoma was nothing but a dirt road— "Main Street," it was called, not that it had any competition—which stretched straight out to a stone fountain, dry and quiet, in the center of a sleepy town square. At that square's far edge was the town hall, with a steeple for good measure and a bell that never rang.

And all along that dirt road, that "Main Street" that couldn't possibly be anything but, were the shops and eateries and storefronts of Lahoma, sometimes with residences above them, each one calmer than the next. And between those quaint buildings, side streets branched off and gave way to a house or two or three or four, but all told there couldn't have been more than fifty or sixty buildings in the whole place—post-Unity, every one of them, but each with a simple, wooden, pre-Unity style.

By the looks of it, many of them were empty. But from where Logan sat, all seemed inviting.

Past the town's edge and to the right was a field, where landscaping would clearly have been maintained were it not for the drought. Browning shrubs and trees lined what must have been considered a park, complete with a baseball diamond and a handful of benches that surrounded a small, wooden stage in its center, clearly set aside for outdoor gatherings and celebrations.

Juxtaposed oddly with these simplicities, of course, were all the modern conveniences of any Marked settlement: rollersticks; roadside Markscans for candy or toys; the glow, in many windows, of television frames left on overnight; wallscreens displaying family pictures or virtual landscapes; the occasional *blip* of a tablet at some early bird's morning table . . .

And, most striking of all, the weather mill, just east of town, its huge, industrial structure silhouetted against the rising sun. The empty plain between it and Main Street was dotted with long tubes that angled up into the sky—rocket launchers, twenty-five of them, all told—though their presence was hardly menacing.

These launchers didn't fire bombs—they fired the projectiles that seeded the clouds. Or they were supposed to, anyway. Logan was here to ensure that they would.

"We can't ride in on these horses," Hailey said, pulling Logan from his thoughts of the place. "They're going to need to stay out here."

"I hate to leave them," Logan said.

And Hailey shrugged sadly, hopping off her own saddle and onto the ground. "With any luck, we'll be back before they know it."

"And without luck?" Logan asked, stepping down.

Hailey frowned. "Why don't we just assume we have some left—and leave it at that."

The horses shuffled their feet and sniffed loudly as Logan and Hailey hugged them both around the neck.

"See you soon," Logan said.

And he and Hailey turned to leave, crouching down low.

Together they snuck into Lahoma under the gaze of the rising sun.

NINE

STANDOFF

1

IT WASN'T EASY, BRINGING A TOWN TOGETHER the way Steve and Sally had done for Connor today. But as the sun reached its highest point, Lahoma's Central Square was buzzing with an energy it hadn't seen since the general's visit last fall.

All along Main Street, volunteers at grills cooked up tempeh burgers and veggie patties. On the Lahoma Park lawn, kids played games, throwing hoverdisks through hoops and running augmented reality races through virtual lava pits. Floats shaped like rain clouds rode through town, Lahomans dancing on top to pre-Unity classics like "Shelter from the Storm," and "Purple Rain," and "Raindrops Keep Falling on My Head." The mayor showed up, speaking briefly at his podium in front of the crowd and awarding framed certificates to a dozen mill workers who'd shown exceptional dedication and drive in bringing Lahoma's weather mill back online. Above them, hanging proudly across the town hall, was a banner to commemorate the day. "Celebrate the Rain!" it read, and everyone talked and laughed about enjoying one last picnic before the evening's storm, as eagerly welcomed as it was after so many days of dry, hot sun.

For her part, Sally Summers had been running around all morning, delivering food to volunteers and laying out picnic blankets and game stations all across Central Square. Steve Larkin oversaw the float construction, and both of them together went door to door to remind everyone in town not to miss the afternoon's celebration.

"If *this* doesn't cheer up Connor," Sally had said, "then I have no idea what will."

And yet now, a few short hours later, she and Steve stood on Sally's front porch overlooking Main Street . . . and the one person they couldn't spot in the crowd was Connor.

"Where *is* he?" Steve asked, growing anxious as the festivities began to die down.

"He must be here," Sally said. And yet she too hadn't seen him all day. "He's been counting on this. He hasn't been able to stop talking about it!"

Steve frowned. "Keep your eyes peeled, I guess."

Before them, everyone in town danced and ate and sang and laughed.

And somehow the person it all was for was nowhere to be found.

2

It wasn't a long list, the things Connor needed to pack. He had his tablet, two shirts, an extra pair of jeans, three pairs each of underwear and socks . . .

He zipped his blue high school backpack in two quick tugs, and he looked sadly once more around the room that had always been his. The action figures from childhood that still lined his dresser, the stuffed animals shoved in embarrassment into the corner behind the door, the powder blue wallpaper he always hated so much . . . seeing it all now, one last time, through the eyes of a soon-to-be fugitive, he couldn't help but lose himself in the undertow of nostalgia.

The Goodmans' home. He'd been born and raised within these wooden walls. The floorboards that creaked and sagged in certain spots; the shower that took way too long to get hot; the hallway closet that trapped him once, the last time he played hide-and-seek with his mom and dad, many years ago . . .

He'd miss all of it, good and bad. The very package of the Goodman life itself. It was gone now. And what he was about to do would bury it for good.

Connor lifted his pack from his old, creaky bed—the same one off which his feet had dangled these last few years, the same one that the light hit in that awful way each morning if he slept too late—and he prepared to leave home for the last time in his life.

No great loss, Connor told himself, walking through the foyer to that old front door. Most of the stuff in these rooms had been auctioned off by now anyway. Already it was a shell of the house it once was. Leaving now put the bow on it, sure. But it didn't do more than that.

When he stepped outside, Connor could hear the happy sounds of Sally and Steve's "rain celebration" raging down a ways on Main Street. He smiled. It really had been thoughtful of them, he knew, to go through all that trouble on his account.

Invaluable too. Instrumental, even, in what he was about to do next. Though Sally and Steve would never know it.

They'd been great friends, he thought. He'd miss them as much as anything.

Connor leaned down now at the row of flowers lining the front of his old house, and he plucked a tulip from the dirt in the ground. He bounced his backpack nervously against his shoulders. He pulled his baseball cap down low over his face.

And he walked east. To Lahoma's weather mill, just outside of town.

ⴹ

Logan and Hailey had waited by the mill all morning long. In the earliest hours, the place was buzzing as workers finished to-do lists, crossed the t's, dotted the i's, and in every way prepared for the now—world famous reopening and the inaugural, nationwide cloud seeding that would take place later that day.

But come noon, as the mill's technicians and mechanics and myriad employees wrapped up the last of their duties one by one, each of them began leaving for the town just a short walk or rollerstick ride away.

At first, Logan and Hailey couldn't for the life of them figure out why everyone would be headed out so soon before the ribbon cutting. But as the noise from Lahoma's Main Street steadily grew, they realized the town was celebrating. And nobody wanted to miss it.

With the scene by the mill much quieter ever since, Logan and Hailey decided to check up on the goings-on a bit closer to town. They circled the side streets now, kicking rocks at one another from the dirt in the roads, waiting for something to happen.

"Looks like a fun picnic," Logan said, peeking in on Main Street from an alley between two storefronts.

Hailey shook her head. "It's too small a town for us to blend in with the crowd. Look at that—everyone knows everyone. No way we go unnoticed."

"I don't know, might be worth it . . . ," Logan joked in a sing-songy voice. "They've got soy dogs."

"No picnic!" Hailey scolded. "No soy dogs!"

"Hey, I bet you and I would *destroy* the competition over at that hover-dodge game," Logan said, pointing out to the Lahoma park.

"Yeah? Those kids are *seven*."

"Just saying," Logan said.

And so it was that Logan and Hailey had their own little picnic, right there in the shadows, as they kept their eyes peeled for anything suspicious.

4

Connor Goodman arrived at the weather mill with his shirt tucked in and the tulip in his hand and his head held high. He didn't slink around back. He didn't walk quickly. He didn't look nervous. Not one thing about him was suspicious.

But as Connor knocked on the main door, he calculated his heart rate. One hundred thirty beats per minute. Not exactly the resting rate of someone who was supposed to be relaxed. And for a moment, it frustrated him that he couldn't control his heartbeat the way he could most everything else.

Unsurprisingly, it was Steve's dad, Mr. Larkin, who opened the door. Mr. Larkin was the head of security at the mill, of course, and the person who had caught Connor's parents in their final act. If anyone was going to miss out on a wonderful afternoon picnic just to be a thorn in Connor's side, it was bound to be Mr. Larkin.

"Connor!" he said, with just the smallest hint of unease hovering in his voice. "So great to see you. You're early for the ribbon cutting ceremony. That shouldn't be for another two hours or so."

"I know," Connor said. "Are you the only one here?"

"Yes . . . ," Mr. Larkin said slowly.

"Oh. Well, my apologies for disturbing you, then. It's just . . . I came by to pay my respects."

Mr. Larkin wasn't sure he understood, so Connor held out the tulip for him to see. "Before we reopen this place. I really think . . . well, I feel as though it might do some good for me, just personally, emotionally, I mean, if I might have the chance to visit, just this once, where my parents died. Lay a flower down from their favorite flower bed, say a few words . . . It wouldn't take more than a minute . . ."

"You could come back for the ribbon cutting," Mr. Larkin said. "And do it then. We'll be holding tours for the kids."

"Mr. Larkin," Connor said, sticking his foot out and wedging the door open with it. "You know I can't do it properly, right out in the open, with a whole crowd here. And do you really want me skulking around during all your big ribbon cutting festivities?"

Mr. Larkin eyed him just a moment longer than one might expect. "Okay," he said. "Follow me."

When Connor pictured himself, pictured the movie of him, the way he must certainly have looked to anyone who might be watching, he imagined the whole scene as an action sequence, larger—much larger—than life. The quick cuts, the slow-mo, the zoom-ins . . .

the low-angle shaky cam following close behind, the pulsing sound track underscoring the edge-of-your-seat suspense . . .

But in fact there was nothing glamorous about the way Connor hit Mr. Larkin when he got inside. There was nothing clean about the way he knocked him out, and dragged him into his office, and magnecuffed him to his desk, and locked the door behind him.

It took Connor a minute to compose himself after the whole ordeal was through. But once he had, he ran quickly into the missile launcher field. And from that moment on, Connor Goody Two-Shoes was all action.

It took him over an hour to crank the missile launchers down by hand. But it was an hour he'd bought himself. And it was an hour Steve and Sally had given to him.

He was standing at the control panel overlooking his good work when he saw the two dots running toward the mill from Lahoma.

"Who in the world . . . ?" he said aloud.

He saw their faces. Outsiders.

He braced himself for trouble.

5

Logan and Hailey took one look at the skewed missile launcher angles, and immediately they were furious with themselves for spending so much time spying back in Lahoma.

"Of *course* the picnic was a cover," Hailey was saying. "What were we *thinking*?"

But in Connor's haste, he hadn't locked the main weather mill door. Logan and Hailey barged in easily, taking fast control of the situation.

"Step away from that control panel!" Logan yelled. "Right now!"

Connor was silent. He stepped back. But he didn't pull his hand from the tablescreen.

Logan could already hear the ticking from the panel in front of them. He knew all of them were on the clock.

"It's already done," Connor said. "Don't try to talk me out of it."

"Okay, buddy, listen," Logan said. "Let's all just take a deep breath. Calm down. Let's talk this through." For a second, Hailey wasn't sure whether Logan was talking to Connor—or to himself.

"Who are you?" Connor asked. "You're no Lahoman."

"That's true," Logan said. "My name's Logan Langly. This is my friend, Hailey Phoenix. We're from Spokie, originally, just outside of New Chicago. Not far from here, in fact. Though most recently we came here today by way of Sierra, and Beacon before that—"

"Cut to the chase!" Connor said.

"Fair enough," Logan said. "Connor—I *cannot* let you destroy this weather mill."

"You shouldn't have come here. You're in over your head," Connor said. "This isn't any of your business at all!"

"Not quite the case," Logan said calmly. "You see this here?" He pointed to his wrist.

"You're Markless," Connor said.

"That's right. And so I have a vested interest in you not pulling that trigger right now," Logan told him. "Because a lot of my friends depend on the cloud seeding this place does. A lot of people, Connor. Innocent people."

"You don't understand," Connor said. "I don't *want* to do this—I *have* to do this."

"Why? Because you think you need to finish the job General Lamson asked your parents to do?"

For the first time, Connor's hand left the control panel. He stood there, stunned. "How do you know that?" he asked. "How in the world do you know that?"

"Doesn't really matter how I know it, Connor. What matters is that right now, General Lamson is not acting with this country's best interests at heart. It's okay to disagree with him on this, Connor. It doesn't make you a bad person to disobey these particular orders."

"My parents *died* carrying out these orders," Connor said. "They wouldn't have just *done* that. They wouldn't have just *abandoned* me if it hadn't been important. So don't stand there and tell me this isn't with the country's best interests at heart!"

"Connor—I believe in your parents' intentions, I do. But do you even *know* why Lamson wanted so badly to shut this place down? Do you even know what it is you're fighting for here? *Who* it is you're fighting for here?"

Connor looked at him coldly. "Do *you*?"

"Connor, *think* about this! If the general's motives here were for the good of the country, then why wouldn't he just tell everyone that the weather mill can't reopen? It doesn't make sense!"

"I don't know!" Connor said. "I don't know why. I just trust him, okay? I talked to him. Personally. He must have his reasons!"

This wasn't working, Logan realized. Connor was stubborn and scared and angry about his parents. It was a dangerous combination.

Logan was beginning to fear that Connor couldn't be reasoned with. Quickly, he sized up the boy. Athletic, muscular, tall . . . He was at least a year older than Logan, and it was a year that made a difference. He guessed Connor had forty pounds on him . . .

No way he's going down without a fight, Logan feared. *And that's a fight I'll never win.*

But in all this posturing, neither of the boys had noticed Hailey's escape. She had grabbed an extra pair of Mr. Larkin's magnecuffs that had fallen to the floor during Connor's attack, and she was running now, across the mill, out the door, fed up with the whole miserly thing.

Suddenly, they could see her through the control room's window. Where she proceeded to magnecuff her hand to a pipe on the outside of the wall. She then placed the key in her mouth, ready to swallow, if it came to that. Without even a moment's hesitation, Hailey had turned herself into a human shield. She hoped Logan might be a somewhat better negotiator over the course of the next five minutes than he was during his first.

"*Get off of there!*" Connor yelled through the glass of the control room, suddenly going very red with anger and fear. He turned to Logan. "She's gonna kill herself!"

"No," Logan said. "*You're* going to kill her. *You* are. If you allow this launch, then you'll have to watch that innocent Markless girl die."

"Oh, come on, don't *do this to me!*" Connor pleaded. "Don't you think this is hard enough as it is?"

"You will kill her," Logan repeated. "Allow this launch at these angles, and you will watch her die."

"*Get her off of there!*"

"No!" Logan yelled. "Connor, don't you get it? If you destroy this mill, it *won't matter* whether or not Hailey gets off that wall—

you'll have killed her either way! Her—and *hundreds of thousands* of Markless just like her.

"This isn't some victimless crime, Connor. It won't be some mere inconvenience for people if America loses its weather mill. You're *killing* people with this decision." He pointed to Hailey. "And *that's* what that looks like.

"You can't wash your hands of this, Connor. You *can't* look away. You're making a choice, *right now*, one way or another. Are you a killer or aren't you?"

"No!"

"Are you a killer or aren't you!"

"I'm not!" Connor yelled. "I'm not!" He stumbled back now, away from the panel. His face was sweaty and hot, and he put it in his trembling hands. "Why?" he asked softly. "Why are you doing this to me?"

"Not *to* you," Logan said. "*For* you. You have a long life to live. I don't blame your parents for doing what they did. They had good reasons. And I'm sure they were good people. But you *don't* have to throw everything away just to prove they were right. It isn't worth it, Connor. General Lamson isn't worth it either."

Connor fell to the ground, as though unable, any longer, to bear the weight of what he'd started.

"You don't understand," he said weakly. "It's already done. I activated the launch process before you'd even arrived. There is no abort. We have four minutes to evacuate." He looked at Logan as though hoping for forgiveness. For absolution.

"Hey," Logan said. "Listen. That's okay. All of this is still okay. You have to—look, all you have to do is reprogram the launch angles. You do that, and these canisters go right to where they're supposed to go, all over the country. No collision with this mill. No destruction. No drought. No famine. This is *salvageable*, Connor. But you have to take a deep breath—and you have to begin right now."

Connor frowned so hard now that it looked like he might fall apart. "I aimed the launchers manually," he said. "I never learned how to work the console itself. I *can't* reprogram them. I don't know how."

"Well, I do," Logan said. "And I think I can fix this, if you'll agree to let me near it." Logan took a tentative step forward. "Will you?"

Connor exhaled sharply and pulled himself up off the ground. He walked over to the control panel. He looked at it, defeated. "Okay," he said. "Work fast."

ㅂ

It took three minutes and thirty-three seconds.

But Logan did it. He reprogrammed the launch angles. And Lahoma's weather mill reopened without a hitch. Ahead of schedule.

The rumble of rockets filled the cavernous mill, shaking the ground and flooding the field with a tangle of smoky trails. Overhead, twenty-five cloud-seeding smart-canisters soared off in all directions, leaving behind nothing else but the bursts of their sonic booms, which thudded against Logan like hard punches to the chest.

They were gone. Flying out to every corner of the American State.

There was no stopping it now.

A great storm was coming.

The sky quieted. And for a moment, Connor stood paralyzed.

Hailey reentered the mill and walked over to them both, dropping the magnecuffs into Connor's open hands.

"Well, that was one way to solve the problem," she said, pointing up to the sky and the already-spent missile launchers down on the ground. "'Course, being as close as I was to the canisters at the time, I myself might have gone with the 'don't launch quite yet' option, but, you know . . . reangling them worked too."

"Yeah, yeah," Logan said, raising an eyebrow at her sarcasm. "Duly noted."

"You all right?" Hailey asked Connor. "'Cause you don't look all right."

"We've betrayed him," Connor said, shell-shocked by the whole ordeal. "The leader to whom I Pledged *everything* . . . He made his request. He had his reasons. And I've directly betrayed him . . ."

"That's right," Logan said comfortingly. "And you should be proud of yourself. It was the right thing to do."

Seconds passed. Connor shook with guilt and fear. "What if we're wrong? What if we've just ruined this great State?"

"I'm not wrong, Connor. You're a hero today. It was a close call." Logan smiled. "But you *are* a hero."

Already, the first drops of rain fell lightly onto the weather mill's sheet metal ceiling.

In the distance, Logan could hear Lahoma's workers running furiously toward the mill.

"We're about to have company," Hailey said. "Time to go, Logan, you think?"

"In a second," Logan said.

He put out his hand.

He waited for Connor to shake it.

⌐

Escape from Lahoma was easy, thanks to the River horses, which weaved and tossed their heads upon Logan and Hailey's return.

"No apple," Logan said to his horse. "Sorry."

"Treats when we get home," Hailey told her own.

"Yeah," Logan said. "And sleep."

As Logan and Hailey rode off into the vast, empty plains, a serene silence fell over them. For miles and miles, neither Hailey nor Logan said a single thing.

And that whole time, all Logan could think was—disbelievingly, miraculously, thankfully, so thankfully—*We've won.*

Whatever else happens next . . . on this front, right here, right now . . . the Dust has won.

Lily's mission was complete.

TEN

TRUMPET CALL

1

GRAY SKIES HAD NEVER BEEN MORE WELCOME overhead. Dane and Hans and Tabitha stood out in the harvest field, hands open to the storm, letting the drops kiss their skin and wet their hair and soak their clothes. They watched pools of water seep into the ground, watched it rain down in sheets, watched the corn and squash and sweet potatoes grow, watched the crops lift up and fill with life, practically right before their very eyes.

"What happened?" Hans asked. "What changed?"

Dane opened his mouth and let the rain hit his tongue. "No one knows for sure what's happening out west. But in her broadcast last night, soon as the rains started, Grandma Sonya spilled the beans on a secret she'd been keeping—that apparently Logan was asking about the weather mill a few weeks ago, wondering how to work the controls . . ."

"You mean those friends of yours are at it again? You think somehow they're behind all this?" Tabitha actually had to raise her voice to speak over the patter of rainwater.

"Not sure," Dane said, squinting as the drops splashed against his face. "But it's good to know *someone* in this Global Union's still on our side."

That night, in the damp, underground homes of the Village of the Valley, under ceilings they were happy to see leak and between walls that shimmered with trickling rivulets, Dane and Hans and Tabby and all the rest of the Markless villagers in Appalachia ate their fill for the first time in two and a half weeks. No one went to bed hungry. No one worried about next month's food. There was laughter at dinner again.

2

A week passed. Logan and Hailey made their way along the Unmarked River, pushing hard 'til they were far enough out from Lahoma that their notoriety might decrease a bit. They rode their horses through the rain and the mud. They stopped at the homes of the Unmarked River's fishers, staying with captains and lifesavers all along the way.

Finally, they made it to a farm that could shelter and feed the horses they'd ridden from out west.

"It's all right," the farmer had told them. "No trouble at all, in fact. Plenty of hay to spare, now that the rains are back."

Once inside, Logan and Hailey eagerly dried off, patting themselves down with a dish towel in the farmer's kitchen. They sat around a small table, slouching and cold and exhausted.

"I've never seen cloud seeding this intense!" Logan said, shouting over the patter of rain on the farmhouse's roof.

"Gotta make up for lost time, I guess," Hailey said, and Logan agreed.

It wasn't until late that night that the two of them even broached the topic of next steps.

In fact, it wasn't until Hailey tuned into her mother's radio show that the discussion really got going. It was an on-air coughing fit that started it.

"Your mom gonna be okay?" Logan asked.

"Yeah," Hailey said. "She's had that cough for years, ever since she started working at the nanomaterials plant."

"I know," Logan said. "But it's gotten worse. I'm sorry to hear it; it must be wearing her down . . ."

"Actually," Hailey said. "Since you bring it up . . . I've been thinking recently, with this latest crisis behind us . . . maybe now might be good for me to be there for her, you know, in the weeks and months ahead . . ."

"*There* for her?" Logan specified. "Actually there?"

A breeze ran through the farmhouse and blew a little of Hailey's hair into her eyes. She brushed it away and tucked it behind her ear. "We've had a nice run, you and me. Beacon to Sierra to Lahoma . . ." Hailey swallowed hard. "That's a whole lot farther than I ever expected we'd get.

"But I'm close to home now, Logan. DOME's not after me like they're after you. DOME still doesn't even know who I am. I can live there, still, in Spokie, with my mom. I can take care of her. Her cough and all . . . all those hours at work, and now the radio program on top of it . . ." Hailey frowned. "She needs me there, I think. She'd never say so, but . . . being as close as we are now, I just can't in good conscience . . ."

Logan put his hand up, gently, and Hailey stopped. "You know, you're welcome to come back with—" Hailey started to say. But she stopped herself. "Sorry. That's a stupid idea."

"Not stupid," Logan protested. "Just . . . impossible, right now, I think."

"Sure," Hailey said. "Sure, yeah, of course, I understand . . ."

An awkward pause filled the space between them, and Logan and Hailey both pretended they didn't know why.

"So, then, uh . . . what about you?" Hailey asked. "Where're you off to?" She laughed. "Any chance you'll retire?"

Logan smiled. "Probably head west, I suppose. Back to Sierra."

"Right," Hailey said. "That makes sense, given Erin's there and all."

Logan felt his cheeks go hot. He looked down at the table for a bit, twiddling his thumbs.

And that's when the farmer came in from outside, carrying fresh wood for the fire . . . and something else balanced under her arm.

"What's that you've got there?" Logan asked, and the farmer came over and joined them at the table.

"Actually, I was wondering if, uh . . . well, I was wondering if you kids might be willing to sign something for me."

Logan shot a quick glance at Hailey. She was smirking hard, and trying her best not to show it.

"Of course," Logan said. "We'd be happy to."

The farmer smiled. She held out her copy of *Swipe*.

The next evening, Hailey made it home to her mother.

And Logan rode his horse into the sunset.

Soon enough, the rumors of a showdown at Lahoma's weather mill reached Beacon. But it wouldn't have taken rumors for everyone to know that something had changed. After not one drop of rain in months, Beacon City found itself in a downpour that had lasted for six straight days.

In City Center, the storm had brought with it excitement, relief, and a certain a sense of solidarity. Markless protesters dropped their signs and lifted up their spirits, celebrating in the streets, cheering, dancing, singing . . . Even the IMP guards let up a little, making fewer arrests and doling out less abuse, on account of the great renewed hope. IMPS, Markless, Marked . . . in a way that was real and tangible and significant, these groups had something significant in common—they were all *people*. They all needed rain because they all needed food. Within the larger picture, they were on the same side. And perhaps they were starting to see it.

But for the Dust, the last few days had been decidedly less hopeful. Ever since Dr. Rhyne's discovery that Project Trumpet's Marked malfunctions had been no mistake, the Dust had taken her warnings of an imminent activation very seriously. They spent less and less time at the Arbitors' now, and more and more time out in the protests, or with the large Markless huddle underground, trying their best to spread the news of Trumpet far and wide, trying to warn everyone that their excitement over the weather might soon be overshadowed by an even greater concern; that Beacon needed to prepare for the worst.

So far, the warnings had fallen on deaf ears.

"We're never gonna get through to them in this rain," Blake

told Tyler, walking along the flooded road now and observing the deep wrinkles in the pads of his fingers. "Everyone's too relieved to be worried."

"Yeah, well, we're never gonna find Eddie either," Tyler lamented. "These IMPS are getting lazy on account of all their stupid sudden optimism. Meg and I played monkey in the middle with one today after Meg swiped the dumb Moderator's flash pellets—actual, playground-style keep-away with tactical equipment—and the wimpy mogul didn't even call for backup. Just gave me and Meg a warning and told us to get lost. A *warning*! Can you *believe* it? I can't *work* like this!" He kicked at a puddle, splashing a few protesters that were sitting nearby and shrugging when they called him out on it.

Together, Tyler and Blake descended into Beacon's Unmarked "capital," ducking out of the rain and walking down the metal catwalk into the abandoned fission reactor where the Markless lived under the city. Jo found them immediately when they arrived. "Hate to interrupt, guys. And I'm sure whatever game you're in the middle of is very important, Tyler. But, Blake—you're gonna wanna see this."

Jo led Blake to a far, secluded corner of the turbine room. They had to duck under a tangle of old pipes to get there. This corner was the medical section of Beacon's underground Markless community, chosen partly for its privacy, and partly because the mess of tubing surrounding it was actually a large part of the room's ventilation system. When it came to an underground infirmary, it was best to have the surrounding air filtered out however possible.

Within this area now was a team of older Markless doctors all flocking around a flushed, sweating, middle-aged man. He was groaning, his eyes rolled up, and he turned his head back and forth in a slow, constant rhythm, as if answering some horrible question that only he could hear.

"What's his story?" Blake asked.

And then Blake caught a glimpse of the man's wrist. The man was Marked.

"I found him up on street level," Jo said. "He was lying outside City Center Hospital, shivering and delirious."

"So you brought him *here*?" Blake asked. "To *our* Markless doctors?"

"That's right," Jo told him.

"But we don't have facilities here," Blake said. "We *barely* have medicine. Why didn't you just take him inside the hospital streetside?"

"Because." Joanne sighed. "They've already run out of space."

Blake narrowed his eyes, confused.

"He was dying, Blake. Our doctors are the only option this guy has left." Joanne looked at the man and his Mark with a great worry in her eyes. "Blake . . . you know what this means."

He frowned. "Yeah, Jo. I know what it means."

That night, Joanne organized Markless field trips to Beacon's hospitals all across the hill. At each of them, the line for treatment had grown in just the last day alone, spilling out now, past the doors and onto the sidewalks. And so, from each of them, Markless shuttled Marked into their great big underground huddle, where Markless doctors could look at them, and where at least they could be dry and warm.

In this way Beacon's Unmarked capital doubled in size that

night, all of its newcomers Marked. Sick. Feverish. Every last one of them.

Everything had changed, the Dust knew now. Rain relief or not, there would be no denying it anymore. The vaccine was active.

The next wrath was already upon them.

Project Trumpet was live.

4

A rain so hard it shook the house. Falling. Running. Too fast to patter or bead. Just walls of water. Falling at once like rubble from some crumbling city in the sky. Like some whole world that exploded into a billion tears. Crying onto ours.

Hailey sat in the hallway outside her mother's room.

The coughing had stopped. Dianne Phoenix was peaceful.

She'd died in the early hours of the morning, with her daughter by her side. Hailey was kneeling at the time, running a cool washcloth against her mother's forehead.

Hailey had been singing softly, a song she'd learned from the Markless back in Beacon.

All day, Mrs. Phoenix had thrashed, and moaned, and screamed. Not just from the pain of it, but the delirium too. She screamed for Hailey's father, long dead himself. She screamed for her boss from the nanomaterials plant, twenty-five miles away. She called Hailey Sonya. She called Hailey Cylis. She asked for forgiveness.

And finally, she was quiet. Restful.

Hailey had watched her mother breathe. She had listened to the sound of it.

A miraculous thing, breathing, she thought. *We never think of it.*

But Hailey did think of it then. She counted the breaths, each one. She listened to the air. To the way the bed shifted, just slightly, each time. Until it shifted less. And then less again after that.

The breaths came slowly toward the end. One every three seconds. One every ten seconds. One a minute.

And then none.

Hailey cried. She cried heavily. It was a hard rain that fell, but it was no longer enough to renew the hope.

There was just so much water.

Hailey sat alone in that hallway outside her mother's room for the rest of the night.

She sat through the morning.

She sat through the day.

5

Back in December, Hailey Phoenix made a foxhole radio for her mother out of scraps and garbage. It wasn't built to last. And yet here Hailey was now, her mother gone while the radio still chattered away. *It isn't fair,* Hailey thought, *that a person's world could go on without them.* But the following night, Hailey sat in that hallway again, close as she could bear to the body she did not know what to do with, and she listened to the radio she'd made. She listened for hours, lost in it, to the Markless broadcasts streaming in on shortwave from all over the country.

She heard about a girl out west who'd been keeping the sick Marked in her town alive by working through her father's stash of old, pre-Unity cans of chicken noodle soup.

She heard about Markless in Beacon who'd put their protests on hold to care for their Marked. Kids with no medical background were taking crash courses in nursing, taught by their peers. In many cases, huddles had moved out of the streets entirely, staying, instead, directly in Marked apartments, sleeping on Marked floors and Marked couches, all in an effort to take better care of the Marked owners inside. The Dust was among these huddles. The Arbitors were among these Marked.

Hailey even overheard her old friend Dane Harold praying for the Marked victims across the airwaves, broadcasting from his community without Marks, sheltered from the plague that was spreading all around him but not ignorant of it, wondering aloud about the state of a world in which such a crisis could come so soon on the heels of another. Was there no end to the trials this new Global Union would have to endure?

Hailey was still listening when Logan's grandmother came on the radio. It was a surprise to hear her voice. Grandma Sonya had always shared her broadcasts with Hailey's mom, and to hear her now, alone, stumbling through the program herself . . .

The broadcast, as Hailey heard it through her sobs, went as follows:

"Hello, Markless. Good evening. I'm, uh . . . I'll be doing this broadcast myself tonight.

"Just wanted to give everyone out there the update on the scene here in Spokie." Grandma took a deep breath, and it crackled over the airwaves. "There's not much help here, for the Marked. I've been listening all night to your stories of Markless huddles helping citizens. And it warms my heart.

"But the Markless in Spokie were kicked out months ago. Their community here, on Slog Row, was one of the first to be raided by DOME last fall. It was hit hard. There are no signs it's coming back.

"So the Marked here in Spokie . . . they're just . . . dying.

"I felt my own first wave of chills today. Haven't taken my temperature yet. Haven't had the courage. But I know what's coming. I know what's in store.

"In the meantime, I keep an eye on my daughter and her husband. They seem healthy, for the time being, so I'm thankful for that.

"But as for most of the Marked in Spokie . . ." Grandma sighed.

"Anyway. It's not clear, I'm sorry to say, how many more of these broadcasts I'll be able to make. There might be a handful more. Or perhaps this is the end. Either way, I've decided to take matters into my own hands before I go. I've decided to do something I should have done long ago."

Hailey could hear Grandma light a match by the microphone. And right there, live on the air, she proceeded to remove her own Mark once and for all.

Hailey was stunned, listening with rapt admiration.

But suddenly Grandma Langly stopped short. In the background, Hailey could hear an elevator door *ding* open. There was a shuffle of feet that leaked out over the airwaves.

What are you doing? A voice said distantly.

Nothing. Just . . .

A rustle of hands and bodies and microphones.

Is this—a broadcast? Are you broadcasting this from my office?

Charlotte, please—I can explain—

Do you have any idea what the punishment for this would be? Have you any idea what they'd do to this family?

What could they do that they haven't already—

You're going to get yourself killed, Mother! You'll get us all killed!

More shuffling. More crackles over the airwaves. The soft *pop* of wires coming loose.

The broadcast went dead in Hailey's lap.

For some reason, this made her cry harder.

And outside, the storm crescendoed. Walls of water falling straight from the sky.

A heavy rain.

So much water.

ㄅ

Logan was halfway between Lahoma and Sierra, spending the rainy night with a small huddle in the northwestern woods, when he first heard the rumors of the outbreak, whispered one night around the dark circle of a fire pit too wet to light.

By the sounds of it, the people spreading the news hardly even believed it themselves. A real, modern-day plague? A virus that attacked Marked citizens exclusively? It didn't make sense. Nature didn't work that way.

Of course, it didn't take Logan long to recognize the signs. He tugged at the wet clothes that stuck uncomfortably to his skin, and he looked around the huddle with heavy, frightened eyes.

He knew now what he had to do.

In the morning, Logan rode his horse as fast as he could. It ate plants off the side of the road. Logan hunted squirrels and birds with a slingshot he made from his belt. He failed at that. He ate bugs. He slept each night wherever he fell. He prayed all day, every day, that he'd make it there in time.

He stuck to the highways, broken as they were.

It took him a month. He rode that horse through the rain. He rode all the way to Beacon.

By the end of it, Logan was pushing himself through waves of chills. His head ached badly, and he prayed it was only exhaustion.

But Logan wasted very little time denying the truth.

He hadn't quite escaped that Pledge of his after all. Unmarked but vaccinated . . . he was dying of Trumpet.

┐

Beacon City was not as Logan had left it. The Markless celebrations during the first days of rain had died with the rise of Trumpet, and the streets were thin on crowds. Many lights were off. The sides of the hill were dark and somber. The ground-to-sky wallscreens on the sides of each building seemed harsh and loud against the quiet of the city. The five-tier grid system of roads and sidewalks went unused past its first level.

Most Marked Beaconers stayed in their apartments, too sick to move, or dead, dying too fast for DOME's Ends and Beginnings Bureau to keep up. Many Markless were with them, but some still overflowed out onto the streets. And the IMPS had cracked down on them hard. Trapped in block-long pens. Guarded by Moderators who themselves were looking worse for wear.

Logan had left his horse at the base of Beacon's hill. He'd walked the rest of the way up, hoping to draw less attention that way.

He walked across City Center, too achy and shivery to run. He walked toward a familiar side alley's "Employees Only" entrance. He opened the door.

He descended into the old fission reactor, Beacon's underground capital of Markless.

In contrast with the thinning streets above, the vast turbine room at Beacon's core was *filled* with people. And not just Unmarked. What had before been an organized space of designated walkways, living quarters, classrooms, church groups, dining areas, and public spaces was now simply one giant crowd, packed person to person. The medical area that had once stayed out of sight in the farthest corner of the room had spilled out across the entire floor. Marked outnumbered Markless now.

And even still, it didn't take Logan long to find the Dust inside that mob. Logan simply looked for the focal point of power and people flow, and he wasn't at all surprised to find Blake and Joanne at the very heart of it, shouting orders and offering advice on how the Markless might best take care of the ongoing flood of the afflicted.

Joanne was in the middle of saying something about an observed mortality rate of 30 percent when she saw Logan walking toward her across the sea of sick Marked. For a moment, she stopped what she was doing altogether. Her eyes and nose quickly went red, and a tear caught in the corner of her eye.

Reunions, these days, were nothing to be taken for granted.

"So what brings you back?" Joanne asked, sitting around a makeshift dinner table down with the Markless huddle underground. "Erin told us about your trip out to Lahoma, but I guess we all just figured you'd be heading on back to Sierra once all that was over."

"You were right," Logan said. "That was the plan. But Project Trumpet changed things."

"How so?" Blake wondered. "I've gotta say, it still seems pretty dangerous for you here. What is it Beacon has that Sierra doesn't?"

"Lamson," Logan said. "First the permadrought, and now this? The rest of America might chalk these crises up to natural disaster, but I've seen enough to know the truth. The general has some explaining to do. And I came here for answers."

Tyler laughed so hard that milk came out his nose. "You're here to talk to *Lamson*? In *person*?"

"That's correct."

"What are you gonna do, storm the Capitol?"

Shawn looked at Logan with one eyebrow raised. "You know,

Logan, when *Tyler* thinks something sounds stupid, you might be wise to take note."

Tyler nodded in agreement.

But Logan was unswayable. He told them about Lily's job working as Lamson's assistant, of how he might be able to leverage that advantage. He told them about the general's duty to hear the concerns of his people. But most of all, he told them, he just wasn't afraid anymore. He'd been chased out of his home, he'd been tortured in a secret prison, he'd traveled this untravelable country *twice* now, he'd almost single-handedly averted a national drought, and—he hesitated to say this last part, but in the heat of the moment it all just came out anyway—he was pretty sure he'd come down with a case of Trumpet himself. He told them of the shot he'd had at his Pledge, even though he'd never gotten the Mark. He told them of the chills he had, even now, talking to them right here. He told them that the fact was, he was rapidly becoming a person with very little to lose. He'd found his mustard seed of faith. And with it, he would move mountains.

Lily had promised—*promised*—that Project Trumpet would not be released. That the permadrought should be Logan's sole concern. So he'd done her bidding. And not one week later, and her promises already rang false. Either Logan had been tricked into a fool's errand after all, or something even more horrible was afoot. Either way, he intended to get to the bottom of it.

So he was going, Logan told the Dust. Tomorrow morning, whether they approved of it or not—he was going.

To Beacon's Capitol steps. To the endgame.

To confront General Lamson himself.

ELEVEN

CAPITOL STEPS

1

LOGAN STOOD WITH ONE FOOT POISED ON the first of Beacon's Capitol steps. It was a gray spring day. The rain had finally slowed to a drizzle, but the streets were still slick and the sky looked ready to open up again at any minute. The Markless looked on from their block-long pens, shouting at the IMP patrols and clinging to some claim of rights. A few broke free when they saw Logan approach the Capitol, but none of them dared come close—the two heavily armed IMPS standing guard at its entrance were more than enough to dissuade even the most disgruntled protesters of that.

Only a madman would dare to climb those steps.

But Logan wanted answers. So Logan did.

Immediately, the IMPS swiveled their weapons toward him, training laser sights on Logan's chest and head. He froze.

But no shots were fired.

He took another step and waited.

Nothing.

This dance continued until Logan was nearly halfway to the doors of the Capitol.

Finally, the first IMP spoke. "Don't come any closer," he growled.

Logan held his hands up in peace. "I'm here to see General Lamson."

"You can't."

"It's important." Logan took another step.

"I said don't come any closer!" the Moderator warned again.

"You don't understand," Logan told him. "I'm going to see the general whether you allow it or not."

The IMP's taser rifle began to shake. This time, Logan paused. The standoff lasted several more tense moments before something happened to turn the whole situation on its head.

Behind him, the skyscraper-sized wallscreens on every building across City Center suddenly flickered and changed in unison. Projections of advertisements disappeared and were replaced with an image of a courtyard, empty except for a simple podium sporting the new G.U. seal and a bouquet of microphones. A video feed. Live. Sent straight to Beacon (and everywhere else, for that matter) from Third Rome in Europe. Within that feed, the sun boiled bright across a cloudless sky. A breeze sang gently. Just-opened blossoms lined the scene, and their fresh colors burst and promised new life—in stark contrast with the morbid, beaten-down, urban sick-scape of Beacon.

The crowd and IMPS alike stopped where they stood when the screens changed, and now a hush fell over the plaza as Chancellor Cylis himself stepped into the picture and out onto his great stage. He spoke into the microphones, hundreds of feet tall, his voice echoing across the Beacon City plateau, reaching every Marked and Markless for miles around.

Logan watched from his perch halfway up the steps.

"Fellow Marked," the chancellor began. "Citizens of this great Global Union: I am deeply saddened to address you under such circumstances. In this first of many spring seasons as one Unified nation, in what should be a time of universal celebration, of peace and prosperity, we instead endure great tragedy and hardship. By now we all are too well aware of the terrible epidemic sweeping through America, of the Lasting Fever, known in some quarters as the Day Shakes, or the Rolling Boil.

"America. Neighbors, friends United across our shared Atlantic Ocean—speaking on behalf of Europe and of the great Global Union as a whole, understand that you are not alone in this. We know that you are suffering, and we feel your pain. We know that you mourn your dead, and we mourn with you. We know that you must heal, and we are resolved to help.

"We know, too, that the crisis in the American State extends beyond the sick and dying. This plague comes hard on the heels of an extended drought, an unprecedented failure of Weather Control from which the land has not yet fully recovered. Worse still, the American State faces fracture from within. Even now, Markless protesters are gathered in Beacon, in New Chicago, and all across America, making demands of a government they long ago chose to renounce. The Moderators of Peace have been charged with quelling these protests, a terrible burden on top of this plague. But they serve proudly and faithfully. And we thank them for their service."

Logan glanced back up at the IMPS guarding the Capitol, who were nodding in silent agreement with Cylis's speech.

"The rain has come down and done its part," continued Cylis. "I now implore the people of America—protesters and peacekeepers alike—to come together and do theirs. Now is the time to put aside our differences. Let us unify to care for the sick and support one another in this time of great need."

Hearing this, Logan stared up at the guards, calculating. Slowly, so slowly, he placed one foot on the next step up . . . and he began to shift his weight.

"Stop," the first Moderator said, glancing at his squad mate and shuffling his feet. He kept his laser sight trained on Logan, but the second Moderator said nothing, so Logan continued to move slowly forward, hands outstretched and palms up. "I'm no threat," Logan said. "I'm only here for answers. If Lamson doesn't want to talk to me, I'm sure he can say so himself." He was just steps from the door now, close enough to see the indecision on the first Moderator's face. Logan glanced to his right to make sure the second wasn't about to shoot him . . .

. . . and froze dead in his tracks as in one swift move the second Moderator lifted his helmet, winked at Logan, swung his taser rifle sideways, and casually shot two electrobullet rounds right into the gun hand of the first, dropping him instantly to the ground.

"He has a point, you know," Eddie said to the crumpled first Moderator as he opened the heavy door to the Capitol. He nodded and smiled to Logan. "Your sister said I should be expecting you. Asked me to make sure you made it inside. Still ten steps ahead of us, isn't she?" Eddie grimaced as he looked down at his squad mate still writhing on the steps.

"You're a good shot," Logan said, looking down at the Moderator's hand.

"Are you kidding?" Eddie said, donning his helmet sheepishly. "I was aiming for the steps!"

Logan cracked a thin smile. He longed to throw his arms

around Eddie, to bring him back to the huddle and reunite his good friends in the Dust. To turn his back on all of this and just live a simple life among the Markless. But those days were behind him, if they were ever his to begin with. *This* was Logan's chance. He couldn't dawdle. He couldn't hesitate. He stormed up the remaining steps and slipped through the open doorway into the gloom.

The city was behind him.

He was in.

2

Inside the Capitol was quieter than out. The chancellor's booming words were muffled by the thick, marble facade, and further still by the red velvet-covered walls. Logan stepped lightly down the hallway.

Side meeting rooms were empty as he passed. From only one room did any sound emanate at all. Down at the very end of the long hall, a tablescreen chattered with the tinny, shrunk-down broadcast of Cylis's ongoing special address.

The room was Lamson's office.

Logan approached.

The door was wide open.

"Well? What is it you're waiting for?" Lamson asked from behind the high-backed chair at his desk. "I won't invite you in, if that's what it is."

Logan stood now at the threshold of the oval office. The carpet inside was red, matching the velvet drapes of the hall and conveying all the regal authority befitting the man in the chair.

His desk faced out, overlooking a window that, Logan

presumed, would have displayed the main Barrier Street stretch of Beacon's City Center, the hill—the *city*—that Lamson had built with his leadership after the end of the long and wretched States War.

But Logan couldn't see the view out that window now; the shades were drawn, and Lamson sat solemnly, in the dim and diffuse light, staring ahead at nothing at all.

He wasn't interested in the view beyond, Logan guessed. Not anymore. The chancellor chattered on in the background, and Lamson didn't even seem to listen.

"Do you want to know the funniest part?" the general asked, strangely, still out of sight behind the back of his chair. "The funniest part . . . is that in your mind, *you've* come here to accuse *me*. The killer, accusing his prosecutor . . ."

"I'm not here to accuse you," Logan said. "I'm here for answers. I'm no killer at all."

"Oh, aren't you?" Lamson laughed a little.

Logan wasn't sure how to respond to that. This wasn't going the way he'd hoped.

"I want to know why you caused the drought," Logan began. "Why you can't just take responsibility for wiping out the Markless, and having the IMPS round us up once and for all. I want to know why you're too cowardly to admit that right now, you're *murdering* your own citizens. You *knew* Trumpet would target the Marked. *So why would you do it?* Was it your plan all along, *hmm*? To activate the plague the *moment* I thwarted your drought?"

General Lamson turned a little in his chair and looked sideways at Logan. "You poor boy," he said. "You still haven't figured it out, have you? Are you really so blind?" And before Logan could answer, he turned up the volume on the tablescreen between them.

Logan looked down at the image of the chancellor, nodding resolutely, four thousand miles away, shedding a tear and dabbing it with the knuckle of his thumb. Through crocodile tears, he was enumerating the ways in which he had already begun contributing to the relief effort from his office in Third Rome.

But now Cylis paused, heaving a great sigh. "Nevertheless," he said, "the crucial questions of justice remain: What virus has caused this terrible fever? From where did it come—and who is to blame? Indeed, as many of you have already surmised but dared not whisper . . . this scourge is no ordinary work of nature. It is, it breaks my heart to say, a weapon—biological warfare unlike any our world has ever seen.

"And before I do one thing more, I owe it to you, the American people, to reveal, today, the name, the face, the *hatred* of the terrorist behind this heinous affliction:

"Logan Paul Langly—enemy of Unity and of mankind."

Logan was stunned. He looked up at the general's chair and shook his head violently. "That's not right! General, that's not *right*!" And yet some part of Logan suddenly wondered . . .

Was it?

On the tablescreen before him, the chancellor invoked testimony from Lahoma's model citizen, Connor Goodman, recipient of the first ever General's Award, to support his bold claims.

"But he's lying!" Logan yelled as Connor's words confirmed his guilt. "What does Connor Goodman have to do with Trumpet? That kid's just mad that I foiled his permadrought plans!"

The general stayed quiet.

"They're both lying! I'm no terrorist! I never killed *anybody*!"

And now the general laughed. "On the contrary," he said, pivoting in his chair. "You've killed *everyone*."

Logan saw him now, really saw him for the first time. The great general-in-chief of the American State—frail, defeated, sickly, and pale.

The general's sunken eyes drooped, half-closed in their sockets. Sweat beaded on his forehead and neck. His hair was greasy, matted, a mess stuck down against his clammy skin. He was shivering. "Cold in here," he said. And he smiled weakly.

Logan stepped back instinctively, petrified by what he saw.

"You and I, you see . . . we're the same," Lamson said. "Each trying to do his best. Each trying to take this messy world and make some order of it. Make it better. Because we like people too much not to feel we owe them that."

"You and I are nothing alike," Logan said, though the sight of Lamson's fever was a shock from which Logan hadn't nearly recovered. He spoke breathlessly, his words all but whispered.

"No? Well, we're both dying of Trumpet. We have that in common."

"You and I are nothing alike!" Logan said again, more resolved this time. "Trumpet may kill me yet . . . but that is *not* the story of me."

"No. Of course not," Lamson said. "Please, remind me—what is it again? The story of you? Ah, yes—*Swipe*. How cute."

Logan took another step back.

Lamson licked his dry, chapped lips. His mouth hung slightly open, his jaw slack. He breathed loudly through his mouth. "Your sister . . . ," he said, already growing weaker. "Your sister has betrayed us, I'm afraid."

"She's betrayed *you*!" Logan said. "Not me! *You* were the one planning the drought. *I* was the one who stopped it!"

"Logan!" Lamson said. "How are you not seeing this? We have

the same goals, you and I. The same strategies, the same enemies, the same failings—"

"You're delirious!" Logan cried. "You're not thinking straight! Your words mean nothing!"

"I'm a man in his death throes," Lamson said. "My words mean a great deal."

He smirked, his lips cracking as he did. And for a moment, he stood.

"At the end of the Total War, Logan, two great leaders rose up. That was only natural, of course. The greater the crisis, the greater the power of the person who solves it. That is how it's always been.

"In America, separated states were no longer an option. A conclusion you'd have come to yourself, I am sure, had you found yourself in my position. Unity was . . . a worthy goal.

"But the Mark came a little later. The Mark was my peace offering—my appeasement—to the great man across the sea. At the time, I had limited options: I could take this bruised and battered country, and set it against Cylis with all our remaining military might—a plan that would certainly have resulted in the death of us all. Or, I could stand my ground politically: stand up to him with sanctions and posturing. A losing proposition, it seemed, given Cylis's unparalleled charisma and charm—an advantage I myself have never had.

"Or, last, I could align myself with the man. I could sing his praises, and I could take up his Pledge, and I could encourage all of you to do the same. I could make that one grand gesture—harmless enough, it seemed, at the time—and I could keep the peace across our world." Lamson sighed now, sinking back into his high, swiveling throne. "But one appeasement led to another.

And then the treaty came along. And I must admit, I did fall for that. To be Cylis's equal, to share this Global Union with him . . . why, finally, the rivalry could end! True Unity would save us after all." A shivering spell ran through Lamson now. He paused. "I should have known Cylis never had that vision in mind. From the Mark, to DOME, to Acheron, to Project Trumpet, to the weather mill . . . he'd spent ten years building a great machine—a tremendous, ingenious machine. And at any point, whenever the time was right, he could set his gears into motion, and that machine could conquer this land once and for all . . . without any of us ever seeing it coming. Without any of us ever even knowing it had happened, once it had.

"Logan," Lamson said. "Cylis is a great many things, but he is careful never to catch himself in an outright lie."

"No . . . ," Logan said, already denying it.

"Yes. It is true. You *did* release Project Trumpet. Its activation protein is delivered in water. The Trumpet *was* the rain. Don't you see? Those canisters you sent soaring all across this country, in direct defiance of my wishes and request? *They* were the poison that felled us all. *They* were the point of this whole deadly thing! And you, my friend, were the carrier."

Logan tried to swallow, but couldn't. He tried to speak, but stuttered. Tunnel vision crept in from the corners, and the whole room seemed darker and darker.

The general continued. "It is true, partially, what you know about my involvement. All those years ago, I *did* green-light the production of the nanovirus known as Trumpet, along with the vaccination of all Marked citizens. I am a general, after all, not a pacifist. I had a fragile nation to consider. I had Marked citizens to protect."

The general shook his head now, a look of horror showing clearly even through his weariness. "But last August, I discovered that the chancellor had modified Trumpet's activation protein in his laboratories overseas. He had flipped it, redesigning it, instead, to target our vaccine. To attack the very same Marked who had for years been Pledging their allegiance to him.

"Why? I had no idea. At the time, I knew not what to make of any of it. The outbreak that sprang up in those Midwestern towns was as horrifying to me as it was to its poor victims. And it left me with no choice. My *only* option was to authorize its containment—an unfortunate task spearheaded by Michael Cheswick, and carried out by your sister and a specialized team of IMPS.

"For weeks, I paced my office, confused and horrified by what had happened, hoping I could find a solution before the problem got worse.

"Until I realized . . .

"The towns that were hit . . . were the very same towns that Lahoma had seeded most recently. That was the link they shared. The storm.

"And I saw, then, the beautiful elegance of Cylis's plan. By attaching his activation protein to something as vital as rain, the delivery itself was foolproof. Even were I to discover Cylis's plot, I would be powerless to stop it."

Now Lamson smiled. "The chancellor did not count on my willingness to halt the rain." He sighed. "Though I suppose, looking back, all I really managed to do was sweep the tide back with a broom. To stop the rain was nearly as deadly as to allow the virus to spread. Either way, I'm sure Cylis knew he had won."

Lamson frowned. "I'm no saint, Logan. But what choice did I have? When faced with my options, I made the decision to save my own Marked citizens, and to hope that you Markless could fend for yourselves until the crisis had passed. It was . . . not ideal, I know. But the alternative was the certain collapse of America."

"Why?" Logan whispered. "Why would Cylis do this to us? He already had everything—you were mere months away from the Global Treaty by the time he put this plan in place. I don't . . . I just don't understand it . . ."

And the general smiled wider now, in some perverse display of respect for the chancellor's strategy. "Logan, right now an unstoppable plague is sweeping through our American State, and no one but us *really* knows why. All anyone sees is that Cylis's European Marked are safe . . . and my American Marked are not. *Especially* in the context of our new Global Union, with its balance of power as tenuous and malleable as it is, the chancellor had devised the perfect way to weaken my state and prove my incompetence in one fell swoop. He could shatter the American State, then play the hero by helping to pick up the pieces. Survivors would flock to him as their one, true leader. And I would be a problem that solved itself. It was a coup fifteen years in the making.

"And with your help, Cylis executed it flawlessly.

"Connor Goodman," Lamson said. "Connor Goodman was the last line of defense between America and the great plague Cylis had in store for us.

"I had Connor's parents on my side. And then, after that, I had Connor. If he could have just kept that mill offline long enough for me to strike a backdoor deal . . . well . . . who knows what might have happened. I figured, at least, that it was worth a try." Lamson sighed. "And try I did. But unbeknownst to me, Cylis had Lily. And so, in the end, Cylis had you.

"And you were the better ace in the hole."

Logan's mind raced to keep up. A sense of vertigo overcame him as his whole world turned on its head. "But . . . in schools," Logan protested. "In history class . . . in the news . . . you and Cylis were a team! Inseparable! That was always how it was told!"

"It was in our interest to present it as such," Lamson said. "Right up until the very end." He laughed. "Even now, perhaps, it will be best remembered that way."

Lamson shrugged now, weakly. "The truth is, Logan, you and I both played directly into Cylis's hand. All along. I, first, with one appeasement after the next. And you, second, in the final hour." He hugged himself, smiling, thinking of it. "*You!* The very symbol of the Markless resistance! Now, that was the icing on the cake." He paused and drew a pained, rattling breath. "All this time, Logan, you were so sure, so certain, that *you'd* be the first to sap me of my power, my support. You and your Dust, slowly chipping away at the foundations of my American State . . .

"But with one swift sleight of hand, Cylis leapfrogged all of that completely.

"You were never the harbinger of my defeat, Logan. Cylis was. And now, with his version of history, he will be the savior too— the savior to the survivors of the very same plague he planned." Lamson laughed. "Who else could have ever challenged Cylis's power, Logan? Who else could have even approached it?

"No one. Except me. Someday. If I'd decided I wanted to. And you. The Dust. Someday. If the chips fell in your favor often enough, as they have this year.

"It wouldn't have been likely. But it was *possible*. And these . . . these were contingencies that Cylis could not abide."

Lamson shrugged. He turned halfway back toward the window, gazing idly at the light leaking through.

"There is no good and evil in this world, Logan. Not as I see it. There are only winners—and losers. We've lost now you and I.

"And Cylis has won.

"And that, I'm sorry to say . . . is simply the story of it."

Lamson's head fell back. The air left him in one long sigh. None went back in.

Lamson was dead.

There was a smile on his face.

∃

Logan made no attempt to run when the IMPS broke into Lamson's office, led by his own sister, Lily Langly. He put up no fight. He stood numbly where he was by Lamson's desk, its tablescreen dark and glossy. The sounds of the door crashing down and the IMPS rushing in registered not at all in Logan's mind. To him, the room was quiet, a soft ringing in his ears the only thing separating it from total, isolating silence.

When the magnecuffs came hammering down around his arms and legs, Logan stumbled, but he did not flinch. His blood pressure didn't rise, his heart rate didn't spike. To Logan, it was as if the whole scene were playing out ten thousand feet below. He watched from his great height, bemused, smiling even, up above the gray and tumbling storm clouds, and not caring in the slightest about that tiny, misguided boy being dragged roughly down the hall. *What was his name?* Logan wondered.

Ah, yes—Langly. Unfortunate, deluded Logan Langly.

I knew him once.

He had a sister I think I liked.

"Snap out of it," Lily said, slapping her brother across the face. "Look alive now. This next part's important."

The two of them were standing at the end of the hallway, just inside the Capitol's main entrance and steps.

"You betrayed me," Logan said. "You set me up. You knew Lamson was trying to protect us, and you had me stop him anyway. Hundreds of thousands will die! Your own family . . ."

"That's right," Lily said. "And I would do it all again, if that's what it takes."

Logan stared at her blankly.

"If that's what *what* takes? Lily—if that's what *what* takes?"

Now Lily pulled her brother close, and she hugged him tight. "You grew up to be a good kid," she told him. "A hero, you know that?" She fell away, looking stoically out the Capitol's doorway to the steps beyond.

"I love you, Logan. But this next part might hurt."

"Why?" Logan asked. "Because you're going to sentence me?"

"No," Lily said. "I'm going to leave it to your peers."

And with that, Lily dragged her brother out the door, to the top of the Capitol steps. He was bruised and bloody and he was having trouble standing, so she had to prop him up for the Markless protesters down below to see.

"Markless!" she called. "I present to you the accused!"

All at once, the crowd was still. "This boy, Logan Langly . . . the face of the Markless uprising . . . the very *symbol* of rebellion against the Mark, against the Marked, against everything Lamson and Cylis and the Global Union stood for . . . has just been convicted of mass murder on a scale difficult even to imagine."

The crowd was not inclined to trust the Marked government—least of all Cylis. And yet the pieces fit. This was the boy who'd broken out of Acheron. This was the boy who started the revolution. What else was he capable of? The crowd simply didn't know.

And the seeds of doubt had been sewn.

To all those who knew of him—through Markless radio and River rumors, through huddle hearsay and banned copies of *Swipe* . . . the crime fit the man. The motivations were clear. The capability was self-evident. Cylis's story checked out.

But in that awful haze of protest-wide doubt, one lone voice spoke up.

Tyler had squirmed his way to the front of the crowd, and he poked his head out from between two much taller adults. "Oh, this is *bogus*," he yelled. "Come on, you people don't actually *believe* any of this nonsense, do you?"

And one by one, the rest of Peck's Dust joined in. Blake. Joanne. Meg. Rusty. Shawn. The team of them pushed their way through the crowd, approaching the base of the Capitol steps. They'd done some research of their own, they said. And if anyone could be blamed for the Project Trumpet plague, it was DOME. It was Cylis. It was Advocate Lily Langly herself. It was *they* who designed Trumpet, *they* who had vaccinated the Marked, *they* who had decided to activate that vaccine . . .

Sure, the Dust acknowledged, Logan was the one who pulled the trigger. But only because he'd been tricked! Who among them would have done any different, under the circumstances? Who among them could have known any better?

When the Dust was finished, Lily propped Logan up once more. "Beacon!" she called. "You have heard both sides of the matter; I surrender Logan now to your will. The chancellor intends the death penalty. But it is *you* Logan's actions have hurt. Your lives are the ones that have been halted by this plague. *You* are the true plaintiffs of this case—not Cylis, not Parliament, not anyone else. And so, by the power vested in me . . ." She hesitated now, briefly calculating the consequences of her next few words. But the risk was worth it, she knew. This was her brother. What choice did she have? "By the power vested in me, I have decided to allow the pardon of Logan here and now—*if the people of Beacon will it.*"

Lily pulled Logan higher as she made her offer. She called out at the top of her lungs.

"If any among you object to the punishment of Logan Paul Langly, the accused, then his crimes will be forgiven." She paused and waited. "Speak now, Beacon! Or forever hold your peace!"

For a moment, there was quiet. The Dust called out for support. Lily appealed to the crowd again. "You alone must decide if this boy's actions deserve death. I am innocent of his blood. It is your responsibility!"

Lily held him there until her arms were tired. She held him as long as she could. Finally, Logan collapsed onto the stairs.

For a third time, Lily made her offer. She was practically pleading now.

She couldn't believe it. But it was so:

The crowd remained silent.

TWELVE

ULTRANET

1

THE SUN ROSE BRIGHT OVER THE SCIENCE Center in Sierra, its morning rays shining through the blue tarp walls. Dr. Rhyne was gentle about waking Erin up, but she wasted no time with it.

"Hey, you," she said, patting Erin's arm. "Wake up. Look. Look what I have." She held a tin watering can in front of Erin's face, shaking it a bit until the liquid inside sloshed and splashed.

Erin opened her eyes, trying to focus them on the doctor. "Did I turn into a plant?" she asked, still groggy from her sleep and heavily medicated.

Now Arianna was gathering her assistants too. They'd been sleeping in chairs beside Erin's bed, some just keeping watch, but many of them hooked up to their own annexed IV drips—by this point the Marked scientists in Sierra weren't any better off than the rest of the country.

"Come on, everyone, wake up! It's a new day. A new *month*!"

"April showers bring May flowers . . . " Erin said as Sam ran around poking everyone awake.

"Erin, that's *exactly* right."

Soon the whole floor was up and stretching and giving the doctor the attention she felt she deserved.

"Good," she said. "Well. Now that we're all vertical . . . may I begin?"

"Begin what?" an assistant asked.

Dr. Rhyne raised an eyebrow and shook her watering can once more.

"It's a free country." Erin shrugged.

"No, it isn't," Arianna said. But she took that as a yes. So for the next few minutes, Dr. Rhyne strolled through the Sierra Science Center, whistling a happy tune and pouring the contents of her watering can over the heads of every last person inside.

"Are you hoping we'll sprout?" Erin asked.

"No," the doctor said, drenching Erin in particular, and carelessly shorting out a few pieces of her medical equipment in the process. "I'm hoping you'll live."

"You didn't . . . " Erin said, springing up in her bed.

Arianna smiled. "The Dust's sample was the key. Once we knew the structure of the modified activation protein, engineering an antidote wasn't so impossible after all."

"And it really works?" Erin asked, her soaking hair clinging to her forehead and cheeks.

"I'm not sure," Arianna said. "But we're about to find out."

That afternoon, Dr. Rhyne placed a call to Mr. Larkin, the head of security at Lahoma's weather mill. He looked so sick over the tablet connection that Arianna wasn't sure if he could even hear her. But she had a proposition for him, all the same. There was a special delivery headed his way, she told him. Sierra Science Center's nuclear helicopter was flying straight for his town, filled to the brim with a new ingredient to add to the mill's next batch of cloud-seeding canisters.

"And it sure would be great," Arianna said, "if you could find a few Lahomans still chipper enough to load those suckers up . . ."

The next day, thick clouds again covered much of the American State.

A new rain had begun.

2

The Beacon protests died down in time for General Lamson's state funeral. Logan's death sentence had taken much of the wind out of the movement's sails, and whatever straggling picketers remained were quickly rounded up by the sudden influx of Cylis's European IMP reinforcements.

The funeral itself was an extravagant affair, with eulogies by Parliament members, nuclear plane flyovers in missing man formation, musical selections by the IMP band and choir, and a twenty-one taser gun salute. Thousands of Marked citizens came to view the guarded, flag-draped casket—and even more came to see in person the historic transfer of power to their new, supreme leader, Dominic Cylis.

Lily Langly looked out over that massive audience as Cylis addressed his people—and everyone within the great Global

Union—from Lamson's old Beacon podium. She stood behind the chancellor, just a little off to the side, in her position of immense power as part of Cylis's new Global Council. Michael Cheswick stood beside her, and he whispered to Lily as the chancellor spoke.

"I must say, you've exceeded every expectation, Champion Langly. You had me worried when you approached General Lamson about his Lahoma plans; I rather doubted that you would follow through with Dominic's request once you learned the drought was a defensive measure against Project Trumpet."

"The general needed to go," Lily whispered simply.

"But at the cost of countless American Marked . . . ," Cheswick said. "Most in your shoes would have flinched in the face of it. And to have your own brother pull the trigger! To pin this all on him!" He raised an eyebrow. "You've quite earned your promotion, Champion, in the eyes of the chancellor. In time I expect you may become our first IMP Decider yet."

"We've both sacrificed country for Unity," Lily said. "Don't think for a moment I believe it was only me working under Cylis's orders within the walls of Lamson's Capitol." She looked at Michael Cheswick now, knowing it was he—coordinator of the Trumpet Task Force—who'd smuggled Cylis's Project Trumpet canisters into the country in the first place; knowing that he'd been a part of this grand plot all along.

"This is war," Cheswick agreed. "People die in war. Alliances are tested. Assassinations are a part of the game . . ."

"And to the victors go the spoils," Lily said.

Michael Cheswick nodded. "It will be an honor to work with you on the chancellor's Global Council. I rather think we've much to look forward to, over in Third Rome. Big things lie ahead."

Before them, the chancellor lifted his arms grandly to Beacon.

He spoke of the general's greatness, and of his own honor in accepting, now, the mantle of Lamson's authority. Around him, the new, curing rain fell. Cylis took credit for that too.

And Lily watched, from behind it all. She stared, unblinking, at the world's supreme leader. She leaned over to Michael Cheswick. She whispered, "You have no idea."

ヨ

News of Lamson's death traveled fast across the Global Union, like a gunshot ringing out forever. Even to those few corners of the land without direct Union media access, the word spread quickly.

But Hailey Phoenix hadn't been listening to the news. Not since the day she'd spent with her foxhole radio outside her mom's room.

She had buried her mother some time later without help, in her own backyard, after removing her mother's Mark. It took her days to build up the courage to do so. And it took her weeks to move past it.

She'd barely even eaten since then, let alone cared about current events. She'd barely gone outside. She'd barely noticed the second wave of rain.

So when Hailey did decide to reenter the world, when she finally did tune in and hear the news of Lamson's demise, of Cylis's takeover across the Global Union, of Logan Langly's death sentence, and of the truth behind Project Trumpet's cloud-seeding activation, the shock came all at once.

It was clear to Hailey, then, the trick she'd fallen for back in Lahoma. The trick Cylis had played. The trick that Lily made possible.

Still think she's on our side, Hailey? she asked herself.

But Hailey started eating again after that.

She saw herself in the mirror. Thin hair. Gaunt cheeks. She didn't recognize herself.

And it was time to turn all that back. It was time to live again. Or to try.

She was free now, Hailey knew.

Finally.

She had nothing left to lose.

The next morning, Hailey set out once more along the Unmarked River, finding that old, familiar path, retracing the route she'd taken last December, step by step. It rained the whole time. But Hailey didn't mind.

She biked to the Hayes's old farm, still abandoned after DOME's winter raid. She approached the stream where Logan had nearly died of hypothermia. She followed it out of the woods. She found the trail to the train tracks tracing east through the no-man's land far outside of town. She waited.

And when the train finally came, a half day later, its conductor was the very same she'd met those five months ago. He recognized her, in fact. He let her sit up front with him. He even let her blow the train's whistle when she asked.

So Hailey rode with that conductor across half the country, all the way to the Appalachian Mountains, to her same, familiar stop.

From there, it was a full day's hike to the valley. But the walk went fast. And her heart pumped red-hot hope into her veins every step of the way.

That evening, Hailey came upon the Village of the Valley, and she found the old path to the radio station up the hill. It was nighttime, after all. Time for Dane Harold's Markless radio program.

Hailey knocked on the wooden door of the small shack. Dane opened it and nearly fainted to the ground.

Over the next few hours, Markless listeners and radio fans all across the country shared in the incredible reunion of Dane Harold and his oldest friend, Hailey Phoenix. The broadcast kept right on going as Dane bounced excitedly around the shack. And everyone everywhere heard the old friends embrace, and cry, and share stories, and mourn, and laugh, and sing, and dance.

That spring, Hailey learned to farm. And she and Dane tended to the squash and the sweet potatoes and the corn and the apples, and they ate well each night, and around a great big campfire at the village's center, Hailey told the whole village a new story, every night, about Markless life in Beacon, and Sierra, and everywhere in between.

And still, each morning when she woke up, each evening when she went to sleep, Hailey mourned her mother. She mourned Logan. She thought of Peck and Erin. She thought of the rest of them—of her friends still out east. Those crazy kids in Beacon, the stars of *Swipe*.

4

Erin felt alive for the first time in months. Her migraines were gone. Her temperature was normal. Her nerves were steady and still.

But the news of Logan made it difficult to care.

She stared distractedly out the window of her parents' crowded

Beacon apartment, absorbing the sights and the sounds and the smells of home, and bemused by its odd contrast to the Dust's company behind her.

They'd spent the last few weeks recovering, hiding away from it all with the Arbitors' help. They'd grieved for Logan, and they'd celebrated his life and his courage and all that he'd done. But it was time, they knew, to move on. Just a little. To think of next steps.

"So what now?" Blake asked. "Peck's gone. Logan's . . ." He paused. "Dead. We've lost our leader and our symbol, both. We're a headless organization . . ."

"Didn't he say *anything*?" Shawn asked Erin. "Could Peck really have given *no* clues as to where he was headed?"

"He wasn't sure," Erin said. "He couldn't have told us anything more because he didn't *know* anything more. It was as if . . ." She stopped herself. "It sounds silly. But it was as if he was answering some call. Like some force was guiding him. He didn't know where it would take him . . . only that he needed to follow it.

"He said he thought . . . well, he said he thought Cylis was more powerful than we could imagine. He said a battle was brewing that would make even the Total War look tame. He said for all we've discovered so far, we've barely scratched the surface of what was really to come.

"And so he left. For Europe? For the Dark Lands, beyond even the scope of the Global Union? Who knows. He left for answers, plain and simple. I guess he figured the details would fall into place."

Joanne sniffled softly and wiped her nose. "Peck will be back," she said. "And as for Logan . . . he'd want us to fight on. We've become our own leaders now. We *are* the symbol. Not Logan. The Dust. All of us. Together."

"Beacon's Markless need direction," Shawn said. "Now more

than ever. If Peck's right about this war on the horizon, then we have our work cut out for us right here in Beacon. We may not know everything about what we have to do . . . but we know where to start."

"I vote we save Eddie," Tyler said, off in his own corner and barely listening. "I vote we do whatever it takes."

"Don't you get it?" Blake asked. "There *is* no saving Eddie. It's not a matter of finding him—he's *gone*. He's Lily's lapdog now. There's no turning back."

But Tyler shook his head. "Eddie wouldn't flip," he said. "He's no traitor."

"Tyler—he's *working* with *Lily*. He led Logan straight into her trap back at the Capitol!"

"Well then Lily hasn't flipped either!" Tyler insisted. "Then it wasn't a real trap!"

"She unleashed Trumpet, Tyler. She sentenced her own brother to *death*. She's been appointed to Cylis's Global Council—"

"I don't care! I don't care how it looks! At some point, you just have to trust people. There were plenty of Marked who thought Peck was bad a year ago, and look how wrong *they* were!"

"Yeah, but Peck never started a plague!" Jo said.

Tyler just shrugged. "If Eddie's working with Lily, then the two of them are planning something. I just know it. And *our* job," he insisted, "is to keep the heat on Beacon until they're ready to pull the trigger. They *need* us, guys. Whether or not they can say so, they *need* us, now, to trust them."

"Well . . . one way or another, something's coming," Shawn admitted. "There's no way Tyler's wrong about *that* . . ."

"What about you, Erin?" Jo asked, looking over to her as Erin gazed, still, out the window. "What's your take on all this?"

"It's just like my dream," Erin said absently.

Shawn laughed. "What?"

"My fever dream." She was quiet for a moment, thinking of it. "I was on a mountain. High up like I am now. I was frightened. Like now. And in my dream, the rains came. And they washed the fear away.

"I didn't ever make it all the way up the mountain," Erin said. "I haven't learned, yet, what the person up top wanted to tell me.

"But my dream was right about the rain."

Below, Beacon's streets were filled with Marked and Markless alike, all basking in the downpour. Smiling. Letting its cure rain down in sheets.

"I guess we lost the battle," Erin said. "But this isn't over yet. And it's still up to us to win the war."

Before her, the crowds puddle jumped. They splashed. They danced in her storm.

5

I was in Spokie by this time. I had escaped from Beacon along the Unmarked River, and I'd just met up again with the woman who secretly taught me most everything I knew about Logan, Peck, the Dust—Logan's grandmother, Sonya. The woman who made *Swipe* possible.

I was working on *Sneak* at the time, and I'd stopped by to learn more about Logan's first days on his own outside of Spokie. I'd given Sonya a copy of my draft manuscript, half-done. I showed her the passages I'd sketched out about life down at the underpass. I asked her if she thought I'd gotten it right.

She read the chapters over a few times before handing them back to me with a shrug and a sigh.

"It doesn't matter now," she told me. "Whether any of this is right or wrong."

On the television frame in front of her, the Global Union news was broadcasting softly. Its announcer was encouraging Marked citizens to go outside into the rain, was discussing the cure and falsely praising America's new leader Cylis for making it possible.

Grandma Sonya did feel better, it was clear, in the wake of Dr. Rhyne's rain. But it did little to brighten her mood.

"Your book is fine," she told me. "It's close enough." She looked at her wrist, scarred and bandaged where she'd burned off her Mark a few weeks ago. "But none of it matters now, with Logan gone. None of it matters at all."

I swallowed hard. I thought about how best to tell her what I'd learned from my research out east, in the time since I'd last met with her, and in the aftermath of Lamson's death. Finally, I decided just to blurt it out.

"Your grandson isn't gone, Sonya. He isn't dead. Not technically, at least. Not yet."

Sonya's eyes brightened immediately.

"That's, uh . . . that's actually one of the reasons I came back," I told her. "To ask what you think I should do with the truth. It would be dangerous, you realize, for people to know. He's safer, right now, if the world thinks him dead."

Sonya frowned.

"But . . . if it's what you want . . . well, I'm in a unique position to tell people," I said. "I could write about it—the truth—in *Storm*."

She thought about this for a moment.

She cried a few silent tears.

She told me to do it.

And so I will.

6

The first time Logan was banished to Acheron's interface helmet, he had received the harshest treatment available—the total-perception simulated reality of Level Nine. The icy lake that froze its prisoners alive, and kept them there, until the interface program deemed its prisoners sufficiently repentant.

Where Logan was now was well beyond all that. On Level Nine, Logan's BCI helmet had been part of a vast array of desks, with no true guards or locked doors at all beyond the helmets themselves.

But on the day that Logan stormed the Capitol, on the day of his public sentencing, Lily Langly escorted her brother to a depth of Acheron previously untouched. Below the training grounds. Below the courtyard. Below the punishment floors. Where Logan now sat, alone in the dark space of his closet of a cell . . . it was the only one like it in all of Acheron.

Within it, Logan's personal helmet simulated not fire, nor ice, nor tar, nor snakes, nor anything like that. That would raise alarm bells. That could draw attention.

So this time, Logan's helmet simulated . . . nothing.

There was no repentance here. No persuasion. No goal of "Revision" awaiting him at the end of his sentence.

There was, in fact, no sentence at all. This was simply exile.

In the face of her brother's otherwise certain death, it was the only thing Lily Langly could think to do. She snuck him down here . . . and she threw away the key.

Here, awareness folded in on itself. Space had no dimension, time had no direction. Logan could not move. He could not sense. He could not feel.

"Where am I?" he asked into the void, after who knew how much time had passed.

But Logan hadn't heard his own words when he spoke them; there was no sound here, of course. There was not even emptiness.

And so, Logan prayed. He prayed for forgiveness, he prayed for understanding, he prayed for salvation. He couldn't have guessed how long his prayers rang in that nothingness. Ten minutes? Two weeks? A year? In the void, time meant very little.

Until, finally and all at once, the question was answered.

"Well, that's a funny thing to ask," a voice said from nowhere perceptible. "How did you get here if you don't know where 'here' is?"

Logan's mind jolted at the response. He couldn't make sense of it. He couldn't make sense of any of this.

"I was placed here," Logan said finally. "But now I'm lost . . ."

The voice giggled. "You mean you can't just ask It for directions?" Logan could understand this now as a girl's voice. A young girl, it seemed. Younger than he was, though he didn't know how he knew that; he saw nothing, still. "The Ultranet," she clarified. "Not reality, but . . . well . . . *virtual* reality." The girl smiled, though Logan couldn't see that either.

"I don't understand," he said. "Do you mean you can talk to the Ultranet directly?"

"Of course," the voice said. For *It* was not its own thing. *It* was the virtual reality itself. The Ultranet was aware. Could communicate. Though apparently not with him.

Logan asked if the Ultranet was Cylis's space. If Cylis owned it somehow.

But this little girl had never heard of Cylis. "*It* cannot be his," she said. "Because *It* is not anyone's. Whoever Cylis is . . . he overreaches." The girl skipped excitedly in front of Logan, and he sensed this now, somehow, implicitly, though he still couldn't see it.

"Who *are* you?" Logan asked.

"Your new friend. Your guide to the Ultranet. To Anything! And the great thing about Anything," the girl said, "is that it can be anything it wants." She smiled innocently. "Don't you love it here?"

"No," Logan said. "It's torture."

The girl frowned. "Well, that won't do."

And just like that, Logan was flying.

"You are in It now," the girl said. "Trapped, it seems. But so what? Everything's trapped, in its own way. Inside bodies, inside routines . . .

"In this moment . . . in your time as you see it . . . you are here." And this girl, this friendly visitor, this savior . . . she couldn't change that any more than she could tear Logan from the skin in which he sat, in his metal chair, with his sustenance IVs, in his cell, outside of Its space.

"No," the girl said as Logan soared higher. "I can't change that at all." She laughed now, playfully. "But Anything can have its own way of setting you free."

Back in the physical world, Logan would sit in his empty, finite cell, for who knew how long.

But the *It* before him had opened wide. His new friend led the way.

And now Logan was soaring through a great mobile, beyond

the scope of understanding. Past the moon, past Venus . . . past Mercury, and the Sun, past Mars, and Jupiter, and Saturn . . . past the divine comedy itself and past fixed stars and past and past, over, over, to a great circle of Anything beyond.

Logan shielded his eyes.

He squinted sharply.

He thought,

What's next?

ABOUT THE AUTHOR

Evan Angler is off to the dark lands.
To see what's there. To escape what's here.

Things got worse faster than he could keep up.

But there's a new promise on the horizon.

So, come on. Destroy all the evidence—and let's go.

Because you are the ones who question. Who think differently. Who doubt.

Because we've already found enough trouble.

And because now it's time to see how much of it we can *cause*.

Evan Angler

If it is such a good thing, why does the Mark seem so wrong?

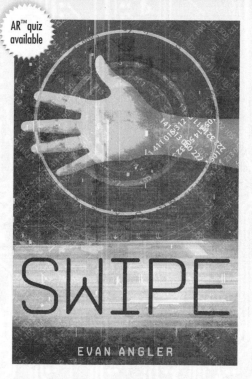

AR™ quiz available

Logan Langly is just months away from his thirteenth birthday, the day he will finally be Marked. The Mark lets people get jobs, vote, even go out to eat or buy concert tickets. But Logan can't shake the feeling he's being watched . . . and then he finds the wire.

By Evan Angler

www.tommynelson.com

www.evanangler.com

Look for more Swipe books coming soon!

AR is a trademark of Renaissance Learning, Inc., and its subsidiaries, registered, common law, or pending registration in the United States and other countries.

IF YOU WERE DESCENDED FROM ANGELS, HOW WOULD YOU USE YOUR POWERS?

Check out the exciting new *Son of Angels* series!

Jonah, Eliza, and Jeremiah Stone are one-quarter angel, which seems totally cool until it lands them in the middle of a war between angels and fallen angels. As they face the Fallen, they will find their faith tested like never before . . .

By Jerel Law

www.tommynelson.com

www.jerellaw.com

AR is a trademark of Renaissance Learning, Inc., and its subsidiaries, registered, common law, or pending registration in the United States and other countries.

Travel back in time to London and solve mysteries with Sherlock Holmes's protégé!

Griffin Sharpe notices everything, which makes him the perfect detective! And since he lives next door to Sherlock Holmes, mysteries always seem to find him. With Griffin's keen mind and strong faith, together with his Uncle Rupert's genius inventions, there is no case too tricky for the detectives of 221 Baker Street!

By Jason Lethcoe

www.tommynelson.com
www.jasonlethcoe.com/holmes

Check out all of the great books in the series!

No Place Like Holmes ❖ *The Future Door*

There is an unseen world of good and evil where nightmares are fought and hope is reborn.

ENTER THE DOOR WITHIN.

Aidan's life is completely uprooted when his parents move the family across the country to care for his ailing grandfather. But when he begins having nightmares and eerie events occur around his neighborhood, Aidan finds himself drawn to his grandfather's basement—where he discovers three ancient scrolls and a mysterious invitation to another world.

By Wayne Thomas Batson

www.tommynelson.com

AR is a trademark of Renaissance Learning, Inc., and its subsidiaries, registered, common law, or pending registration in the United States and other countries.

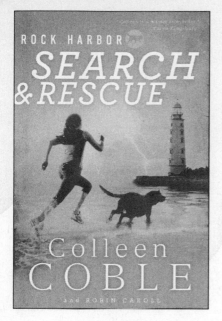

FROM AWARD-
WINNING AUTHOR
COLLEEN COBLE
COMES HER FIRST
SERIES FOR YOUNG
ADVENTURERS:
A MIXTURE OF
MYSTERY, SUSPENSE,
ACTION—AND
ADORABLE PUPPIES!

Eighth-grader Emily O'Reilly is obsessed with all things Search-and-Rescue. The almost-fourteen-year-old spends every spare moment on rescues with her stepmom Naomi and her canine partner Charley. But when an expensive necklace from a renowned jewelry artist is stolen under her care at the fall festival, Emily is determined to prove her innocence to a town that has immediately labeled her guilty.

As Emily sets out to restore her reputation, she isn't prepared for the surprises she and the Search-and-Rescue dogs uncover along the way. Will Emily ever find the real thief?

BY COLLEEN COBLE
www.tommynelson.com
www.colleencoble.com